# Gathering Moondust

An Anthology

edited by

## Libby Belle

Pure Luck Press

Gathering Moondust
An Anthology edited and compiled by Libby Belle



Published by Pure Luck Press
LibbyBelle.com
Austin, Texas



ISBN: 978-0-9985165-9-2 (eBook)
ISBN: 978-0-9985165-8-5 (Print)
Printed in the United States of America

# Contents

*To the child within us
who still believes in stories*

To hell with facts!
We need stories!


Ken Kesey
Author of *One Flew Over the Cuckoo's Nest*

## BY LIBBY BELLE

In this eclectic caboodle of stories you will meet hopeful, confused, opinionated, funny, murderous, innocent, and incorrigible human beings. Oh yes, and two dogs who think they are human. Their experiences are vastly different and like a good story, they are written to resonate emotionally with the reader. Expect to be delighted, amused, deeply moved, surprised, and cozily horrified. Above all, enjoy being entertained.

I am a storyteller and the gatherer of these fine writers and their stories. How I found them is a story in itself.

One day at my desk, staring at the black screen, feeling alone with my craft, I decided to reach out to other writers. Who else but another writer could understand why we choose this artform and the joy and suffering thereof. I needed comradery, inspiration, and a safe place to gripe. Little did I know the good folks I reached out to would be the catalyst for this anthology of love for the ever-lasting short story.

When I whispered my silent wish to the literary gods, they sent me Don Tassone, storyteller extraordinaire. He had read my first collection of stories and liked them. I nearly cried when he asked me to write a blurb for *Snapshots*, his seventh book featuring 75 remarkable short stories inviting his readers to pause and think more deeply. Seeing how easily he made friends with other writers was just the inspiration I needed. We have been writing buddies ever since.

Soon, I met authors, Monika Martyn and Kenneth Robbins through an unsettling, although eye-opening experience with the publisher of our books, at the time. Instead of wasting our energy on a losing battle, Monika suggested that we "add vodka to the lemon juice," and share, enjoy, and support each other's work. So we did! Monika's debut novel is a beautifully written page-turner. It's not surprising that her short stories, allowing us to engage our darker halves, are also as intriguing.

Award winning, Kenneth Robbins holds nothing back in his long career of published stories, novels, and stage and radio plays. His charming Southern style, witty and unfiltered humor is refreshingly honest.

I learned by sheer curiosity that some of my friends are natural writers. Patricia Lebo, a fan of my work, shared a tender story with me that immediately tugged at my heartstrings. I was not surprised to learn that this adorable tiny dancer had more.

While visiting us from Atlanta, our longtime friend Gerald Gaul was completing his first short story after publishing a humdinger of a novel. I convinced him, over a hearty breakfast and a cheerful evening with wine, to submit his funny, intelligent, and insightful story.

Who would have thought that my favorite bartender, Jacob Surles, was enrolled in a creative writing class. He willingly shared his first ever stories that jolted me out of my comfort zone. I still shiver when reading them, all the while strangely enjoying the uncomfortable thrill of getting inside the heads of seemingly innocent characters and their underlying depraved intentions.

C. Marshall Rea, my mentor, older, wiser, much more educated brother is a natural storyteller loved by all. With the promise of a cheeseburger, he dug out some of his old stories. I had to add a chili dog to get him to release them and the heart melting song he wrote.

Cute as a bug, Carol Beth Anderson is an amazing fantasy author and an expert in book formatting. Not only did she format this anthology, but she also contributed an unforgettable and magical story that lovingly speaks to our imperfections.

Rob Radmer, my editor and muse finally confessed that he had written stories over his lifetime and with much coaxing, they were resurrected from dusty old cardboard boxes that haven't seen the light in decades. Who knew that a classical conductor, guitar playing fool, songwriter, strings teacher and Doctor of Viola Performance could write so genuinely, and with pure ease portray a young man's formative years of life in the Midwest.

I had originally decided on ten authors for this anthology, but after reading two of John Young's excellent novels, I broke the mold and invited writer #11 to the fun. His well-told, down-to-earth, often comical stories are enjoyable and easy to believe.

So the literary gods heard my plea, and that, dear reader, is how this anthology you now hold in your hand came to life

—by reaching out, believing, and simply asking. A grateful and warm thank you to these marvelous contributors for sharing your precious stories. I am most pleased to be tucked in between these pages with you in *Gathering Moondust*.

"I think this is the beginning of a beautiful friendship."

# Carol Beth Anderson

Carol Beth Anderson was born and raised in the Arizona desert, where she played make-believe games with her siblings, transforming blankets into princess capes and her mother's dresses into fine gowns. Almost as soon as she learned to write words, she began turning them into stories.

Beth graduated from college with a degree in theatre/drama. As an adult, she moved to the Austin, Texas area, where she periodically returned to creative writing. For decades, she said she wanted to write a book "someday."

In 2017, *someday* turned into *now*. Beth met a local author, read her book, and thought, "I could do that." Hours later, she started brainstorming a young-adult (YA) fantasy series, the Sun-Blessed Trilogy. She published it in late 2018.

Beth published The Magic Eaters Trilogy, an upper-YA fantasy series, in 2020 – 2021. Blogger Sara Cleveland reviewed Book 1, saying, "Anderson's characters are wonderfully imperfect creations…. *The Frost Eater* is hands down the best YA book I have read in a long time. Maybe ever."

Beth has also published a book of fifty-word stories titled *The Curio Cabinet* and a guide for fellow independent authors called *Early Readers Catch the Worms: How Alpha, Beta, and ARC Readers Can Help You Publish a Better Novel.*

These days, Beth spends much of her time narrating audiobooks for fellow authors. She also enjoys baking sourdough bread, reading too late at night, and hanging out with her teenage kids, husband, and miniature schnauzer.

# Dog House

BY CAROL BETH ANDERSON

I t started with a sorcerer.

Don't tune me out, please—I get it. I didn't believe in them either. Until one cast a spell on me.

I'd lived selfishly, exceptionally so. Affairs, betrayed friendships, and a decades-long history of littering. It's a boring story, really, and not the one I'm here to tell.

I was lying in bed in a public hospital after eighty-four years of narcissism that had left me quite alone, when a nurse with curly, black hair and green eyes showed up. "Hello, Mr. Lewis. I'm a sorcerer."

"Not a sorceress?" I'm not sure why that's the question that pushed itself through my dry lips, but there's a lot about the man I was that I'll never understand.

"We've gone to gender-neutral titles." She proceeded to inform me that, due to my supreme selfishness, I would spend my next life as a dog.

She lifted her hands and spoke several words I'd never heard.

And then I died.

I don't remember being born. I came to awareness while drinking warm, sweet milk from the teat of a tired dog.

All at once, I knew who I was, what I'd done, and the punishment I'd been sentenced to. I stopped eating and looked around.

That woman hadn't just made me a dog, she'd made me one of a litter of nine mutts, all with stubby legs, boring brown fur, and ridiculously floppy ears. And she hadn't sent me to live with a family. I was surrounded by chain link, barks, and stink. An animal shelter.

Damn sorcerer.

I shoved one of my siblings to the side and latched on to my mother, puppy instincts warring with human fury.

Once I was no longer hungry, my mind cleared. The sorcerer might've set me up for failure, but I was in control of my own life now. I'd go for what I wanted. The way I always had.

The next day, when people came to look for pets, I sat up straight, wagged my whip-like tail and let my tongue hang out of the side of my mouth.

It worked.

A young woman and her husband fell in love with my brown eyes and lolling tongue. I listened as they discussed me with the staff. Weeks later, Ed and Sheila brought me to live at their little house in the city. They named me Moby, after the whale. (My belly was quite round.)

I expected to live a life of ease in my new home. Quickly, I realized my error.

A dog has little control over his existence. Ed taught me to ring a little bell with my nose when I wanted to go outside. All his high-pitched praise couldn't take away the humiliation of ringing a bell to ask permission to piss.

And the food—how to describe it? Dog food is like greasy, meat-based dry cereal. It tasted better than I expected, but eating it day after day was torture. I wanted to growl at Sheila, "Do you have any idea how many five-star meals I've eaten? And you give me this?"

Anxiety slithered into my little gut. Would they ever forget to feed me? What if I ventured into the bathroom, accidentally bumped the door closed, and got stuck? And the big birds I occasionally saw outside—would one snatch me from the yard and make me its breakfast?

As I became daily more aware of my lack of agency, I swear my sensitive canine ears heard the sorcerer's high-pitched cackle.

I responded the same way I would've when I was human. I took what I wanted instead of waiting for someone to give it to me. If the front door opened, I darted out to mark as many neighbors' mailboxes as I could. I jumped on the one chair that was off limits. Its upholstery was rough on my skin, but I still napped on it for hours when my owners were at work. I chewed on leather shoes (a surprisingly delicious habit).

Sheila and Ed became more and more frustrated. "Why, Moby?" they'd ask as they chased me through the neighborhood or held up another ruined shoe.

If I were capable of laughing, I would've. However, their sighs and chiding words affected me, despite myself. Sometimes I caught my ears drooping, and my tail tucked itself between my legs. I never would've admitted it, but I missed their smiles and cooing words.

Then, one day, I smelled it—my very favorite scent. Sheila was cooking chicken.

You don't realize, you can't understand, how meat smells to a dog. I don't care how many incredible restaurants you've been to, with French-trained chefs and creamy sauces and buttery desserts. I don't care what delectable odors wafted from your grandmother's Thanksgiving table. Nothing you've smelled as a human can compare to the scent of sizzling chicken when you're a dog. Drool collected in my mouth as soon as I caught a whiff.

I stood there, tongue darting out repeatedly, eyes wide, tail twitching, silently begging Sheila for a bite.

She was in a hurry, ingredients and pans scattered over the kitchen as she worked on the chicken and a variety of less interesting dishes. "When do your parents get here?" she called as she swept the back of her hand over her flushed forehead.

"Fifteen minutes!" Ed replied from where he was frantically dusting the living-room furniture.

Sheila cursed, then muttered under her breath, her fears emerging in short phrases: "They won't like it." "They don't like me." "I'll mess this up." Not once did she look at me, sitting there with hope written all over my little body.

She finished the chicken and set it on the dining table in the next room. When she went to the entryway to welcome her in-laws, a quick hop brought me onto a chair. Another jump, and I was on the table.

Then I was in heaven, tearing into the chicken, gulping down huge bites of it. It was savory and moist and altogether perfect. I got through a breast and two thighs before Sheila and Ed appeared, leading his parents into the room. I froze. My traitorous tail slipped between my legs.

Ed's mother let out a soft gasp.

A sob burst from Sheila's mouth, echoing off the walls, followed by the pounding of her feet as she ran into the kitchen.

My gaze met Ed's. He'd never laid a violent hand on me, but I truly believed I could smell his fury. A single leap, and I hit the floor, my feet skidding in four directions on the slick wood. I recovered and followed Sheila into the kitchen.

I'm not sure why I didn't run straight through the room and find a quiet corner to sit in. I saw Sheila sitting on the tile floor, muffling her cries with her hands, and found myself walking to her and sitting in front of her. The tile was cold on my little rump, but I stayed there, waiting.

Sheila looked up. "Oh, Moby," she choked out. "Why?"

Something squeezed at my heart, something I didn't remember ever feeling.

Regret.

The chicken got heavy in my belly. More than ever, I wished I could talk. Since I couldn't, I leaped onto Sheila's lap. I nuzzled her neck, and my tongue found her cheeks and kissed away her salty tears.

She held me close to her soft chest for a long time, then pulled back and met my gaze. "I forgive you," she whispered.

No one had ever told me that before. I guess it was a day for firsts.

Things changed after that. I changed. I didn't run out the door or sit on the forbidden chair. I didn't steal leather shoes or food. (Not often, anyway.)

Ed and Sheila frequently scratched behind my ears and called me a good boy, and I could tell they meant it.

At last, I truly settled into my role as a pet. In many ways it remained uncomfortable, being totally dependent on others and having such limited communication skills. But there was a certain beauty to the simplicity: playing and eating, walking and napping.

I stopped growing and was pleased to find my head had reached the level of my owners' knees. Not too long after that, Sheila began to grow. She and Ed had one baby, then another two years later. I got less attention from the adults and sometimes too much from the toddlers in the house.

Months passed, then years, full of the crunch of boring dog food and the petting of hands big and little and the divine smell of cooking chicken (and, when I was lucky, the taste of it).

One day, when the kids were at school and Sheila and Ed were at work, I lay in a band of warm sunlight on the wooden floor of the living room, watching dust motes and listening to the gentle whoosh of the fish-tank pump. I'd learned to appreciate those times of relative quiet, even though my ears perked up at every small noise as I waited for someone to return home. In that lazy space between sleep and alertness, I considered my unique role in this house.

When Ed, Sheila, and the kids left for work and school, I remained. In those times, I was the only one to hear the thunk of packages on the front porch. When the family went out to dinner, I alone admired the purple-and-salmon sunset through our back window.

Being canine, I detected scents that the humans in the house were unaware of. A home, especially one with children, is a wonderful place for a dog's nose. The house was full of the odors of dropped food and dirty laundry, along with the intriguing, slightly jealousy-inducing scents brought back by anyone who'd been socializing with other dogs.

And in becoming a dog, I'd lost my human inhibitions. If something smelled amazing, I'd taste it, at least once. I was the only one in the home to know the flavors of dirty socks and crumpled tissues and that one sticky spot on the kitchen tile that sat for weeks before getting mopped up. (Don't knock any of it until you try it.)

Most importantly, the members of the household felt safe around me. I heard the parents' quiet conversations about their kids, and I heard the scheming of the kids planning to pull something over on their parents. When someone was angry and didn't want to be touched by human family members, their hands found me, burying in my fur, scratching that wonderful spot on my neck. I was party to more interactions in this place than anyone—I was the quiet observer, the secret keeper, the comforter.

A home, I thought as I lay in the sunlight, belongs more to a pet than to their humans. The honor of that, the wonder of it, made my eyes heavy with something that would've been tears if I could produce them.

This was my home. It was full of the scent of cooking chicken and the taste of dropped crumbs. It featured beaming faces and the click of my toenails. It was lush with the promise of warm hands reaching out for soft fur.

My home.

The kids are in elementary and middle school now. Ed's going bald, and Sheila's embracing her first strands of gray hair. I suspect this canine life is coming to an end before long.

Sheila told Ed this morning that my vet retired, and the new one will do house calls for an extra fee. She kneels next to me. "Wanna get your checkup here or at the office?"

I used to love occasional rides in the car. But now, the area rug on the floor feels cozier than ever. I roll on my back, and Sheila laughs and pets my belly. "I'll ask her to come here."

When the doorbell rings, I don't run to it like I used to. My ears perk up and my tail thumps as I wait. There are murmurs in the entryway, and as they come closer, I make out a few of the visitor's words: "Sounds like he's earned these restful days." The voice is vaguely familiar.

"He's a good boy," Sheila says.

They enter the living room, where I'm lounging. All at once, my entire body stiffens.

The smiling vet has curly, black hair and green eyes.

The sorcerer.

She kneels and says, "It's okay, Moby. I'm not here to hurt you."

For some reason, I believe her. I relax and let her examine me.

When she's done, she speaks to Sheila, but she's still looking at me. "I think you've still got some time with him." Her voice is gentle. "And I think this life with you is just what he needed."

I give her a little nod. Her lips twitch with a half-smile, and for the first time, I consider what it will mean to leave my home. To find rest at last.

I think I'm almost ready.

Libby Belle Bryer is a mother of six, grandmother of twelve and a stranger to no one. "I came from a one bathroom family, and there were five of us! Need I say more?"

She lives in Austin, Texas, a city that thrives on weirdness—a perfect place to nurture her vivid imagination.

Anytime, anywhere, and especially during the witching hour, she has written over 100 stories, many collected in four published books, *The Juicy Parts, A Woman Always Knows, Humble Fumble* and *Happy Hour Fools*.

*Gathering Moondust* features her wonderful fellow writers. Her debut novel, *Box of Secrets,* predestined to be a movie filmed in Austin, is in the making.

"I even write in my dreams," she says. "It's a wonderful curse."

# Sparkles

BY LIBBY BELLE

Her name was Maude in that other life, long before she changed it to Sparkles. Back when they were blessed with three fine daughters, a four-bedroom home, a Cadillac in the garage and a Ford Pick-up in the driveway, keys to the community pool, Friday night cookouts, Saturday nights at the dance hall, (Maude so loved to dance), and Sunday morning vigilance—you get the picture. "Living the dream," her husband used to say until the little weasel decided to step out of that dream and seek pleasure elsewhere. And not just once, she would learn from the neighbors, but more than enough to wreck a marriage and keep her searching for guilt in the eyes of every woman she passed in the grocery store aisles. How fooled she had been, and it hurt like hell.

The daughters were well on their way to their own lives when the divorce was finalized, and Maude soon found herself miserably alone in a house too large for just one lonely divorcee. At the time, she was still a vivacious forty-five-year-old, but there was no getting rid of the sour taste in her mouth as long as she stayed in that neighborhood with all that judgment surrounding her. When opportunity knocked, and just in the nick of time, she sold the house and joined up with a group of like-minded people seeking adventure in Alaska. Towanda! Four men to every woman! Men who were most eager to help her recover from the humiliation of a cheating husband did wonders to restore Maude's confidence. Many would say, including herself, that she went wild. Hog wild!

When her girls started having babies and begged for mama to come home and do the natural grandparent thing, Maude abandoned the geographical cure of "The Last Frontier" and dutifully returned to an ordinary life. In her spare time, she enhanced her culinary skills, and soon her sexual appetite and any foolish thoughts of love were replaced with countless new recipes devoured in front of old movies. Stuck in this routine, she gained an ungodly amount of weight—sixty-five pounds, if you really want to know. "E-gads!" her ninety-two-year-old mother exclaimed, after calling her by her dead aunt's name. "Geez, Louise, that's a buttload of fat!"

Nothing hurts quite like a mother's ridicule except for watching her ex-husband, with his ridiculous facelift and bad hair weave, marry three more times—her daughters embracing each new skinny wife right in front of her. Soon Maude was filled to the brim with shame and resentment, blaming it all on the father of her children and the boatload (not buttload, she informed her ill-mannered mother) of extra fat she carried around for the next ten years.

Of course, the grandchildren in their selfish teens went in different directions, leaving Maude purposeless and trapped in the daily grunge of her tedious job. Eventually, she moved to the outskirts of the city into a small condo with a long-distance view of the Houston skyline she was glad to leave behind. Even with a change of scenery, designer clothing, pedicures and manicures, hair coloring, teeth whitening and the finest Mary Kay make-up, depression was just inches from her doorstep. Death lurked closely behind. And men? Ha! Nada! Zilch!

Often, while lying in bed, immersed in the soft light of the candy swirl lava lamp, she would imagine her broken heart giving out in the middle of the night and how they would find an overfed, pathetically lonely woman lying dead in between 600-count sheets, above her taped to the ceiling a poster of Burt Reynolds stretched out in the nude smiling wickedly on a bearskin rug. At the foot of the bed on a feather-filled euro sham covered with silk scarves, her little Yorkie, Brando would be playfully licking his master's toes in a vain attempt to revive her. "Farewell, cruel world!" she cried to Burt on those long, lonely nights.

But each morning like clockwork, Maude would awake at the break of dawn, alive and well and always hungry.

Sixty-five hit like a stifling hot August wind off the Galveston coastline. Most women who face the Medicare age surrender to their body's betrayal, but not Maude. Something had to give. The answer came from her hairdresser who told her a story about a miserable obese man who had elected to have a gastric bypass at the age of sixty. Sixty! So what if he died on the operating table, at least he was courageous enough to do something, anything, no matter the consequences. The story motivated Maude to have the same operation and by the very same surgeon. Finally, a way out! She couldn't make the arrangements fast enough.

Several cancellations had just been entered into the

system, and the day for surgery was soon upon her. Perfect! No time for second thoughts. With her place all tidied up and a handwritten will set out on the kitchen table, she gave Brando to another lonely and needy neighbor and took a final step toward the beginning of a new life, or a quick ending to the old one, however destiny saw fit.

As scheduled, she was lying on the gurney in her birthday suit by midafternoon. "A stretcher on wheels, how clever," she teased the doctor. "Made to roll you right out of surgery and straight to the morgue. One-stop shopping." Maude laughed, and a bit too loud. The nurse chuckled behind his facemask. The doctor stared straight ahead.

So convinced she would die while under the knife, she told Dr. Nankin not to feel bad that his skills may be in question when it was all over, but this time he could rest assured that her death would be in fate's hands and not his. The fretful doctor nervously patted her leg and weakly promised she would awaken to a brand-new life, and he would be there to serve her Jello. "Oh? So, you're going to heaven with me, too, Dr. Napkin?" was the last thing Maude said when the stage curtains fell before her eyes.

But something magical happened while under anesthesia. Maude had a vision. She saw herself being carried in a man's arms. She was laughing. She was happy. And to her surprise, when she opened her eyes, destiny had decided to send her back to earth.

It was said that right after the surgery Dr. Nankin was so overwhelmed with the outcome, he rushed to the nearest bar. A woozy, but vigilant Maude, yelled from the recovery room, "Hey, Dr. Napkin, where's my Jello?"

The transformation that occurred in the following year was simply amazing, and with each pound shed Maude became more of the sexy, exciting woman she was while living in Alaska twenty years earlier. As far as she was concerned, not a day could be wasted, as love was now at her thin fingertips.

Quick weight loss required a necessary tummy tuck and the bags removed from beneath her eyes, followed by contact lenses. The urge to gratify the newly restored sexual impulses flashed in her glazed-over pupils. But if one cared to look closer, they'd see hidden behind that thin veil of lust something entirely different.

A co-worker gladly showed her how to get back in the groove by using an online dating site. She also advised her to use a pseudonym. Because Maude adored jewelry and never left the house without wearing some, she named herself Sparkles. Within a week she had a slew of men lined up. She would tackle each of them one by one, starting with a man guarding a diamond mine in Botswana who wooed her with the perfect words, although often misspelled. 'How perfectly appropoo you name is Sparklee, like my dimonds,' he wrote. He promised they would spend the rest of their young lives making love in sparkling champagne and African diamonds. A mere four thousand dollars was all that he needed from her to fly him across the ocean and into her arms by the end of the month. So be it!

She waited with the excitement of a new bride. When the next month came and another flew by, and the flirty dog mysteriously dropped from sight on the internet, she was convinced that he had faced his biggest fear: (KIA) killed in action.

When she told the outlandish story to the ladies in her book club, not one had the heart to contradict her. Her daughters, however, were not as kind. Their harsh demands that she act her age ricocheted right off Maude's' glossy gullible exterior. She flippantly quoted from an old movie, "Oh my, how the world still dearly loves a cage," and left them with an emphatic, "I will not go back to mine!"

"You're doing it all wrong," her co-worker lambasted her after Maude described in detail the bizarre online affair.

"But it was fun pretending," she explained. "No real harm done. Everyone has the right to make an ass of themselves. You just can't let the world judge you too much."

"Well, fine, but you have to actually date them first before you do anything as crazy as giving them money. Let's get you on a better dating site. You'll have to pay for this one, but honestly, Maude, as much as you love to dress up, it'll be a cinch. Start with dinner first. It may take a half dozen or so to get used to it, and then you can move on to drinks, and dancing, and after that ... well."

"OK, but my name is Sparkles now. For real. You can call me Sparkles."

With newfound courage and a new identity, new outfits were bought, and regular dates were set up. It was much easier than Sparkles had thought it would be, but it certainly had its flaws.

The first date appeared to be a regular sort until he got down on his knees, crawled under the table and begged her to show him her feet right when dessert was served. Feigning the need to powder her nose, Sparkles hid in the restaurant's kitchen where she donned an apron and helped scrub the dishes until the date finally gave up and left. The nut with a foot fetish not only ate his dessert, he ate hers, too.

A four-foot-tall man who claimed he was over six feet *before* the accident, nearly had her talked into a second date until he stood on a chair and begged her for a kiss.

Some dates never got past the menu, ending abruptly after the first drink with a standard, "Sorry, we're just not a fit." The men who eventually confessed, right in the middle of dinner, that they were married were the cruelest. Their excuses and stories about their lame wives made Sparkles cringe. Rather than waste the nice meal, she'd wait until the check was paid and the boxed-up leftovers in her hands before going separate ways after firmly announcing, "Just for the record, buster, I used to be one of those lame wives!"

Disenchanted, she put men aside long enough to read more books and watch old movies that spoke to her heart. Fueled with a fresh attitude, more clever one-liners, and ready to face the opposite sex again, she gave dating one last chance.

The place was packed. She'd heard from others that The Jackalope Restaurant bar was always full of executives on their way home from work. A good sign, Sparkles thought, if this date turns out to be a dud. She had dressed in a tight link-strapped sequin knit dress. A fur collar wrap sat delicately on her shoulders. Her shoes were strapless with a rim of rhinestones around the heel. Layers of delicate silver chains draped from her neck; one with a white swan pendant landing right in the middle of her cleavage. The Aurora Borealis drop earrings complimented the azure sky contact lenses floating on her eyes. Rings on two fingers, one on the middle toe, and bangle bracelets on each arm completed the ensemble. She was more excited than usual about this new date. He was a retired firefighter. And a firefighter who loved to dance.

Dreading the three-block walk in high heels and not

willing to trust the valet with her freshly painted 1980 Cadillac Seville, she squeezed her car in an empty space between a backhoe and a pile of lumber on a construction site right across the street from the restaurant.

A striking resemblance to Shirley MacLaine, she noted while examining her face in the visor mirror and singing along with Frankie Valli on the radio. When the song ended, she eased out of the car and discovered that her dress had slipped up to her crotch. Two construction workers nearby were standing next to each other ogling. One yelled out a cat call.

Sparkles stood up tall, stretched, and shimmied the dress back into position. Now, both men were whistling and egging her on. So absorbed in the attention, she hadn't noticed the eighteen-wheeler that had parked just a few feet from her car. Strutting toward it, eyes peeled on the men, she tripped over a piece of metal jutting out from the construction fence and fell face forward. Her feet flew out of her backless shoes, and her purse soared into the air and landed elsewhere.

The workers quickly turned their backs and carried on with their digging. Stunned, Sparkles pulled herself up to a sitting position and stretched out her legs. Checking for broken bones, bruises, cuts, and, oh dear Venus, please no rips in my dress, she didn't realize she was sitting within inches of the eighteen-wheeler. Just when she pulled her knees to her chest to try and stand, the rig began to move. Right before her eyes a huge set of tires rolled over her bare foot. Mortified, she fell back on her elbows and watched the monstrous truck move sluggishly past her.

A delayed, "Ouch!" flew from her mouth once she realized what had happened. "Ouch!" she yelled again. "You ran over my foot!" The truck came to a complete stop, and the driver frantically flew out of the cab and ran in her direction.

"Oh my God, lady, are you alright?" he asked in a panic, kneeling next to her, scoping out her body for mangled bones and blood.

"My foot, my foot! That giant tire ran over my foot!" She held it up in the air, surprised that there was no sign of damage of any kind, other than a black line of tire tread smeared across her big toe. Dazed and temporarily confused, she sat staring at the polished toenails, still sparkling even in the soft dusky sunlight. Then for no apparent reason, she started laughing.

The driver stepped back at a distance and waited until she finished before offering his hand to help her up. Too shaken to pull herself to a stand, he wrapped his arms around her waist and hoisted her to her feet.

"Ohh!" Sparkles squealed. "You're strong."

"Can you walk?" he asked with an anxious smile while awkwardly tugging at her dress that had climbed up her thighs.

"Maybe, but where are my shoes, and oh dear, my purse?" Realizing they were not in plain view, she freaked out. "I can't see out of my right eye! My contact has fallen down into my eyelid!"

"Here they are, here's your shoes, and, oh, look, there's your purse, hanging on the No Parking sign." He nervously gathered them up.

Sparkles placed her hand on his shoulder and steadied herself, while he slipped her heels back on her feet. From her good eye, she glared at the construction workers apparently quite entertained at her expense. "Cowards!"

"What?"

"Those men over there," she said, pointing their direction, "they didn't even bother to help me."

The driver looked their way and flipped them the bird. The workers dropped their cheesy smiles, turned around and went back to work. Sparkles muffled a laugh. "Thank you."

"Do you want me to take you to the hospital?" he asked, allowing her to lean on his arm.

"No, I've seen enough of those. But I'm certainly not in any state to be in public now. Geesh, my hair is a mess!" She blew at a lock of loose curls. "Do you live close by?"

"Not too far from here." He gave her a confused look. "Why?"

"If I could just sit quietly for a while, get this contact back in my eye, I'm sure I can determine if my foot is broken or not. And then you can take me to the hospital, if need be. I imagine your company would expect you to do that," she implied with a sudden formal demeanor. "By the way, what's your name?"

"Harry. I, uh, well, what's your name?"

"Sparkles. You can call me Sparkles," she said almost dreamily. Then she lowered her voice to sound more official. "I should get your driver's license number next. I think that's protocol after an accident."

"OK, I'll give it to you when I get you settled in your car."

"I'd prefer now, if you don't mind," she demanded, but not in a harsh way, more like parental chiding.

Harry presented his license, and he knew at that moment he was at this woman's discretion. He must be careful. This was not his first infraction, and he needed to keep the job. Sparkles stuffed the license in her purse and the car keys in his hand. Relieved that she didn't call the cops, he picked her up and carried her to her car.

"Oh my, I can't remember the last time I was swept off my feet," she giggled. The feeling of déjà vu stayed with her all the way to Harry's home.

The story was a long one, she had warned him. Nevertheless, Harry was determined to hear her out. After all, it was me who ran over her foot, he admitted to himself, while hurriedly scrubbing three days of grime from his body before the hot water ran out in the shower.

Refreshed, but still a little skeptical about the stranger sitting on his sofa, he returned to the living room and poured her another glass of Pinot Grigio from the bottle left behind by Bernadette, the girlfriend who never came back.

"You clean up nice," Sparkles said, sipping the cheap wine like a real lady, her pinky waving at the same time her eyebrows lifted in flirtatious approval at seeing him out of the soiled overalls and in a nice clean shirt and cargo pants.

Harry dropped his head to his chest and soaked up the compliment. His eyes roamed the room looking for the beer he had started earlier. He spotted it dripping condensation all over a poem he had been writing. He snatched it up, wiped it off on his pants and hid the poem behind his back. When he swallowed the last of the warm beverage, his stomach growled. Turning to his guest, he asked, "Are you hungry? I could rustle up something while you rest your foot and finish telling me all about yourself."

"That would be wonderful. I was supposed to have escargot if I hadn't ended up here," she said, with a hint of disappointment. "It would have been a first. I love firsts, don't you, Harry?"

"Firsts … oh, sure … but I'm afraid I don't have much in

the fridge. I'm rarely here." He opened the pantry, slipped the poem under a four-roll pack of toilet paper, and sorted through the goods. "Tuna, chicken spread, a big can of peaches, half a bag of elbow macaroni, and what do we have here … a package of Saltines."

"Now that I think about it, swallowing slimy snails is rather disgusting. Let's have a smorgasbord and open them all, Harry. I'll hobble over to your cute little bar and help you prepare it." When Sparkles tried to stand, she fell right back down on the sofa. "Ow, it hurts even more now. I guess there will be no dancing for me in the near future. That's a shame. I so love to dance."

Harry stood over his guest looking down at her shimmering gold toenails. The big toe was now accentuated by a mound of pink puffy flesh and the tire tread marks were still there. "You're right, it is swollen," he observed, guiltily. "Keep it elevated. I'll make you an ice pack."

While Harry popped out the ice cubes from the plastic tray, Sparkles leaned her head back, closed her eyes, and sang a Cat Stevens tune. So deep in the moment, she did not know he was standing over her with the baggie full of ice watching her bosom rise and fall as she sang. "If you want to sing out, sing out, and if you want to be free, be free … there's a million things to be, you know that there are." The swan pendant caught in her cleavage looked as if it was struggling to get free.

Nice rack for an old gal, he thought. I wonder how old she is. Got to be older than my mom. Uncomfortable with his impure thoughts, he cleared his throat and woke the woman from her reverie. He placed the ice next to her with a subtle suggestion that she should apply it herself and went back to the kitchen to prepare the appetizers.

In between nibbles, upon Sparkle's insistence, Harry told

her a little about himself, his short stint with Bernadette, and the two years of college ten years back when the world was his oyster. "I inherited this rusty old mobile home from my grandfather. Mobile? Ha!" he said jokingly, "this metal box has never gone mo-bile."

He confessed he'd never been out of Texas, either. Pasadena is where he rests his stiff muscles after weeklong trips delivering heavy equipment from one end of the state to the other. Uncomfortably aware that he sounded pathetic, he went back to the task at hand—spreading canned chicken across a piece of frozen white bread. "You were going to tell me how you got the name, Sparkles," he reminded her.

Transfixed by Harry's meticulous distribution of the pasty spread, making sure each corner was filled perfectly to the edge of the crust, Sparkles felt the alcohol kick in. She sighed wistfully and answered in a mellow voice, "Better brace yourself, Harry, it's a long, long story. It all began the day I stopped backing away from life …."

She rambled through chapters as far back as she could and surprisingly without tears. "There's so much more I can tell you, Harry, but it seems my glass is empty." Sparkles nudged the sleeping prince at the other end of the sofa.

Harry had not realized he had drifted off, his face smashed against the lumpy cushion that smelled like his grandfather's Vicks VapoRub, until he felt Sparkle's fingers tickling his side. "Oh, sure, yes, of course."

Glad to be rid of the last reminder of Bernadette, he cheerfully uncorked the wine.

Feeling more at ease with Sparkles, he sat down next to her and popped open another beer. "So, after all that, you're still online dating and still single."

"Yes, and thanks to Dr. Napkin's skilled hands, I'm still

shapely," she said, gliding her hand seductively along her hip down to her thigh.

Harry gave her a thumbs up along with a cutely bashful smile.

"How about you, Harry? Are you dating?"

He ran his fingers through his damp hair and thoughtfully rubbed his chin. "Nah, I've been giving it a rest. Pretty busy doing other things these days."

"Like writing poetry?" she ruefully suggested.

"Oh, you read my poem, huh?" Harry folded his hands together and waited glumly for her critique.

"Couldn't resist. It's good, Harry. You must really love her."

"Love who?" He looked at her curiously.

"The girl in the poem."

"No, no, there's no girl. It's just kind of how I see me loving someone someday. A perfect girl like her probably doesn't even exist … anymore."

"Not even Bernadette?"

"Not even," he sighed. "She was, let's say, a trial run."

"Well, you know Harry, it's best not to be too moral, you cheat yourself out of too much life." She removed the melting ice bag from her foot and stretched out her leg.

Harry sat quietly considering Sparkles' vaguely familiar words. He refrained from telling her that the girl of his dreams had died while he was in college, and she was the real reason he quit school and why no one could take her place. Afraid he'd lose his composure if he even said her name, he tried to subdue his feelings. He did not hear himself let out an exasperated moan.

Rescuing Harry from his apparent agony, Sparkles placed her foot gently on his thigh. "Look, the ice is helping with the swelling."

He forced himself to focus on her jiggling toe. "Guess it's not broken," he surmised. When she didn't move her foot, Harry picked it up and placed it next to the other one. "Maybe you should be taking me back soon to get my truck. You can drive, right?"

"I'm not sure I can. Let's just give it a little more time. Pass the peaches, please."

"I just have to say," Harry began, placing his hand over his heart, "that I am really sorry I ran over your foot. I didn't see you there. Just how was it you were so close to my rig?" He had been holding back this question, worried that Sparkles might sue him, but now tipsy with wine and in his entrusted care, he felt more comfortable asking.

"I was leading up to that earlier … until you fell asleep," she teased, lightly shoving his shoulder. "I'll spare you the details again, and there were a lot of them, some you shouldn't have missed."

"I'm sorry. These trips take a lot out of a man. I usually go straight to bed when I get home."

"Ohh?" Sparkles gave him a slow wink over the rim of the plastic wine glass.

"Ahem," he mumbled, trying to hold back his smile. She had such a youthful air about her, he found he was easily charmed. "But I'm all ears now. So, you were standing so close to my truck for *what* reason?"

"I was meeting a date at the Jackalope, right across the street. I could not find one lousy parking spot, and I drove forty miles for this guy. I thought it was a good sign that I found that spot until you ran over me."

Sparkles heartily laughed after reliving their unusual introduction. She threw her head back on the sofa cushion and proclaimed, "I might be the only person alive that can say I was run over by an eighteen-wheeler and lived to tell the story."

Harry laughed with her. She was a good sport after all. Although, he saw in her demeanor a sadness he had not seen before—a refreshing vulnerability hiding behind her laugh. Somehow it made it easier for him to tell her personal things about himself.

"Harry's my nickname. I'm not that crazy about my real name, so I'm guilty of using Harry a lot."

"Well, sure can't be any worse than Maude."

"Maude?" Harry choked on his laugh. "I'm sorry, it's just that I have an Aunt Maude … she's, well, she kind of resembles a fullback with a bad attitude. If you don't mind, I'll just call you Sparkles."

"And I'll just call you, Harry. And that's the end of that." They clinked their glasses together in a pact.

"I used to be like your Aunt Maude," Sparkles spoke softly, reflecting on unhappy times. She shook off the impending sadness with an exaggerated shiver of her shoulders. Later, after sharing much more, the tears were harder to shake.

In the still of the night, hesitant to wake his guest sleeping so soundly next to him, Harry was left to contemplate his own dull existence. Eventually, he had let his weary head land on the soft furry wrap resting on her shoulders, and soon the low, contented hum of her snoring lulled him to sleep. It was like cuddling up to a mama bear.

The next morning, back at the scene of the accident, Sparkles placed her fur wrap around Harry's neck and thanked him for a lovely evening.

"My girlfriends are going to be so jealous when they find out I had a sleepover with a handsome young truck driver," she teased.

"Ha, you're funny, Sparkles," he said, defusing the comment. "My mom called it a pajama party in her day."

"Well, that's somewhat true. But back then, we actually wore pajamas." She pulled her sunglasses down her crinkled-up nose and gave him another one of her mischievous smiles.

"You're the queen of hoots!" Harry decreed, removing the furry wrap and placing it back on her bare shoulders. He didn't have the heart to tell her about the rip in the back of her dress.

Inside the car, Sparkles held her arm out and dropped her hand, gesturing to Harry that he may kiss the hand of the queen. So, he did. "Go and love some more, Harry," she said, tossing the fur wrap in his direction. She jerked the gear into reverse and backed out so quickly she nearly rolled over his foot.

The construction workers leaning on their shovels had been watching them with big dopey grins. "Run over a woman and she takes you home with her," one said to the other. "I'll have to try that on Mary Jo at the office."

"Aye yi yi," the other one crooned.

The doctor said that it was merely a fracture, too small to worry about, although Sparkles had to wear an ugly boot for five days. "You're messing with my style," she told him.

He laughed, until he realized she really meant it. "Well, look at it this way young lady, you can take full advantage of the sympathy."

"Oh, you're absolutely right." Sparkles' frown switched to a wicked grin. She whispered in the doc's ear, "Maybe I'll wear it five extra days. Or better yet, keep it in the car when I need it."

From there, she drove straight to the salon and had her toenails painted blue—the color of the boot mixed with a dash of silver glitter. During the entire session she told the whole story about the eighteen-wheeler and the very handsome driver. She had the technicians and the customers in stitches. When she ended it with the pajama party, less the pajamas, and passed Harry's driver's license around so that there would be no doubt of her story's validity, the laughter changed to barely audible sniggers.

Harry had felt a kind of muddled relief watching Sparkles drive away. The whole thing seemed too close for comfort, yet she had managed to tug at his heartstrings. Never had he met someone who shared so easily and spoke so clearly with little reserve. Her life was an open book. She had a father that used his hand more than his brain. "Poor soul died before he could apologize. Apologies are very healing." The divorce had scarred her heart forever. "Scars remind us that we've truly lived." Dating wasn't nearly as much fun as she thought it would be. "But they sure do bring zing to my stories."

She had said that finding a companion was nearly impossible, and he didn't even have to be particularly angelic or handsome like everyone expects, just witty and kind and one who notices things around him, like the differences in flowers.

So charmed by her, Harry had forgotten the thirty-five-year difference. He even found himself talking about the girl of his dreams who was killed in a skiing accident. In between tears and laughter, they had talked for hours until the last thing Sparkles said while falling asleep in Harry's arms: "I'd like just one honest kiss before I die. I'm lonely, Harry."

Throughout the day an unexpected chuckle would burst out when reviving those scenes. Giving Sparkles a fake phone number, Harry convinced himself, was the right thing to do. Forgetting to get his license back from her was just pure stupidity. Or was it? What were the odds he'd ever run into her again?

He went to bed alone with his thoughts and Sparkles' furry wrap on the pillow beneath his head. Meeting her had been an interesting, no, an extraordinary event, and there was no one he could trust to share it with.

The next day, Harry met a woman squeezing avocados in the produce section of the grocery store. While trying to find the perfect avocado, they chatted about the disparity of the poor fruit, unjustly named a vegetable. He surprised himself when he accepted her brazen invitation to meet for drinks the following Friday. But he was even more surprised when at that precise moment he thought of Sparkles and her challenging words of encouragement, "Reach out, take a chance, get hurt, even. But play as well as you can."

After hearing Sparkles' unusual but entertaining excuse, the retired firefighter was very understanding about being stood up and agreed to meet again, same time, same place.

Sparkles would not risk being run over by anything with more than four wheels and parked in one of the five empty handicap spaces at the Jackalope restaurant. She left the big blue boot on the dashboard as proof of her disability.

The place was packed with drinks all around. The patrons were smiling and seemed relaxed, eager to begin the weekend. Suits and loosened ties were everywhere — about two men to every woman. Sparkles nearly swooned.

She pressed her way through the crowd to the bar. Noticing how the women looked dainty drinking from fancy glasses, she dropped the idea of a hearty whisky and ordered a lemon-drop martini. Delicately pinching the stem between her fingers, she scoped out the men, hoping to recognize the firefighter. From his online picture, she looked for broad shoulders, a thick neck and rippling muscles, a head held high with pride. She wondered if his pores still carried the scent of burnt forest.

Across the way, she spotted Harry sitting alone in a booth for two. An enormous smile seized her face, and she found herself advancing toward him.

"Oh my, if it isn't the man who almost killed me," she embellished, clinking her glass against Harry's beer mug.

"Sparkles!" He acknowledged her with a boyish grin.

"Yes, tis' I," she said, accepting his cheery smile as an invitation to sit down across from him. "So good to see you, Harry. *Really* good."

"Good to see you, too. What a nice surprise," he said meaningfully.

"What brings you here?"

"ME," a woman announced flatly, seeming to appear out of nowhere.

"Oh, yes, Sparkles, this is Reba. Reba, this is Sparkles."

Harry stood up to give Reba his seat. She huffed while claiming it. Harry stood awkwardly without a place to sit.

"Here, Harry, sit by me. I can squeeze you in." Sparkles patted the cushioned seat with such enthusiasm, Harry obeyed. He looked over at his date who was not smiling, apparently uncomfortable with the change of events. Sparkles noticed her discontent and said, "Oh don't worry honey, he's an old friend. Matter of fact let me tell you the story of how we met. Harry ran me over with his eighteen-wheeler…."

Teetering on the edge of the seat, Harry nervously laughed in between gulps of beer, while Reba maintained a look of irritation. When Sparkles got to the part about falling asleep in his arms, his laughter came to a halt. Reba looked at Harry in disgust. Her face crumpled as if a festering boil had suddenly appeared on his nose. She turned to Sparkles. "Aren't you kind of old for him. I mean come on lady, you have to be at least twice his age. And you, Harry, have you always slept with older … elderly women?"

"I didn't sleep with her," he protested. "I was just being kind. I mean, after all, I did roll over her foot."

"Just being kind?" Sparkles reached for Harry's arm and gazed into his eyes. "You *are* kind, but I thought we liked each other, Harry. I mean, we did share a lot that night."

"I think this date is over!" Reba slammed her drink on the table and stood up. "Next time you see me at the grocery store, pretend you don't know me, Harry. And you," she leaned in and said directly to Sparkles, "why don't you find somebody your own age? You look like his mother!" She rolled her eyes in a slow condescending manner. "Sparkles! How ridiculous!"

Harry moved quickly to stand up and slipped off the cushion onto the floor. Humiliated, he picked himself up and rushed after Reba, not looking back once at Sparkles' doleful eyes.

The cruel and worthless words Reba had said dissolved in the air like soap bubbles. But Harry's reaction wounded her heart. Profoundly disappointed, Sparkles considered leaving, until she spotted her date at the bar. At least she thought it was him. He was the only man in the room with a handle-bar mustache. She mustered up the courage to greet him.

"Are you by chance a firefighter?" she asked, tapping the man on the shoulder who swung around on the stool to address the question.

"Depends on who's asking," he said, looking Sparkles up and down, expressionless.

"Well, I was supposed to meet an online date here, and I have only a distant picture of him, but you sure do have the muscles for a firefighter. Are you Phil?"

"I am, and I was supposed to meet a woman here, too, but she is, well … no offense, but how old are you anyway?"

"Not old enough to be your mother," Sparkles retaliated. "How old are you? You look to be in your sixties." She sized him up with one raised eyebrow.

"I suppose I am, but I only date women of a certain age. I think there's been a mistake. You can't be the woman I met online. Are you … are you Sparkles?"

The look on his face almost made Sparkles deny her identity. But she would not cower, not now, not ever. "I am … but right now with the way you're looking at me, I wish I weren't."

"Well, I should probably at least buy you a drink for the trouble. You're a nice-looking lady, but I just don't have an attraction for…."

"Women your own age?" Sparkles challenged him.

"Yes, I guess you're right. But hey, tell my lady friends here about being run over by an eighteen-wheeler. That was a seriously funny story!"

Sparkles' lower lip went slack. Telling the story to Reba had taken the fun out of it. Even though it was so worth repeating, she hesitated, noticing the younger women huddling at the bar listening to the conversation and rudely whispering behind cupped hands. They snubbed Sparkles and sat up taller upon seeing the good-looking man who suddenly appeared behind her. The man placed his hand on Sparkle's shoulder. Startled, Sparkles turned to see who was getting all the attention, as well as taking the liberty to touch her.

Harry kissed her on the cheek. "I'm so glad you waited for me," he said. "Can I buy you a drink?"

"Oh!" Sparkles eyes widened and every rotten feeling up to then dissipated. Bolstered by Harry's timely rescue, she gave them all a bashful smile. "Phil has first dibs on buying me a drink. Don't you Phil?" Before Phil could respond, she turned to Harry, "But you can buy the next one."

Through a round of drinks, Harry, himself, told the story of how he and Sparkles had met. He ended it with them falling asleep on the sofa and leaving that tidbit for his captive audience to digest, he whisked Sparkles away. Before they reached the exit, she pulled away from him, went straight up to the firefighter, leaned in, and like a dog, she sniffed his neck. "Yeah, I thought so!" she said with a smirk. Holding her head high, she linked arms with Harry, and they casually strolled out of the establishment.

In the parking lot, Harry remarked, "You sure do have a way with people."

"Well, they're my species! Like it or not."

Looking at her sideways, Harry was visibly puzzled. "What was that sniffing all about?"

"I wanted to see if he smelled like burning forest. He did not. He smelled like cheap cologne. Firefighter, my foot!" She opened her purse and added more lipstick to her lemon infused lips. "Hey, what you did back there ... that was very sweet of you, Harry. What made you do it? What about Reba?"

"Besides telling me she doesn't date truck drivers, Reba was wrong to treat you like that. I pretty much told her so." He paused and added sheepishly, "Although, I kind of wish you hadn't told the part about falling asleep together."

"Well ... you told it back there to Phil and his harem."

"Yes, I know. I did that for you. You do know nothing happened between us, don't you?"

Sparkles looked down at the ground and pinched her dress. "Yes, I know that. It just felt so good pretending that someone liked me, especially someone kind and vibrant like you. I'm sorry I made you so uncomfortable."

"And I am sorry I'm so uncomfortable with the idea of being with an older woman. I really don't know why that is, but it is."

"A much older woman," Sparkles conceded. "If I were to be really honest with myself, Harry, I probably *should* be uncomfortable with the idea of being with a much younger man. Weird, huh?" She fished through her purse again and held up his driver's license. "I tried to get this to you earlier, HAROLD, but I guess you wrote down the wrong phone number."

Harry looked away in shame.

"It's probably best you don't go in the Golden Nail Salon on Third. Everyone working there knows who you are now." She covered her mouth and giggled. "Good night,

Harry … and thanks again." With a little wave of surrender, and a misty-eyed farewell, she turned to walk away.

"Wait, wait!" Harry frantically stepped toward her. "How's, how's your foot?"

She turned around slowly, surprised to see the anxious look on his face. "Thank you for asking. Working just fine … see?" she said, breaking into a Texas two-step in her fancy high heels. "Too bad the firefighter won't be taking me dancing any time soon."

"It must be great to feel younger than you are. I hope I feel like you do when I'm your age, Sparkles. Well, heck, I'd like to feel like you do right now, at *my* age. And you're so refreshingly bold … and honest. In my opinion, that firefighter is missing out. You're much more fun to be with than any girl I've ever met."

"I am?" Maude sucked in a sniffle.

"Yes, you are." Harry shuffled his feet. "Do you think we could be friends?"

Maude stood silently basking in the request. A playful chuckle leapt from her throat. "Only if you promise not to run over my foot again."

"I'm afraid I can't make that promise. I have two left feet, but I'll try really hard not to step on your foot on the dance floor." Harry cocked his head and offered his most sincere smile.

"And I would really like to ride in your monster rig … wait! Dancing? Did you say dancing?" Sparkle's moist eyes twinkled.

"Yeah, let's go dancing, Maude."

"Oh, what a fine idea … Harold!"

Then it hit them both at the same time. "Harold and Maude!"

"Oh my gosh!" Maude squealed with delight. "That's my all-time favorite movie."

"Mine, too!" Harold bellowed and gave her a high five. "Wait a second, that's who you've been quoting all along!"

"The earth is my body. My head is in the stars!" Maude recited, swirling around in a circle, her arms reaching for the sky. "I've been trying to live the rest of my life like that wonderful character."

"Who sends dead flowers to a funeral? It's absurd." Harold mimicked, looping Maude's arm around his as they walked into the darkness.

"Everyone should be able to make some music. That's the cosmic dance," Maude recounted tenderly.

Harold stopped and looked up at the heavenly stars above.

"Maude?"

"Oh my, I never liked my name until just now hearing you say it like that. Say it again, please, Harold."

"Maude … do you pray?"

"Pray? No, I communicate," she said easily, looking up and joining him in his gaze.

"With God?"

"With life."

And in that perfect illogical moment, Harold gave Maude an honest kiss. And he was not just being kind.

# Wake Up Dorothy!

## BY LIBBY BELLE

Scenes from my life are flashing before me from an old Bell and Howell Super 8 movie projector. Each one flutters by, colorless, a dull patina flattening the images, the camera moving slow, then fast, and then crazy-like as if the person behind the lens wanted to speed up their miserable life. I see my mother, her strained smile and narrowed reproachful eyes, her plump body bouncing around like a balloon being carried by a toddler, her finger wagging, always scolding. My boyfriend Landon is popping his head in and out of the picture frame, making sure he is seen, "What about *me*?" he cries, shaking his long dirty blonde hair wildly like a rock star as he plays air guitar. His fake grin is exposing his pale upper gums, and his top lip is stuck to his braces. No, he's not a teenager … he's twenty-seven.

Now the camera jerks away and points to the sky and the bare trees and then it suddenly lands on its side filming a line of marching ants, a crashed bicycle wheel—the spokes going around and around—and just beyond that, there's me, running barefoot up a hill in my favorite green hippie dress, in the background an old employee punch-out clock is making that clunky clicking noise over and over again until the scene cracks and the film slowly begins to burn, and I hear a faint voice from faraway.

"Snap out of it, Dorothy!" my co-worker yells again in my ear, and I am jolted back to reality—me at work holding my empty stained coffee cup.

Drifting off like that is not unusual these days because I've been in a strange kind of sleep mode ever since I met Landon. And by the way, my name's not Dorothy, but because of my frequent visits to OZ, they call me that at work. Before Landon came along, I could see clearly, the rich color of butter, children playing in the park, pictures of Paris on my refrigerator, the things I bought with my own hard-earned money. But now, everything seems to be coated in a film of Vaseline, and it's really not his fault. Really.

Landon was special, and although I was the only one who thought so, I convinced myself that given the chance, this ordinary person would eventually meet his full potential all because of my unselfish love. Just watch! I have so much to give, he will blossom right before my eyes, and then everyone will see what I see that they don't see. And just wait until his braces come off!

I'm now working two jobs plus overtime to put this budding human being through college. Quitting school in his second year and wasting away four more years on odd jobs, surfing, and dimwitted girls, Landon confessed, with those flickering blue eyes, that he wanted to go back and get his degree. But at his age, without the means, how could he? And that thing about his attention deficit disorder really pushed my pity button. How lucky for him that I stepped into his miserable life and offered to pave, well, okay, pay the way, as he shamelessly agreed to let me work to the bone for him while he enriched his mind, learned to braid his own hair, and beefed up his pectoral muscles.

Of course, he moved in with me after the arrangement was made. I would pay the rent, the groceries, the utilities, the whole shebang and never mention it or make him feel bad about it. All he had to do was pass his classes in between going to the gym. A bargain for a man with such possibilities! And did I mention his muscles?

On my only night off, we went to parties, always at a student's place. I was embarrassed to hang out with these people nearly eight years younger than me, but Landon explained that they were taking the same classes and there was much for them to talk about since the subjects were fresh in their heads. I tried to fit in, but usually I was so tired from working nonstop, I found myself falling asleep in a chair or, if lucky enough, in the bedroom, if not already occupied by students having wild, random sex while high on their drug of choice.

Jealous, that's what he called me whenever I suggested that we go to a movie instead, or even stay home and have dinner together with music, a game of cards, or that crazy all-white puzzle my mother gave me along with her words of wisdom, "Figure this out, and maybe you'll figure out your own life."

Jealous? Not a word I wanted to sully my list of praiseworthy traits, so from then on, I bowed out gracefully as he cheerily walked out the door with a twenty he had snatched from my purse, so he could at least buy some beer because no one should ever go to a party empty handed. No way, man! Not cool!

The first year of this grueling routine nearly wiped me out, but I never protested once, nor did I tell him that the rent had gone up. Considerably. During that time, he managed to pass his classes, barely, and I managed to get a raise and more hours which allowed us to have a little extra cash for maybe a nice dinner out, or rather, pet bills; because one day while I was slaving away, waiting on tables at the local restaurant, he walked by the plate glass window with a puppy in his arms and waved the little guy's paws at me. The "Can I have him" look was plastered all over his face, and the puppy was as cute and irresistible as a puppy can be, especially in my love's arms. With everyone watching the scene from their tables, their eyes pleading along with Landon's, what else could I do but nod a yes and offer a cheesy smile, which I quickly dropped like a hot hard-boiled egg when turning away from view, knowing full well that having a pet would raise the rent and my blood pressure.

I don't think I ever hated an animal in my entire life, but this canine turned out to be a demon dog. Nothing was spared from Gilligan's razor-sharp teeth, and when he gnawed off the claws of the lion's paws on my grandmother's antique dresser, I cried for the longest, cross-legged on the floor, while the mutt yapped like crazy from behind the bathroom door where I heard him chewing and scratching on the door jamb as if it were coated in melted beef jerky. But even with mangled shoes, the strap of my only good purse wrapped in duct tape, the bristles of my hairbrush stuck between Gilligan's teeth, I would not let this dog from hell distract me from my goal. I will get Landon through school even if it kills me!

Only five more months, Landon reminded me after I threw myself face down on the living room floor and fell fast asleep, waking up in the middle of the night with dog hair stuck to my tongue. A mere hundred and fifty days and Landon will have his degree, and I know that, humbled with gratitude, he'll become the man of the house, get a fabulous job, pay the rent, and I can quit work, stay at home, wear muumuus, and take Gilligan for long walks while my boney white arms get a much-needed tan. But not until then will we finally clinch the deal with those three little unspoken, unrealized, one-syllable words that will make everything perfect, "I love you." We got drunk on cheap wine toasting to his graduation on my Saturday night off, and I was knocked out by nine o'clock while Landon left with his buddies to celebrate passing yet another semester.

Christmas, finally, a three-day weekend with nothing else to do but rig a small tree in the corner of the apartment and watch *Christmas Vacation* in front of my giant poster of a flaming fireplace while Landon went skiing with his brother. My gift. After all, someone had to stay home with the mutt. I'm pathetic, and I know it, so I offered to feed the neighbor's python for extra cash.

She's cute, petite, big-breasted for her size, and her hips couldn't hold up a pair of hip-huggers even with a belt. But she is smart and a great tutor, Landon claimed, and it was necessary that he have help with the final course of the year if he were to graduate. So, while I was at work, stocking Ranch Style beans, he was at home with Luna studying his little heart out. Landon soon reported that he felt adequately prepared for the final exams *all* because of *her.*

Someone at work asked me if I was depressed. I avoided that unsettling question and instead of my usual lunch in the back of the meat section where we could have all the six-day-old cold cuts we could eat, I walked right past the black plastic curtains and out the front door without removing my work apron. I didn't even punch out as regulations required.

I found myself sitting on a park bench reading the carved initials and philosophical sayings etched in its old soft wood. Words like, "The end of the world was yesterday," and "Screw your teacher for an A," stuff like that. I rubbed my fingers across the letters and imagined the young and carefree students who had all that leisurely time to sit there carving into the wood well enough for it to be legible. Never having experienced that life, I felt sadness for myself and my stupidity, and my only goal, to lift Landon to a higher level as I sunk deeper into my ineptness.

Curious, I stood up and looked at the carvings where my bottom had been sitting and saw two letters I recognized— two large L's. I twisted my head around and positioned it just so to read the rest. Luna + Landon. It read just that, Luna + Landon. Hoping no one had seen me, I quickly sat down, looking cautiously around as if I had just found a wallet full of money. What are the odds that there is another Luna and another Landon besides the ones that are under my ass?

Have you ever been so tired that you were too tired to sleep? Tossing and turning was becoming a nightly routine, so naturally I moved to the sofa to allow Landon that precious REM sleep he claimed was necessary to keep him focused. Have you ever been so tired that you didn't notice you were fifteen pounds lighter than your usual weight? So tired that you didn't remember if you had brushed your teeth, filled the gas tank, shut the refrigerator door, took the clothes from the washer to the dryer? I was so tired I didn't even know I was tired. Now that's effing tired!

What's more, I was so weary, I thought that I had dreamed about the L+L names carved in the bench and let that potentially disastrous clue fly right out the window. But when I picked up one of Landon's school books and out dropped a note with a big 'L' in a swoopy loopy font surrounded by a heart, I could not deny that clue number two was more than a figment of my imagination. Matter of fact, that little note that promised more sex like the last time, thrust me into a whole new dimension. But by the time my only day off was right before me, and it just happened to be my twenty-ninth birthday, and poor Landon had to attend his great aunt's funeral, I was relieved that I wouldn't have to challenge him. I slept through the entire day in the same position until I woke up in the middle of the night to a dark empty apartment—a reminder of the denial I was in.

"Happy Birthday to me."

I sat up in bed and had the same recurring vision of me riding my bicycle in my green hippie dress. Then suddenly I'm running barefoot up a path to nowhere. Before I get to the top, the scene fades to black and what remains on the other side is a mystery.

One day I decided to come home for lunch. I don't even remember driving, much less walking up the steps, but I became aware when I heard voices coming from the bathroom. I stood at the door and listened. I heard giggling, then a sudden hush, then a gasp for air and something like a bar of soap dropping to the shower floor with a thud, and then the sound of water hitting the wall in a constant rhythm with sighs or groans, or both, but whatever they were doing in there, I was certain that they weren't scrubbing down the shower together. I could have opened the door and caused a scene, but maybe I didn't want to see what I already saw in my own fuzzy imagination, which was probably not near as good as what I'd actually see.

I went to the refrigerator, took out a chicken leg from dinner two days back and ate it with a wilted salad I found behind a gallon of something green. I sat there eyeing the bathroom door until I heard the water turn off and them moving around, talking. I took my last bite, grabbed an apple next to two oranges coated in mold fuzz and turned to leave. Just when I did, Luna came out of the bathroom wrapped in a towel with my shower cap on her head. She stood there dumbfounded looking at me, and when I smiled at her, she dropped the towel, but not her surprised expression. I took a big crunchy symbolic bite out of the apple, and I left.

I'm guessing we had a quiet understanding between us because none of us ever spoke about that day. It just kind of got pulled into "The Suck Zone," like the other clues, landing some place where secrets and birthdays go to die.

The day of the final exams, I came home early with a serious headache and found Landon pacing the floor in worry. When I asked what was on his mind, he expressed his fear of not passing and what the consequences would mean. He looked nervous when he asked me where we stood if he had to take another year of classes. I didn't have an answer for him because I was frankly feeling too ill to think about the future and what it might hold, for mine was so bland it was not worth considering. And besides, deep down inside, I was in a bizarre way enjoying the unattractive, pitiful anguish on his usually smug face. Instead, I offered to help him study, but he decided that a beer with his buds is really what he needed, so I handed him my wallet, shoved the dog off the sofa, and curled up in my usual fetal position. Oddly enough, my headache went away shortly after I heard the door slam.

I awoke to the big day when I would come home late that evening to hear the verdict. For a moment I nursed a sense of pride that I did not renege on a promise. I truly went into this arrangement with Landon purely from the heart. He had a goal, and I didn't. Why not help this soul achieve his? La dee da, what a wonderful selfless act, and I fulfilled my part without complaints, excuses, or judgement. I'm a saint! Another chapter of my life would begin all based on Landon's success.

I knew when he didn't come home, that he had failed.

I blew out the candles burned down to less than an inch of their life, put the cake and the champagne in the refrigerator, and crawled into bed still wearing my long green hippie dress. It was my favorite, silky and backless with thin spaghetti straps. The full chiffon fabric felt like a fine sheet against my skin. I wrapped my body in it, and with the bed all to myself, and no dog sniffing my feet, I slept like a baby for reasons I would figure out later.

The following morning, it took everything I had to call my mother and give her the news about Landon. I dealt briskly with the delusion that I could handle another year of supporting him. Her silence said it all. "I know what you're thinking, mom … I'm pitiful." I hung up before she could say, "I told you so."

My cruiser bicycle has been used as a clothes rack for much too long, so I removed all the scarves, socks, and panties from its metal protrusions, aired up the tires and took off for a nice long Saturday morning ride to nowhere in particular. Remaining in my green dress, I tied the flowing fabric between my legs. The campus was the last place I wanted to go, but somehow, I ended up there and in my bare feet.

The school grounds were empty; no sign of anyone, anywhere. I enjoyed zooming around the carless spaces, in and out of the 'reserved for teachers only' area and along the vacant sidewalk covered with thousands of black, fried and flattened gum glops carelessly spit out from the mouths of our future leaders. I could almost hear my tires screaming in delight as we flew down the hill toward the park where students studied, or smoked pot, or groped one another in between classes.

Wheeeee!

I rode through the thick woods, dodging tree limbs and squirrels, the sun racing with me through the shadows from the towering limbs overhead. I was beginning to feel and see the beauty around me, so much that I spotted a path leading to the top of a hill, like the one I've been imagining. I jumped off my bike and began running up it. When I got to the top, it hit me! I'm free! Free, at last! I stood there looking down at the new world below. It was then that I knew exactly what I was going to do next, and I felt wonderful, even ecstatic about my decision.

Back down the pathway and back on my bicycle, I took off. Could it be that easy? Yes, yes, yes, I squealed with delight, and when I came out of the woods to the main street, I stepped on the breaks just in time to avoid colliding with a car zipping by right in front of me. What a close call! I could have been killed! I was spared. But why me? Is there another purpose in store for me?

My heart is pounding in my chest. My hands are shaking. My feet are on fire. I'm so fucking alive! Across the street I see Landon and Luna walking down the sidewalk, hand in hand, heads bent as if in a serious conversation, the devil dog lunging ahead of them on a taut leash. I yell, "Landon, Luna, Gilligan! I'm awake!"

Spotting me, they quickly let go of each other's hands and gave me a stiff wave. At least the dog was happy to see me as he broke loose and ran in my direction. I stood up on the pedals and moved toward them, when suddenly a cargo van with a goofy looking giraffe painted on its side panel swerved to keep from running over Gilligan and hit me instead, head on. I was thrown like a beer bottle from the bike to the curb.

Everything went cerulean blue.

I don't know how long I was on my back looking up at the cloudless sky, completely motionless, not a feeling or awareness of my body at all. It was the most marvelous sleep state ever, and when Gilligan's rough tongue licked my nose clean, and Landon and Luna appeared above me, their faces distorted, their eyes full of guilt, and wait a second—when did Landon get his braces taken off? I'm sure that I smiled before I closed my eyes and let the warm light lift me.

"Wake up, Dorothy!" someone whispered from far away.

While I was being rocked in the softest angel's wings, I said my very last words to Landon, loud and bold, as clear as day, words I had kept inside me for two whole years, words that I had practiced over and over just for him that were bursting to come out. Words that meant more to me than anything. Just three little one-syllable words. "The rent's due!"

## Gerald Gaul

Gerald Gaul started his adult life as a doctor. While continuing an active career as an Ophthalmologist, he studied early violin performance and researched the development of the violin bow in the years between 1750 and 1850. This research led to his first book, *The Missing Strad: The Story of the World's Greatest Violin Forgery.* According to Kirkus reviews, the book is "An entertaining ramble through a golden age of violin-playing and violin-faking." Dr. Gaul presently serves as Vice Chairman at the National Music Museum in Vermillion, South Dakota.

He lives in Atlanta Georgia, and in addition to writing, he plays viola in the Georgia Philharmonic Orchestra and the World Doctor's Orchestra. His day job is an optical company, Gaul Ophthalmic Services, LLC.

# The Love Tourist

BY GERALD GAUL

We had been together just a little over a week when Sophie, my Argentine girlfriend, announced that she was no longer in love with me. The day of the announcement we were sightseeing in the Palermo neighborhood of Buenos Aires. I couldn't figure out why she was walking me up the hill and away from the things to see near the Japanese Gardens. It looked to me like we were going to visit one of Sophie's friends. We entered an old apartment building, she introduced me to an old man, and I thought to myself, is this one of Sophie's old boyfriends? We went into the man's library and Sophie took up the spot on a fainting couch while the old man and I sat in comfy chairs across from her. My Spanish is not great, and it took me a while to understand that the old man was Sophie's psychotherapist.

Sophie's therapist took meeting me very seriously. The therapist struggled to put his most important psychological insight into English so that I would understand. "She still loves you, but she's no longer in love with you." Over the years, I'd gotten this news fairly often in the United States. Sophie was the first person to ever deliver it through her therapist.

Sophie explained her situation more thoroughly after the session. The problem boiled down to one thing. Sophie told me that she was a narcissist. She told me that she was incapable of understanding the wants and needs of others. Years of therapy had revealed this truth to her, and she wanted me to understand so that I didn't become too emotionally invested in her.

We agreed that I should return to the United States. Sophie thought I should go right away, but I wanted to wait. I was enjoying the hot January weather. Once the Argentine summer was over, I planned to return to the United States and have another summer fling up there. Surely my Argentine girlfriend could hold back her narcissism for a couple months so I wouldn't have to face up to my seasonal depression back in the United States. Another factor made me want things to work out longer with Sophie—I had met her under the most perfect of Argentine conditions, the New Year's Eve Milonga.

Those not familiar with tango culture cannot possibly understand the New Year's Eve Milonga. Every Argentine woman plans for the New Year's Eve Milonga for months in advance. Red underwear is a must, because it signals hope for a new love in the new year. Even married women buy red panties. Argentine men do not wear red underwear. At least, I don't believe they do; it would show through the traditional light-colored New Year's Eve dress pants. Argentine men put their real effort into picking out nice New Year's Eve Milonga tango shoes. Once at the milonga, a hopeful male dancer must, using subtle signs, indicate from across the room that he wishes to dance with some attractive Argentine woman. Her decision is often made by a quick examination of the man's shoes. A man with pristine new tango shoes is probably a good dancer. A man in sneakers certainly will not be. Men's tango shoes are not comfortable. They are built on faulty assumptions about men's feet—that men's feet are narrow and that the little toe and the big toe have been surgically removed. Any decent man who can feel pain will limp horribly once tango shoes are laced. If a man can smile through the pain of wearing tango shoes, he can probably tolerate the discomforts involved in dating in Argentina.

I had beautiful tango shoes and had learned to put my foot pains out of my mind. I planned to go to the New Year's Eve Milonga in San Telmo, one of the oldest parts of Buenos Aires. One of the charms of San Telmo is that most of the buildings are from the early twentieth century. The milonga venue had clearly once been magnificent. Looking at its limestone facade, I thought that perhaps in happier times it had been a bank. The milonga was being held on the second floor, which in Buenos Aires is called the first floor. The stairway up was painted black and poorly lit, and I briefly had the sense that I was going up to a bordello. The ballroom did very little to contradict the staircase; it had a tin ceiling and ornate wood paneling that had been painted over several times too many.

I was early. It was only ten PM, so nothing had started. It was time for me to drink some Champagne. Not, of course, real Champagne. Chandon, of Moët and Chandon, makes a local Argentine variety of bubbly white wine. It comes in a frustratingly tiny 187 ml bottle. To quench my thirst, I had to return to the bar several times, negotiating the perilous transaction in pesos every time. After my third trip to the bar the music started. I held myself off to the side, as though I didn't really want to dance. The pot-bellied local men found partners right away. There was a tiny group of young women who held back. One of the women looked at my shoes and then looked up at me hopefully. That woman was Sophie.

The wine made me bold, and Sophie was willing. The evening appeared to have promise as we made our way to the dance floor. It was a tango that I knew, although unfortunately, not "Por una Cabesa," the tango that was playing when the blind Al Pacino character danced with the young girl in *Scent of a Woman*. Sophie, who smelled a little bit like sweaty gym socks, was a great dancer. She followed my every move as though we had been born for each other. The crowds in Buenos Aires dance in a great counter-clockwise circle, mimicking the paradoxical Southern Hemisphere rotation of water in a toilet. Sophie and I danced this circle like our own little turd, as though we were ready to head through the sewage system down to the La Plata River, where the right-wing dictatorship used to discard the bodies of its real and imagined enemies.

Too soon, the flush was complete, and the dance ended. Sophie pulled me close, wanting to whisper something in my ear. Everyone was talking. I strained to hear her. I could tell she was choosing her words carefully, not knowing if I understood Spanish. Oh, but I do, I do! Her voice was soft. It smelled a bit like cigarettes. What she said was this: "You are not doing this right."

In my broken Spanish, I carefully explained the subtle differences in how Argentines dance the tango and how the Americans do. Argentine Tango encourages women to make elaborate moves that make their partners feel completely inadequate and American Tango does not. I was more polite in my explanation. Still, Sophie was having none of it. "I speak English perfectly well. My mother taught English in La

Plata. Not only do you have trouble dancing our dance, but you also have problems speaking our speech. Your lack of skill is not in the moves you allow me to perform. Your problem is much more basic. You do not know how to walk."

What she meant was that I did not have the over-bearing gait of the average Argentine. This complaint did not keep her from dancing with me for the rest of the night, nor did it keep her from going back with me to my hotel. She made it clear that she was not interested in sex. My hotel, the Hilton in Puerto Madero, shows up in a lot of Argentine movies and TV shows. She wanted to see it for real. After she had seen the lobby of the hotel, she wanted to see my room. Once there, she plopped herself down on the second queen-sized bed and went right to sleep. I was too polite to wake her up and send her home, so she stayed with me. And that is how Sophie became my Argentine girlfriend.

I was willing to change the way I danced tango. But Sophie's concerns, expressed in more detail on New Year's Day, were more global. She complained about my walking, even out on the street. From her point of view, I walked all hunched over. I did not hold her hand right. Nor did I speak English correctly and my Spanish was hopeless. She explained to me that I spoke Mexican Spanish. The Argentines use a different word for "to drink" and "you." I needed more artful ways of cursing as well. Also, I hesitated too much when I spoke. It sounded like a stutter, or like I was imitating Porky Pig.

Even before we met with her therapist, it was never clear to me if I was the problem or she was. Or perhaps, there was no problem at all. After the visit to her therapist, I suggested to Sophie that perhaps the cultural differences between us were at the root of our conflicts. This idea, in her view, was a sign that I had a serious mental illness, perhaps psychosis.

She was convinced that it was time for me to see my own therapist. She had one all picked out: Dr. Garcia in Monserrat. He spoke English and he practiced not far from Puerto Madero. On top of all that, he looked exactly like Sigmund Freud. I objected to going. She told me that she also knew of a therapist that looked like Carl Jung and one that looked like Alfred Adler. I could have my choice.

The appointment was for me, but Dr. Garcia greeted Sophie with the most enthusiasm. "Miss Sophie Gallo! How nice to see you again. What have you brought in for me this time?"

"Dr. Garcia, this is David Bramley. He's an American tango dancer and he's visiting Buenos Aires for the summer."

"Sophie, it's always the same story, isn't it? You know that your constant attempts to undo the past with a new boyfriend is a defense mechanism against overwhelming anxiety, hmm?"

I found it very strange that Dr. Garcia knew so much about Sophie. I wondered if perhaps Dr. Garcia was her second therapist. Perhaps her first therapist interpreted Sophie's dreams and Dr. Garcia was in charge of figuring out Sophie's love relationships. Or perhaps they were both former boyfriends. Perhaps she just had a thing for shrinks. I could not escape the sense that Sophie was herself studying psychology. Perhaps her doctoral thesis was a careful analysis of the abnormal psychology of American men. Maybe Dr. Garcia was supervising the whole project. Perhaps I was merely a part of an experimental protocol. Before I had a chance to sort out any of this, we were moving towards Dr. Garcia's office.

"Mr. Bramley, come into my study. I have many

questions. Do you mind if Miss Gallo joins us? Of course you don't. She can help you translate."

I did mind that Sophie was going to sit in on the session. I didn't really want to see Dr. Garcia. I didn't want to have Sophie interpreting my every thought like she examined my every move and word. I wondered, did going along with Sophie's craziness make me a crazy person too?

Dr. Garcia did look a lot like Sigmund Freud. His office looked to be a replica of Dr. Freud's Vienna consulting room and was at least as old. There was worn carpet on the floor. There was a big wooden desk by the window. There were tall bookcases with leather bound books. Just like Sophie's other therapist's library, there were two comfortable chairs. Dr. Garcia took one and Sophie took the other. My spot was the fainting couch. The couch was old and worn. It had only a slight elevation at the head end. This head end was the problem. Every part of the upholstery was dirty, but the head end looked greasy, as though a thousand unwashed heads had gotten there before me. I couldn't help but point and ask, "Do you have something to put over this?"

"Mr. Bramley, I'm sorry to report that all my antimacassars are at the cleaners. Ms. Gallo, do you have one?"

"I'm sorry Doctor, I forgot all mine at home."

"Oh dear, it seems that Mr. Bramley has to put his head where others have put their heads. Mr. Bramley, sit down please. That couch belonged to my predecessor. He lost the antimacassar in the 1970s. During the 1980s, he treated the recovering torture victims of the right-wing dictatorship. For those poor men, leaving a stain on the couch was the most they could expect from their miserable lives. And now you can't be bothered to leave your own stain? If it distresses you, I'm sure you have a freshly laundered white handkerchief in your pocket. All obsessive-compulsive men like you have one. Use that."

As a matter of fact, I did have a freshly laundered white handkerchief in my pocket. But I wasn't going to give Dr. Garcia the satisfaction of seeing me use it. I sat down and laid my head back. "Good! Now Mr. Bramley, I want you to relax. You might know that there is a wonderful lake in the south of Argentina, San Carlos de Bariloche. I want you to imagine that you are on a boat on that lake. Perhaps you are fishing or sunning yourself. I want you to feel fully satisfied with how things have worked out for you. You are a success and you own a boat and you are on a beautiful lake and there is no one to bother you. You have no regrets about your past. Imagine that you are guilty of some terrible crime against humanity. Even so, you are perfectly calm. It doesn't bother you that you used to be a Nazi and that now you and your ill-gotten stash of gold reside in Argentina. It doesn't bother you that you introduced an invasive fish species to the lake and that all the sport fish have been replaced by a monoculture of trout. All you are thinking of is the German word for trout, Forelle. Whatever feelings of guilt or anxiety you deserve to have, you only need think of this one word, Forelle, and all is right with the world."

Dr. Garcia made this hypnotic suggestion with an air of longing, as though San Carlos de Bariloche was his happy place and he hoped someday to be an old Nazi there. In spite of myself, I did relax. Trout is my favorite fish. I had never thought of the German word for trout, but it did sound nicer than the Spanish word, trucha.

"Now, Miss Gallo, I have a few questions. What is your psychiatric diagnosis?"

She replied without hesitation, "I'm a narcissist."

"Ah yes, I remember now. And are you still an other-directed perfectionist? Do you still routinely criticize others in order to support your own self-esteem?"

I felt that I had something to say and lifted up my head. "Oh yes, she does. She complains about everything. The way I dance, the way I walk, the way I speak Spanish. I'm fine, but she complains endlessly about me."

Both Dr. Garcia and Sophie glared at me, and I sank back into the oil stain. "Mr. Bramley, Forelle. Think of yourself on the lake and how beautiful that German word is." He turned back towards Sophie. "Miss Gallo, are you still other-directed with your perfectionism?"

"Yes, doctor."

"And how about the Karpman Triangle of Drama? Where do you sit on that?"

"Well, I can play the persecutor or the rescuer, but mostly I feel comfortable in the victim role."

I lifted my head up to look. Both of them were staring at me with contempt. Dr. Garcia slowly shifted his gaze to Sophie. "You know this is why you choose men like Mr. Bramley." I tried to say something, but Dr. Garcia put a hand out and said, "Forelle, Mr. Bramley, Gott im Himmel, Forelle!"

"Now Miss Gallo, what is your classification with the Interpersonal Circumplex?" This sudden move into psychiatric jargon alarmed me. I almost sat up, but I was dealing with my own intrusive thoughts about fishing for invasive trout.

Sophie spoke. "Doctor, do you mean the IAS, the ICL, or the IBI?"

"I know them all. Give me your position on any one of them and I can transpose it."

"Oh, fine. On the 1982 Interpersonal Circumplex I'm

C1, Suspicious and Resentful. I tend to present myself to others as K2, Gullible and Merciful."

"Have you ever been C2, Paranoid and Vindictive?"

"Oh, no doctor. My mother was C2. She once shot my father with a pistol. Fortunately, it was small caliber. My father was highly enabling. He told the police that he accidentally shot his leg as he was cleaning the gun. My mother still has the gun. She would threaten me with it when I was a child. The psychic injury is one of the reasons I'm so narcissistic now. I could never be C2 like my mother."

This exchanged seemed to satisfy Dr. Garcia. He went to the shelf and pulled out a book, La Guía Completa de Relaciones Amorosas Patológicas. He sat down and started paging through the book. After a few minutes of study, he closed the book and addressed me. "Mr. Bramley, you can come home from the lake now. Imagine that a butterfly has floated by and your idyll was interrupted by the German word for butterfly, Schmetterling. Now you are back in Buenos Aires and in my office. You are still relaxed and ready to hear and accept what I have to say."

He paused dramatically, looked at Sophie with a smile and then said to me, "You are a hopeless co-dependent."

This was too much. I sat up from the oil slick. "What kind of phony doctor are you? You haven't talked to me about anything, and already you know what my problem is? Have you ever seriously considered that you might be mentally ill?" Dr. Garcia was genuinely surprised by my outburst. He stared forlornly at the worn carpet in front of his chair.

Sophie spoke almost right away. "Oh, great, David. Now look what you've done! Dr. Garcia is only trying to understand and help you. Your response is to viciously attack him. I'm honestly ashamed of you." She turned towards Dr. Garcia and asked, "Dr. Garcia, are you ok?"

Dr. Garcia raised his head up to look at Sophie. He studied her face and then his eyes became wide and he smiled at her. "Your therapist must think you are the most wonderful patient in the world."

"Doctor, you are too kind. But we're here for David. Remember?"

"Oh yes, Mr. Bramley. I was about to tell him that it is easiest to determine his psychopathology from a determination of his preferred love partner. Because you have so much insight into yourself, I don't actually need to deal with Mr. Bramley and his denial, projection, transference, and so on. You are what you are, and you know what you are. What you are determines who he is. It is as simple as that. Mr. Bramley could be thankful that I've come up with his correct diagnosis in a single session. But his mind is too disorganized for that."

They both looked at me. I was absolutely speechless. I wanted to say, "I'm not the crazy one here," but I was clearly outvoted. Once again, Dr. Garcia looked at Sophie and smiled. "Miss Gallo, Mr. Bramley may suddenly become fully psychotic. Do you have a plan?"

"I don't know. My family is full of neurotics and borderline psychotics. I don't have much experience with psychotic patients. What do you recommend?"

"Try to keep Mr. Bramley from being over-stimulated. Perhaps take him out into the countryside."

Just like that, the session was over. Sophie thanked Dr. Garcia profusely and he gave her a hug and kissed her cheeks as we left. He turned to me and clicked his heels. "Auf Wiedersehen, Herr Bramley. Come back anytime if you need more help."

We walked out of Dr. Garcia's office and into the heat of the late afternoon. I was struck by a sudden, overwhelming desire to be normal, but I could not keep myself from thinking about a boat on a mountain lake. Sophie took my hand and squeezed it. "Forelle, Forelle. Don't worry, this will all turn out fine."

We walked towards the "Pink House," the Argentine equivalent of the United States White House. There was a sightseeing bus stopped right in front of it. These buses constantly run from one end of Buenos Aires to the other and stop at all the local tourist spots along the way. We paid and hopped on. The air conditioning in the bus was a perfect relief from the sweltering heat outside. The bus made its way west. We passed the English Tower, the commuter airport, the large mechanical flower, and the horse track. We sat in silence, looking out the window and watching the video monitor as it explained what we were passing by and what we could see at the next stop. The bus went as far west as the Naval Academy, the buildings where the right-wing dictatorship tortured and murdered people in the early 1980s. Then the bus turned east, back towards the Pink House. We got off at the Recoleta Cemetery in Palermo. It was evening and already cooler. We paid to go into the cemetery and made a beeline to Eva Peron's mausoleum, then wandered silently and aimlessly through the remaining paths.

Finally, I spoke. "Are you really a narcissist?"

"I've always wanted to be. I imagine myself not caring about anyone or anything and think of how nice that would be. Not to care."

"Why do you spend so much of your energy on people like Dr. Garcia? You know that he's crazy and yet you make me pay him to tell me that I'm crazy and that nothing can be done about it. How does that help anything?"

"I feel sorry for Dr. Garcia. Those people who were tortured in the 1980s? They are still around. They were young then, but they are middle aged or older now. The government pays for their therapy with doctors like Dr. Garcia. Those people who disappeared into the Naval Academy when they were young are never going to be normal. They were tortured then and they still are tortured now. Those poor souls can't make sense of it and Dr. Garcia has to find a way to make sense of it for them. He has to be optimistic even when there is no reason to be. He loves seeing patients like you. First, he can afford to tell you that you are hopeless because he knows you won't listen to him. Second, he knows that you are not hopeless at all. He knows that whatever traumatic experiences you have had are nothing. He's well-meaning. But he's angry that Argentina is filled to overflowing with people who can never recover and that places like the United States are filled with people who could recover but won't."

We came back to Evita's tomb. The crowd was less, and we stood in front of the crypt. I turned towards Sophie. "Are you one of those people who will never recover?" She turned towards me and held me close. "David, I've noticed that you are walking better. Thank you for listening to me and fixing yourself. It means a lot."

The embrace surprised me, and as we turned to leave the tomb I slipped and stumbled. Sophie laughed "I guess I spoke too soon. Your walking may be getting worse. Maybe it's better if you go back to walking your stupid American way."

We came out of the shadow of the crypt and walked by the regular tombstones. It was late enough in the day that things had cooled off and it was a pleasant stroll. Sophie stopped me in front a grave. All the tombstone had was a name and dates, but nonetheless Sophie studied it intently. The person had died in the 1940s. I asked, "Do you know this family?"

"Not at all. This gravestone reminds me of my burial plot."

"You have your own grave already?"

"Yes, I saved my money and bought a tombstone years ago. It's at my brother's place out in the country near La Plata. I sometimes go there to have a look at it. I know it seems silly, but I like to imagine the day when that tombstone is all that remains of me. I imagine it wearing down, becoming unreadable, and breaking up into dust. Then that will be the end of me. No one will remember and there won't be anything to remind them. When my life is hard, I think of how hard that stone is and try to be at least that hard. I try to hold on at least that well."

"Does it bother you that while you have to be a stone in La Plata, I get to be a Nazi in Bariloche?"

This joke seemed to please her. "Not at all. Well, maybe a little bit. I have an idea. Let's get away from Buenos Aires and go to the beach. We can drink Fernet and Cola and look out over the ocean."

I hate Fernet and Cola. Fernet is a bitter Italian liquor that the Coca Cola makes only marginally drinkable. I don't like the beach either. But in that moment, I liked Sophie, so I said yes.

Sophie's brother Manuel had just started a limousine service. He had borrowed money from their mother the English teacher and had bought a Peugeot sedan. This was a personal vehicle that he wanted, but could not afford, so he planned to pay back his mother by driving people around. Sophie and I and our trip to the beach at Mar del Plata would be his first job. Manuel had never driven in Puerto Madero and had never seen a hotel as fancy as the Hilton. His car looked fine, but when he got out of the car, he was so sloppily dressed that the doorman tried to chase him away. Sophie came out to argue with the doorman, but the dispute was not settled until I came out and allowed Manuel to put our bags in the trunk.

The trip to Mar del Plata took hours. There was a direct way that was a toll road and an indirect way that was not. The toll would have been trivial, but Manuel insisted on the economy route even though it took us two hours out of our way. I sat in the front seat with Manuel while Sophie played a game on her phone in the back seat. Manuel was irrationally excited about his new car business and wanted to talk about it beyond all reasonable limits. He had a loop of facts. The car was a good investment. It was a top-of-the-line Peugeot. It would become more valuable over time. Driving clients like me just a few days a month could make the car payment. Oh, and the car was a good investment. It was a top-of-the-line Peugeot.

I argued with him right away. The car was not becoming more valuable, it was just that the peso was shrinking. At some point in the future, the scrap paper value in the pesos needed to buy a car would be worth more than the car. But this did not mean the car was getting more valuable. It was a result of the peso getting smaller. This became my circle of conversation and our two circles wrapped around each other until we finally joined the main road to Mar del Plata. Then I made a new conversational gambit. I told him that it would be better if he started buying gold.

Sophie perked up in the back seat. She wedged herself forward between the front seats and whispered in my ear. "If you want to make this trip truly miserable, keep on talking to my brother about investing in gold."

This made me angry. I wanted to know, what makes Argentines so stupid about money? I looked over at the brother, studied his pock-marked face and his greasy long hair. I thought to myself, "You bastard, you're going to charge me a fortune for this trip. And when we get to Mar del Plata, you're going to want go to a bar and drink Fernet and Cola until your diabetic ass runs out of insulin. And then, driving back to Buenos Aires, you're going to run off the road. You'll ruin your car and your health. And all because you were too stupid to put your savings in gold."

I spoke. "I want to know, Manuel, why don't you put your money in gold?"

Sophie called forward from the back seat, "Don't go there. I'm telling you, don't go there. Manuel, you too. Why don't we stop somewhere and get a Fernet and Cola?"

"Manuel, tell me why not gold?"

Sophie, from the back seat, "Shit."

The traffic was bad, and we were almost at a standstill. Everyone was going to the beach. The women were going off to the beach to sun themselves until they developed skin cancer. Men were going to the beach to get paid for driving their personal cars, their precious Peugeots and Renaults. Everyone was going to the beach to drink Fernet and Cola. But I was going to the beach to force Manuel to explain to me in harsh economic terms why he was too stupid to put his money in gold.

He looked ready to cry, but looking straight ahead, he

started his story. "I live in a country." A country is the Argentine way of saying that they live on a larger plot of land in a rural area next to other larger plots. The communities are usually gated to keep the thieves out. "I had a good business buying and selling cars. I was making good money. I had a beautiful girlfriend, Sylvia." I believed every part of this up until the part about the girlfriend. What sort of woman pairs up with a loser like Manuel? "We were very happy, and we were saving up money to move to Nunez. I was a big fan of River and I thought we could rent a box at the stadium."

Nunez is a wealthy suburb in the western reaches of the Buenos Aries. "River" meant River Plate, the soccer team. There are two great soccer teams in Buenos Aires. Boca is in the eastern part and River Plate is in the western part. Boca fans are always fighting. You can recognize the fans because they always have a lot of teeth knocked out and they tend to live in the slums near the Boca Stadium. River fans also have a lot of teeth knocked out, but they have enough money to get implants or dentures. "I was saving money like crazy. I took my money to Corrientes Street and got dollars, then buried them in my yard. But no matter how carefully I wrapped them in plastic, they aways got a little wet and musty. I knew one of my neighbors was ready to buy a place in Buenos Aires. He had gold, but needed dollars, so we made an exchange. He dug up his gold in the middle of the night and we met at his house. It's the most dangerous thing in a country to move gold. People want to steal your dollars, but the idea that you might have gold drives people crazy. I carried the gold to my house in old leather bag. I loved how heavy it felt! It started raining, but I knew I had to get home and bury the gold before anyone found out. And I did get it buried. I buried it just south of my favorite apple tree, so that

I would know exactly where to find it when I needed it. I told no one about the gold, not even my girlfriend."

"Manuel, do you need a tissue, or are you ok?" Sophie from the back seat.

"Thank-you, but I think I'm going to be ok this time." Manuel stared straight ahead at the slowly moving cars ahead of him. "I'm going to get through this." I couldn't tell if Manuel was talking about the traffic, the story, or some other aggravation. "I was smart to have buried the gold so well. Word had gotten out about the money exchange and my neighbor was robbed of the dollars. He'd made the mistake of keeping the money in his house and the thieves had taken some sort of bulldozer to break into the wall of his bedroom. They had guns and forced my neighbor to give them all his dollars."

"Manuel, don't forget to say that he had a brick house."

Manuel shook his head up and down. "Yes, it was a brick house, that's why they needed the bulldozer. They couldn't just go through the wall with a chain saw like the thieves do with wooden houses. But I was happy, thinking of my gold buried ten paces south of my favorite apple tree. I didn't even go to look at the spot. My girlfriend knew that something was up, but I didn't tell her that I had the gold. I started wearing a River Plate jersey around the house. We were never so happy. I waited two weeks before I checked on the gold."

Like a reflex, Sophie handed Manuel a tissue. Even before the next sentence, Manuel's face contorted with pain and became blotchy. "When I finally decided to look to see the spot where I buried the gold. I couldn't find it. I couldn't find the spot. I dug up so many spots around the apple tree, I was certain that the tree would die. But no gold! After a while, I started tearing up all my land! It was almost random, and it was so pointless. After days of this, I took to my bed. Even my girlfriend couldn't cheer me up. I finally told her my problem. She came up with a great idea right away. She had a friend with excavating equipment, Marcos. For not very much money he would dig up the whole yard and find my gold."

Manuel's face had settled down. Traffic was moving again, and he almost seemed happy. "The friend with the excavator looked and looked, but never found anything. I never trusted in gold again. Funny thing was that once I got over losing the gold, I was much happier."

Questions came straight to my mind. "The friend with the excavator. Did he have a whole business?"

Manuel became even more animated. "Oh yes, he became very successful. And he never charged me. Can you imagine that? He worked for three days. He told me that additional work was hopeless and that he would never find the gold. And he put all the dirt back and replaced the sod."

"What happened to your girlfriend?"

We were coming up on a gas oasis. Sophie called out from the back seat. "Manuel, stop here, I need to go to the bathroom." We stopped. She gave Manuel a hug and said, "See, it goes better every time that you tell the story. You're fine!"

Manuel beamed. "I am better!"

"Of course, you are!" I was loitering by the store and Sophie came up to me. She gave me a hug and whispered to me menacingly. "Never bring up this story again."

"But why?"

"Sylvia ran away with Marcos the excavator guy, who was also the bulldozer guy who robbed the man with all the dollars. We never tell Manuel that he was robbed. All that keeps Manuel going is the thought of one day finding the gold and getting his girlfriend back." My girlfriend pushed me back and held me by my shoulders. "And we are never going to take that tiny bit of hope away from him."

It was an easy trip after that. The brother stayed with us for a few hours, and we all drank Fernet and Cola. The taste grows on you. Fernet is extremely bitter. The Cola doesn't make it sweet. Maybe it makes it even more bitter. But it makes the drink go down faster. The service was slow. I drank my Fernet and Cola, and then spent a lot of time chasing the ice cubes in my glass with the straw, while Sophie and Manuel talked in Spanish. I paid Manuel a lot of money for the trip. He tried to give some back. Then he was gone, and we were at the beach house.

I couldn't help but notice that beach house had brick walls and bars on the windows. I had brought a wad of American money with me. I showed it to Sophie. "Is this going to be a problem?"

She took the bills from me. "You idiot! If they know we have this kind of money here the thieves will be here in a minute. Lucky for you, I know where to hide it."

There were two bedrooms, but only one of them was furnished. The other bedroom looked like a landfill. Sophie dug through a pile of old cereal boxes and pop cans and found a tote bag. It was filled to the brim with old pictures. At the bottom of the tote were about a dozen 35 mm film canisters. She took the bills, folded and rolled them and started stuffing them into the canisters. "You could help, you know."

"I'd rather look at pictures." Most of the pictures were of Sophie. They went back all the way to her as a child. In almost every one, she was wearing a swimsuit. And in almost every one she had a rash. There were red spots, welts, swelling, pustules. In a few, Sophie had what appeared to be a cold sore. In more than a few, one eye or the other was swollen up. I showed a swollen eye picture to Sophie.

"I was beautiful, right? Every time I had a rash at the beach here, my mom took a picture. And I always had a rash here. It itched horribly."

"Didn't you have anything to take for it?"

"Antihistamines worked perfectly. But I used to throw them in the toilet. They made my mouth dry and all I wanted to do was sleep. It was better to be awake, itchy, and spending time with my mom and her camera. It was miserable, but I kind of liked it at the same time. Then one day, I had a boyfriend here in Mar del Plata. I still got the rash, but my mom wasn't interested in taking pictures any more. She blamed the rash on the boyfriend."

"I'm so sorry for you."

"Why be sorry? Even with the rash, I was the prettiest girl at the beach, and I always had the best boyfriends."

"How about now? Do you still have the best boyfriend?"

"I'm not pretty like that anymore. And you, even with all your pain-in-the-ass American dollars, are a big downgrade. Let's go out to eat."

The beach house was not close to the beach and was not close to a bar. We hiked into town along the beach road. The spot we chose to eat had only a few tables. Most of the main room was taken up by a large dance floor where tourists were being taught to tango. There was tango music playing and the waitress could not understand my Spanish until I was practically yelling. The waitress knew Sophie and confirmed that she just wanted a hamburger. I was trying to get in a better mood and ordered a Chandon. And then another one. Sophie and I sat silently. After our food arrived, the tourist tango lesson began.

It was a beginner's lesson that seemed to consist entirely

of teaching people to do the easy steps. The tourists formed a large circle, boy, girl, boy, girl. The men moved forward to music and pushed the women backwards. Step. Step. Side-step, slide. The instructor kept them in time by calling out, "T. A. N-G. O." Sophie pointed out one of the men in the class and said, "You see? He knows how to walk. Too bad none of the women do."

I was a bit tired of her passive aggressive criticism of me. "Why don't you see if he can be your boyfriend? Or do you have to have a rash first?" Sophie glared at me. She tossed her half-eaten hamburger on the plate and said, "I've had enough. Enough to eat and enough of listening to you. Take me home."

The amount of time we spent arguing before we left would have been enough time for me to finish my steak. We walked back to the beach house wordlessly. There was nothing to do at the beach house. Sophie went to bed while I watched TV shows that I could not understand. I slept on the couch. When I woke up, Sophie was still asleep. I went out to get groceries. When Sophie woke up, she was in a perfectly happy mood. It was as if none of the argument from the day before had made any impression on her. By the time we made it to the beach, it was hot and clear. I invited Sophie into the water, but she didn't want to come. "I don't swim. I'll just collect sea shells."

There were no sea shells anywhere on the beach. There was just sand, water, and few men with surf boards and a single concrete pier. At first, Sophie walked out on the pier and looked over the water. Then, bored, she went to the beach end of the pier. It was there that she fell into a pit in the sand that had formed from the eddy of surf at the shore. She was in waist deep and studying the sides of the pit as though she had intended to jump into the pit all along. It took me a minute to realize that she was trapped.

I ran to the pit to help her out. Her feet got no traction on the side of the pit. In a flash, I was in the pit with her. I held her for a second, then asked "Why did you decide to jump in here?" Before she could answer, a wave pulled us out of the pit and into the surf along the side of the concrete pier. A strong riptide pulled us away from the beach. We did the logical thing. I faced towards shore and tried to walk onto it. She was facing me and trying to walk backwards. As the waves broke over us, we made some trivial progress towards safety. But after every wave, the riptide came back stronger than before. We performed our strange tango for a long time, always slowly moving out to the sea, deeper into the water, farther away from shore, and ever more consumed with panic.

Soon the waves were breaking over our heads and pulling us up from the sand. Sophie's feet lost contact with the sand. Then mine did. I made swimming motions with my feet while Sophie clutched me around my chest. We were moving more quickly away from safety. She looked at me with crazy eyes. "You have to save yourself. You can get back to shore without me. If you stay with me, we will both drown."

I know what a riptide is and I know how to swim in the ocean, but I had never clearly thought out what it would be like to be in a riptide while being pulled down by an Argentine girlfriend. If I had been alone, I would have swum perpendicular to the riptide to get out of it. But we were still next to the pier. I imagined that we might somehow pull ourselves up to it. Or perhaps someone would run out on the pier and throw us a life preserver.

I was not thinking clearly. I knew that I was a strong

enough swimmer to get myself back to shore, but even if I was planning to abandon Sophie, I wanted to stay with her until the last minute. And if I was going to abandon her, I wanted to say exactly the right thing just before I left. This line of thought took up a lot of my mental energy as I struggled to keep us both above the surf. What I said wouldn't matter to her. She would be carried out to sea. It would matter to me whenever I thought about that time that I lost my Argentine girlfriend in a riptide. I impulsively said, "I love you."

By that point we were past the pier and into the open water, still being pulled out into the ocean. Whatever impulse might have made Sophie pull me down into the ocean with her was ended with my three words. She pushed me away and flailed by herself in the open water.

Suddenly, the crisis was over. One of the men from the beach had gotten to us with a surf board. He managed to get Sophie to lie on top of the surf board. I was already swimming to shore.

By the time we got back to the beach house, Sophie had her rash. She went right to the bedroom to scratch herself to sleep. I wanted to comfort her but did not know how. She tolerated my company briefly, then kicked me out of the bedroom when I pretended to take her picture. She still wasn't speaking to me the next day when her brother came to pick us up. Manuel didn't notice we weren't getting along. He helped us with our bags, we got into the car and drove off. Sophie, red, swollen and furiously scratching, tried to lie down in the back seat. I was stuck talking to Manuel. He wanted to know how the beach was. I didn't know what to say. Did Sophie want me to make it sound like everything was ok? Or did she want me to tell the story of the riptide and the rash?

It was impossible to know what Sophie wanted me to say, but Manuel was not listening anyway. "I have two pieces of really good news!" He worked himself into this line several times, looking through the rearview mirror to get Sophie to respond. She was silent.

We were most of the way back to Buenos Aires before I gave Manuel his opening. "Ok, Manuel. What is your good news?"

"Well first, I had a talk with the manager of your hotel. He took a bunch of my cards and told me that he would help me find clients. This is my big break! One of my friends promised to also drive the Peugeot. I'll be busy every day of the week!"

This comment finally brought Sophie up and around. "Manuel. Stop the car. I need to go to the bathroom. Now." We were not close to a bathroom and the traffic was terrible. Still, Manuel found a way to get to the side of the road. Sophie stayed in the car, came up between the seats and spoke directly into Manuel's ear.

"Manuel. This is not going to work out well for you. Nothing ever does. You should never trust anyone with your car. Having someone to drive your car will not help you. You will never be rich." Manuel stared ahead, saying nothing.

This made Sophie even angrier. "You will have nothing. Do you hear me, nothing."

Manuel was not listening. "No, this time it will all work out."

One of Sophie's eyelids was swelling up. She was screaming now. "Sylvia is never coming back to you. She's happy with Marcos."

There was no evidence from Manuel's face that any of this registered with him. "I know, I know!" he replied.

"No, Manuel. You do not know. Sylvia is never going to

break up with Marcos. She is going to live with Marcos in their fancy house while you drive around this car until the wheels fall off. Sylvia has someone to drive her. She doesn't need you. They are always going to be loaded with money." Manuel took in Sophie's words with calm, it was Sophie's face that was bloated, red and contorted. This made Sophie even more angry. "Sylvia and Marcos love each other. Sylvia fell in love with Marcos while she was still living with you. They stole all your gold. But you were a loser even before Sylvia. You are a loser and you always will be a loser. Because that is who you are."

Manuel turned his head to face Sophie. Sophie tried to pull away, but still stuck between the front seats, there was no room to get more than a few inches away from Manuel's lips. "You always act like I don't know all that. I'm tired of it. Now either get out of the car and take a piss or let me drive my client back to his hotel."

Sophie fell back into the back seat. Manuel pulled back onto the road. There was silence for a few minutes. Then Manuel directed himself to me. His face was bright as though none of the conversation with Sophie had ever happened. "And I have another piece of good news. I'm seeing a therapist now. He says I have Familial Constitutional Inferiority. That means that I'm defective and so is everyone in my family. That is why nothing ever works out for me. He says there is nothing to be done for the disease, but that he can help me cope. I feel so much better already."

With this statement, Manuel stopped talking. We drove up to a service station. Sophie went to the bathroom while Manuel refilled the gas tank. When Sophie came back, she no longer appeared to have a rash. She told me to get into the back seat, and she sat up front with Manuel. They spoke in soft Spanish all the way to my hotel. Manuel helped me out of the car and gave me my things. He said he was very happy to have met me and was grateful for my help. I gave him a film canister of money. Sophie did not get out of the car and Manuel did not take her bag out of the trunk. "Sophie is not feeling well. She's going home with me to my country."

His country. Meaning his house in the middle of nowhere. With the gates and fences that keep the thieves in rather than out. With the dug-up yard and the half-dead apple tree. The first thing he will do there is bury the film canister. He will keep careful track of it this time. Beyond this single event, the burying of the cash, I couldn't predict any future for either one of them. I shook Manuel's hand and wished him the best of luck. I went into the hotel, had a Fernet and Cola at the bar, went up to my room, showered, and went right to sleep. The next day, I made an appointment with my therapist, Dr. Garcia.

"Guten Tag, Herr Bramley, come into my consulting room." He took one of the comfortable chairs and I took the other. For a moment, we both looked at the grease slick on the analytic couch. I took out my handkerchief and wiped my forehead, then put it back. Dr. Garcia spoke first. "So, I see that the co-dependent American has returned to see me! How did it go with Sophie? Let me guess. You tried to push her where she did not want to go. You had hopes of backing her into a corner where you could trap her. But her narcissism was too strong for that. Once you realized that you were not going to win her, you gave up all hope. You knew you needed to abandon her. And right before you abandoned her, you said what you always say. "I love you." At that point, she realized what a horribly toxic person you are, and she pushed you off of her. Better to be abandoned and alone than to be under the control of someone so committed to their psychopathology."

"That's not at all how it went. She went off to a country with her brother."

"She went off to a country with her brother. No, Mr. Bramley, I'm quite sure that I'm right. You did what you always do. You will certainly find a new girlfriend to play out your little game. And the ending will be the same. The shape of your suffering is a perfect circle. And the shape of the suffering of your victims is also a perfect circle. Around and around the two of you go. The faces change but the shape stays the same." Dr. Garcia took off his eyeglasses and caressed his beard. "Mr. Bramley, why do you bother?"

"I don't know what you mean."

"Oh, I think you do. Sophie ended her affair with you and then fled to a country. But you came to Argentina after one of your affairs ended. You also ran away to a country. Both you and Sophie ran away to a country. But she did something convenient. She went a few miles out to be with her family. You did something very inconvenient. You bought an expensive plane ticket. You learned a foreign language. You learned how to tango. You learned how to find shelter and get food in a strange place. You went through a lot of bother for your suffering. You went through a lot more bother than Sophie. What is so compelling about your suffering that you are willing to go to so much bother to experience it?"

I knew that Dr. Garcia was wrong. And I knew, most of all, that I was right and Sophie was wrong. Sophie had found someone who loved her and couldn't tolerate it. I knew that she was psychologically damaged in a way that I was not. But I had no answer to the question of why I had bothered to fall in love with her. I had no good answer to the question of "Why bother?"

I felt I had to say something to Dr. Garcia. "Why did I bother with Sophie? That's a good question. Now let me ask you a question, if I'm so hopeless, why should I bother with therapy? You are telling me I'm a hopeless patient. Why should I bother coming to your office? Why should I bother paying you for something that almost certainly won't do me any good?"

"Maybe you shouldn't bother. If you can't think of any other path forward, maybe the logical thing for you to do put in less effort. At least then you will find a way to be the same kind of failure with less work."

Suddenly, I was very tired. I had used up only a fraction of my hour with Dr. Garcia. But there was no point in more therapy. I had already decided to leave Argentina for good. Dr. Garcia did not disagree with my plan. I got up to leave and Dr. Garcia didn't stop me. I shook his hand at the door and paid him with a film canister. There was nothing else to say.

I had another week left to be in Argentina and I vowed to spend it drinking. Not Chandon, or Fernet and Cola, but beer. Nice cold beer. I knew of no other bars other than the ones that were also milonga venues. But it did not matter. I had a plan to keep the Argentine women away. I had a pair of old tennis shoes.

Whatever assumptions about men's feet these shoes reflected did not matter. After years of wearing them, they fit my feet perfectly. I put on jeans and a T shirt. Before I went out to the bar, I looked in the mirror. I looked like the gringo loser that I am. It took me nearly an hour to walk to the ballroom of the New Year's Eve Milonga and I was a sweaty mess when I arrived. I went up to the bar and ordered a beer.

The oblong toilet of the dance floor had already filled up with turds. Round and round they went. T. A. N-G. O. A handful of young American women were searching the room for potential dance partners. One briefly caught my eye, and I looked away, back at my beer. I looked up the next minute, and she was still looking. I lifted a foot up from the stool and pointed at my shoe while shaking my head "no." And then I looked back at my beer. It occurred to me that I might also be a failure at trying not to date in Argentina. When I looked up, the woman was right in front of me.

"Soy Larisa. Quieres bailer con migo?" Her Spanish was terrible. And the look of hopeful expectation on her face seemed strangely out of place for a woman out for a night of dancing in San Telmo.

"There's no need to speak Spanish. I'm an American."

Her face lit up with this news. "Oh, thank God! It's like no one understands me when I ask for a dance in Spanish."

She threw her arms around me. She was sweaty, but she smelled like soap. I whispered in her ear. "Well, no wonder. You're doing it wrong."

She pulled back and looked at me with mock horror in her eyes. "Oh no! What have I been asking these men to do?"

Larisa pulled up the stool next to me and I ordered her a beer. Her girlfriends came over, and she told them to leave without her. We talked. She had taken the tourist tango lessons several times already and was shocked to learn that she had not developed enough skill to pass for a local. I asked her if she was wearing red panties. She blushed and admitted she was. So at least she got that right.

After the beer, I took her to the dance floor. Round and round we went, doing the most basic tango walk. T. A. N-G. O. My tennis shoes didn't slide quite right, and I'm sure that I didn't walk anything like an Argentine. Larisa didn't care. We went back to the Hilton long before the other turds had been flushed.I had to explain to her that the Hilton was famous for being in movies and TV shows. She had never heard of it.

We flew home from Argentina together. Manuel's employee drove us to the airport, and I paid him with a film canister.

The planes leave Argentina at night, and we rose up out of Argentina just as the lights were coming on in the city. The neighborhoods that make up Buenos Aires are one long line from east to west along the La Plata River. I pointed out Boca, San Telmo, Puerto Madero, Palermo, Nunez, and finally Tigre. Then the plane flew into the darkness, and I had to explain to Larisa that I was no longer sure of where I was.

# Patricia Goitia Lebo

Playing with words has been a joy even before I learned how to write. This ludic passion began in the language of Cervantes as I was born in Mexico and grew up in Peru where I did my schooling. Later, as Dr. Seuss predicted, I was "off to Great Places." Raising a husband and two boys in Texas I obtained an M.A. from The University of Texas at Austin. No time to write a novel so poetry and short stories were my creative snacks. A few were published. Recently, "Hija," won first place in the poetry contest organized by Latino Arts, Culture and Education; and the magazine "Mujer." Today, while dancing with my husband, playing with our grandkids, traveling and reading, I'm having a feast writing my memoirs.

My pen name is Piri. Read "Mr. Wiley" to learn what Piri means.

# The Game



*The heavens declare the glory of God,*
*and the sky above proclaims his handiwork.*
Psalm 19:1 ESV

Lately, as during my pubescent years, I have found myself playing the daisy game. But the mantra I repeat is not "he loves me, he loves me not." Instead, as I pluck the petals of the sacred symbol to Freya, a Norse love goddess, what I recite is "should I do it or should I not." Not that I believe in mythology, legends, or symbolism, but is it serendipitous that daisies abound in my backyard and that they happen to embody innocence and purity?

What about chastity and transformation? According to a Roman myth, Vertumnus, god of seasons and gardens became enamored with Belides, a nymph. He pursues her so relentlessly that the charming maiden turns herself into a daisy in order to guard her virginity. Too late for me.

There is no doubt, the fruit in my womb is burgeoning.

The clinic confirmed it with a blood test and a black and white image produced by an ultrasound. Like the daisy which consists of two flowers in one, a little inner disc and the petals, I have become a unit of two. A garden that waters and nourishes the flower inside me.

My idol has deserted me. Fled or transformed himself into someone else, into a daemon who claims not to be responsible for the seed. But I know the truth. I and only I have the certainty on this side of the universe. Of course DNA can confirm it. But what comfort will it bring? How can it help me? Us? Because I am plural now. So I pluck at the delicate white petals over and over again repeating "Should I do it, or should I not?" I know what my heart wishes for the last petal to say. It's not that I want the flower to speak to me. No. It's the game.

The clinic insisted on extracting the bud inside me as early as possible. They said it is the best way. It is what benefits me … us. The easy, painless, and fast way. The path to a bright future. I can go ahead with all my wonderful plans. Finish my studies in Botany and go on to discover how plants grow under different conditions. Help the environment. Did they think about you, the efflorescence of my womb? You have no voice, you have no choice, and you're at my mercy. At the fate and whim of my decision.

I know better God. I know you. Tonight, I look at the firmament you made with your own hands. The heavenly bodies you created. The moon floating like a yellowish upturned boat or ripe banana in the indigo sky. Tell me, why am I important to you? Why do you even think about me? You made me almost like a goddess. You put me in charge. And even though the ways I've managed my life have been messy, you still love me … and you like to play the game with me.

There are from fifteen to thirty petals in a daisy. I sit next to the birdbath under the goldish light of the moon with the last flower in my hand. One by one the ghostly petals leave my fingers as I intone the repetitious chant, "should I do it or should I not." This decision should not be so difficult. I avoid looking at the balding yellow crown of the plucked blossom. It would be easy to cheat. Change the order of the mantra. Exfoliate once in total silence. But this would be defrauding myself and being dishonest with you. Do I not seek your perfect will, even if it is not what I really, down-deep-in-my-heart want?

"Should I do it or should I not?" I peek at the bud that now looks like a tuft of white feathers on the head of a sick bird.

"Should I do it?" Pluck.

"Should I not?" Pluck.

"Do it!" I sing as I excise the last petal from the naked disc. And as I grin holding hard the final segment of the daisy like a triumphant flag, my eyes are drawn to the shiny surface of the birdbath. There, reflected in the liquid mirror is your smiley face. Your approving, ripe banana lips below two mischievous starry eyes! Oh! How you love me! Oh! How you like to play the game! I shall do it! I will name her Daisy!

# Princess Shoes

BY PIRI

*You are a princess, and your feet are graceful in their sandals.*
Song of Solomon 7:1a CEV

"I'm looking for little feet," chanted our neighbor as she walked down the Mexican-tiled stairs leading to the lower apartment where my husband and I were staying.

It was early afternoon. I was sitting by myself basking in the warm sun and the glorious memories of the morning when I recognized Debbie's friendly voice.

"I'm looking for little feet," she repeated.

"I have little feet," I declared. "Very little feet."

We were in San Carlos helping my in-laws who wintered there. The picturesque town on the northwest coast of Mexico is a paradisiacal beachfront community washed by the blue Sea of Cortez and skirted by copper-colored mountains. At dawn and at sundown sky and clouds ignite turning land and sea into gigantic kaleidoscopes. Catching a moonrise over San Carlos Bay is addictive: You can never have enough and you keep on wanting more. So it is with God's blessings. They come in all shapes, colors and sizes turning up in the most unexpected and unusual places. They show God's favor, energize your life and keep you wanting more.

"I have a pair of princess shoes," said Debbie as she sat across from me.

Every Monday that we were in San Carlos I visited the *ladies at the cereso* (prison) in Guaymas. As I drove there I would visualize the smiley faces, feel the warm hugs, hear the praise voices and anticipate the love I received from them. Like the moonrise over San Carlos, it was always better than I expected, and I could never get enough. That particular Monday was November 16. San Carlos was commemorating the Mexican Revolution. Having had a vision of washing the feet of these ladies the week before, I had made secret arrangements to have a tub of warm water and soap available for this purpose.

"I have a pair of princess shoes," repeated Debbie removing sparkly slippers out of a bag. "They belong to my mom. As you know, she has terminal cancer and will be dancing in heaven soon."

"I have very small and very clean feet," I told Debbie as I tried on the Cinderella shoes and proceeded to relate my morning at the prison and the washing of feet.

From John 13 I shared with the ladies that God had come to serve rather than to be served. I talked about the Mexican Revolution, about how admirable it was and is to fight for human rights, our God given rights. But then I pointed out that the Creator and Master of the universe had forsaken all his rights on a cross to bring reconciliation to all men. We discussed what to do when our mind states that we have a right to demand an apology before forgiving, that we need to hear a confession of wrong before we mend a relationship, that something is not our responsibility or that we cannot abase ourselves to this or that.

Was not washing feet the task of the lowest of servants? Is not the cross by world standards a ridiculous act? And yet, only the cross can cleanse our sin; and the cross continues to be the greatest revolution that keeps loving and freeing people. A gift so simple that confuses the brightest. An act so humble that appears insane to most. When I asked the ladies for the honor and privilege of washing their feet, they gasped. I washed their feet and prayed. They washed my feet and prayed. No words can describe the moonrise over San Carlos and no words can convey the mood after the washing of our feet.

"They fit me perfectly!" I exclaimed jubilantly twirling on the shiny dance shoes.

"Now the only thing you need is the dress and the wedding," said Debbie smiling widely.

"Actually," I reported, "I am going to a very special wedding in Peru this coming May and it will be an honor to wear your mom's shoes!"

"They are princess shoes," Debbie insisted.

Goosebumps on my skin, wonder and joy welling from my heart, I blurted, "I am a princess! The daughter of a King!"

"Really?" Debbie questioned puzzled.

"Yes!" I explained, "I am the daughter of the King of the universe and that makes me His princess!"

# Marfil

BY PIRI

*Your forest-drenched garments are fragrant with mountain breeze.*
*Chamber music—from the throne room—makes you want to dance.*
Psalm 45:8 MSG

**W**  *hat a strange girl*, I thought, as I stood in front of the very blond, almost albino girl that my dad and I had gone to greet at the airport. It was 1960 and I was nine.

"This is Marfil," said my dad. "Aren't you going to tell her hello?"

My dad and I were there with his boss, a tall, strong, energetic man with shiny eyes. He smelled of garlic, smiled broadly showing his teeth, had a loud voice and his speech had a strong Mexican intonation. We were greeting the last members of his family to arrive in Lima from Mexico.

"*Hola* Marfil," I greeted her. I don't recall if she responded. I don't remember the rest of the family. I do see her next to an adult, probably her mom. But in my photographic memory, it is only the image of Marfil that remains vivid and solid. The small, bright copper eyes behind her glasses were perhaps a little crooked but alert, curious and watchful. She was most likely scrutinizing me also. Two thin, pale blond braids framed her serious oval face which appeared to have no eyebrows or lashes at all, being they were so very light colored. Her skin resembled that of a polished elephant tusk splashed with muddy freckles. She was thin and small, a milky-blond reed looking deceptively fragile.

I assumed her name was due to her alabaster complexion. Marfil is the Spanish word for ivory. Many years later I learned that her very pregnant mom, while traveling in Guanajuato, Mexico, with her husband, came into a small, picturesque town called Marfil. This hidden jewel, known for its temple to the Lord of the Water, was the inspiration for her namesake.

Our families gathered together often as Mexican expats. Our parents had much in common and felt a close affinity. They missed their country, their relatives, their friends and their food. They loved music, literature, art, and family. They helped each other adjust to the long, grey, humid winters; and together they enjoyed the short but glorious summers. We celebrated together, reminisced together, ate together, cried together, sang together, drank together, hoped together.

Marfil was not just my best childhood friend. Besides being a story-teller extraordinaire, she was my confidante, encourager, reading companion, college buddy, ally and very especially, my dance partner. Our common interests and views created a bond, a unique friendship, a connection that time, geographical distance and periods of silence were not able to break or even diminish. My sisters and I think of her as another sister, a chosen one.

Though Marfil was the age of my youngest sister then, we became inseparable. What truly tied the knot between us, besides our shared love for reading and more, was our passion for dancing. We dreamt together of becoming artists like Anna Pavlova or Isadora Duncan. Wherever we went, our house, her house, the streets, our neighbors' yards, the green grounds of the country club, the beach … we would dance. Every place was a theater stage for us to perform. We were not shy or embarrassed to spin, twirl, leap or trip in front of an unintended audience. We danced for the joy of dancing. Of course we loved it when we received adulation.

We chose the music from the compositions we knew by heart. "Waltz of the Flowers" from the Nutcracker and the "Dance of the Little Swans" by Tchaikovsky were two of our favorites. We listened to the music in our head, felt it in our heart. We studied our surroundings and used them as sets and props. We collaborated as we choreographed. I don't remember disagreeing at any point. We created our dance, we rehearsed it; we performed it over and over again until we were satisfied with the results. Sometimes we would practice for days on the same stage. One of our favored front yards was also the most challenging. It had steps and beautiful stone planters from which to execute darting or soaring jetés. We paid close attention to the shape we made in the air, critiquing each other to attain perfection. Not only once but many times we were ousted while performing at a neighbor's property. Sometimes we were applauded and praised. Those were the best curtain calls. We did not miss the chance to respond with our deepest gratitude by curtsying repeatedly.

Sleepovers at my house were great opportunities to perform on our terrace. Decked out with colorful, ethereal veils—stolen scarves from my mom's closet—we would dance part of the night away. Like Arthur O'Shaughnessy's "Salome," *we freed and floated on the air our arms, above dim veils that hid our bosom's charms... The veils fell round us like thin coiling mists shot through by topaz suns and amethysts.* Pretending to be Scheherazade and her sister Dinazade in *Arabian Nights*, we would dance unconcluded stories to prevent the prince from killing us in the morning.

Marfil and I also shared a passion for the outdoors. Her family gave us the opportunity to experience nature in wonderful ways. They loved to camp out. Scout new secluded beaches. Dig for clams, clean them and cook them. Gather and classify kauri shells. Track a baby octopus by looking for broken crab shells close to holes or crevices in the rock walls. Spot them in spite of their artful camouflage. Find the perfect bend on the river for swimming and racing on the dry pebbly shore. Observe plants, birds, fishes, tadpoles, frogs and bugs.

*Tío* (uncle) Oscar and his wife, *Tía (aunt)* Pupi, had studied archeology. They were also versed in geology, geography, history, literature and more. They turned our outings into exciting, hands-on outdoor classrooms. Oso, their only son at the time, loved animals, especially bugs and snakes. He shared his dad's adventurous spirit and his mom's curiosity for detail. Their grandma, Maneta, was a woman ahead of her times. She had eloped with her tutor. She and her family survived life in a concentration camp during World War II. Eleni, their first-born, was a lovely and smart adolescent. I aspired to be like her one day. Inés, their nana, was a plump, warm-natured woman from Tehuantepec, Mexico. She always wore a short *huipil* (blouse) and a long skirt. It was the traditional garment of the indigenous women of her region. I loved the different designs woven into the fabric, decorated with embroidery, ribbons and laces. Her long hair was always braided. She adored the family and especially her baby, Marfil. I wanted her to be my nana too.

I missed my *Consue*, my own nana, so much it hurt physically. Nana Inés knew it. Many were the times she welcomed me into her big, comforting warm arms and bosom. Especially when she knew I had been singled for something Marfil had done or instigated. She always found a way for me to cuddle and receive her soothing affection away from eyes that could become jealous. There was also a dog, a wiry short-hair canine with a waggy tail. They were all an extension of our family. I loved them then. I love them now.

Marfil and her family were very fond of animals. Aside from dogs, cats and her brother's reptiles and bugs, they had an assortment of wild creatures living with them now and then. I will never forget Marfil's overflowing joy when back from one of his trips to Brazil her dad gifted her a small baby ocelot. Unfortunately the exotic feline did not survive the habitat change, dying shortly after its arrival in Lima. Marfil's sadness broke my heart.

At one time or another, they also had turtles, canaries and chinchillas. Another exotic animal that Uncle Oscar smuggled into the country was a Kuzumba, also known as Kinkajou or honey bear: a monkey-like creature closely related to the raccoon family. Her big round black eyes told you she was curious and mischievous. She had a very long flexible and versatile tail that she used for grabbing things and hanging from things. Her hands were almost humanlike. Her dexterity was amazing. Unfortunately, it cost her her life. She was a charming little thief who craved honey and alcohol. One day, looking to get tipsy she found a perfume bottle and drank it. Needless to say, we were all devastated.

Then there was this curious fellow, a baby alligator that

had to be fed itsy bits of ground meat by mouth. When the family took a vacation, the wee caiman was left in the care of Grandma Maneta. Woefully, as Maneta held the cute reptile in one hand close to her face to bring it towards the morsel of food in her other hand, the hungry baby mistook Maneta's nose for his supper taking a chunk out of it. Of course, that was the end of the snappy pet who found itself at the local zoo.

Hide-and-seek was another one of our favorite pastimes, together with tag, freeze, dodgeball and more. We played these with our friends in our neighborhoods. When dark or when the weather was not favorable, which was rare, we played hide-and-seek in our rooms.

But the last part of the day with Marfil was the best. Bedtime meant storytelling-time! My sisters and I relished her fairytale inventions. She made the voices of ogres' sound like thunder, the words from lips of princesses sweet as dripping caramel, the admonitions of good fairies convincing, the threats of witches terrifying. We heard of dogs with eyes the size of dinner plates, of cats that transformed into children, of underwater forests that hid treasures untold. She took us to worlds of adventure, mystery, intrigue, peril, rescue and happy endings. She gave wings to our imagination.

The afternoon of Sunday, May 22 of the year, 2022, Marfil placed a period to her earthly story. She metamorphosed—took on wings to flee the wicked witch of pain. To extinguish the fiery cancer dragon. To enter a new world of adventure, unveil the mystery, be the princess who was rescued, live happily ever after. Three thousand miles away from her, a gentle breeze like the flutter of veils or butterflies' wings sprinkled with pixie dust, whispered something into my heart: *How exquisite your love, O God! How eager we are to run under your wings,* (Psalm 36:7 MSG).

Farewell Marfilinha. Dance away.

> *You did it: you changed wild lament into whirling dance;*
> Psalm 30:11a MSG

# Mr. Wiley

BY PIRI

*The fear of man brings a snare,*
*But one who trusts in the Lord will be protected.*
*Proverbs 29:25 NASB*

"Piri," Mr. Wiley repeated slowly.

He was trying to pronounce the Spanish simple "r" correctly but was failing.

"What kind of a name is Piri?"

It had not been easy to get the courage to meet the man sitting across the table from me. He had finally stopped talking about himself to inquire about my name. I was uncomfortable. Fear wrapped in inadequacy was making my heart beat faster. It was my first time dining with a total stranger—one introduced to me by my aunt two nights before at the bar of the hotel where we had been staying. He said he was a wealthy businessman from Louisiana attending important meetings in Bangkok. Middle-aged, of average height and build. Pleasant.

"My niece is staying in town for a few more days after I depart tomorrow. Will you keep an eye on her? She's only twenty-one and will be on her own."

That's how I had accepted his invitation to dinner and a Thai-dance show.

"I will see you safely back where you'll be staying," Mr. Wiley had promised.

No more fancy accommodations, especially guided tours or expensive restaurants. The afternoon my aunt left I started on a student's budget. The taxi ride from the luxurious hotel, where I had spent wonderful days with her, to the youth hostel had been surreal. The rain was coming down slowly and gray mirroring the state of my heart when I arrived at the weather-beaten orange façade of the Bangkok Youth Hostel. The bare room at the end of a poorly lit corridor. The bed, uninviting. The prospect of sharing a bathroom with other women and men looming in my mind like an unwelcome guest that refuses to leave. The rest of the day was a blur. The rain grew thicker and louder as night fell. It reached my heart echoing the sighing wind, finally welling through my eyes in torrents of miserable dread. *I can just go home tomorrow.* This thought had appeased me. Still crying but comforted by the remembrance of my open-ended airline-ticket, Hypnos, the god of sleep, found me.

The morning after, sunlight greeted me with warm fingers of promise. With the airline ticket in my purse and an almost song in my step I went for a walk. The streets were busy, lively, filled with sounds, people, voices and aromas of food. Realizing I was hungry I stopped at a small restaurant. A friendly attendant helped me order a delicious dish of noodles, vegetables and chicken. *That wasn't too bad*, I thought. I don't know how long I walked, but the longer my feet moved, and my senses absorbed my surroundings, the more at ease I became. I found myself outside the offices of Air India. Ah! India! The country of my dreams. A land I was familiar with from the slides my dad had shown us and the stories he had told us. One of the reasons I had always wanted to travel! Why not? I went inside. The place was busy. There were no free agents at the counter. I sat down to wait my turn. Two minutes later an attractive young woman about my age, wearing a sari, came through the door. After looking around she walked towards me.

"Is this seat taken?" she asked.

I motioned for her to sit next to me.

"Are you going to India?" she added.

"I'm thinking about it." I replied.

"Are you traveling by yourself?" she asked and quickly volunteered, "My name is Naoi. I'm travelling by myself also. I'm going back to school. I live in Bangkok but study in New Delhi."

By the time I was called to the counter, we had agreed to travel together. I would be going with her to Delhi. There she would connect me with an uncle who managed a small hotel and was in the tourism business. Her cousin would be happy to drive me on his motorcycle to bus stops and pick me up after my outings to the Taj Mahal, The Red Fort and other wonders of the country. The family also rented houseboats in Srinagar, Kashmir.

At this point in my life I had lost my virginity and my religion. The first one recently, the latter years ago. But I did know there was a God. I could feel His Hand on me, guiding my steps, protecting me from dangers, from my unwise ways and from my worries. His Hand was painting a rainbow in my heart after the rain. I was looking forward to finally setting foot in the magical kingdom I had learned to love through my father.

Walking back to the youth hostel, after parting with my new friend, I had decided to kill two fears with one stone—ride the bus to the hotel and meet Mr. Wiley for dinner.

"Mr. Wiley, you've told me all about your work, but you haven't told me your first name," I said, as I observed his tanned, dimpled-face, sculpted features, wide smile and eyes that twinkled.

"My first name is famous because I'm named after a very popular brand of cigarettes," was his response.

"Really?"

"Yes. Can you guess what it is?"

My mind searched my memory bank for all the cigarette brands I knew—Winston, Kent, Philip, Raleigh, Benson, Carlton… He dismissed every guess with a winning grin and a head shake.

"I give up," I blurted out defeated.

With a triumphant sparkle in his eye he said, "Maurice!"

"Maurice? I've never heard of Maurice cigarettes."

"Philip Morris. They are world known."

"But Morris and Maurice are not the same," I said disapproving of his deceitfulness. "Besides Morris is a last name!"

"You're a sore loser," he said. Diverting the conversation, he asked, "What kind of a name is Piri?"

"My real name is Patricia. Piri is my nickname. It is short for *Pirinola*."

"*Pirinola*? Am I saying it right? What does it mean?"

"Well … yes. A *pirinola* is a small octagonal spinning top. My *tíos abuelos* (great aunt and great uncle) Candido and Paz gave me the moniker when I was a toddler. They thought it suited me because I was teeny, ran fast and spun round and round."

"I can picture your whirling around ... and much more," said Maurice with a twisted smile.

I felt ill at ease. My body tensed even more. Thankfully the lights flickered to announce the beginning of the dance performance. Between bites of the tender minced pork with holy basil, I sipped my wine with nervous apprehension. As I waited for the show to commence, I chewed on the unsavory intentions of Maurice Wiley.

The stage was small, but lighting was good. We had an unobstructed view of the dance platform. Two female dancers in bright scintillating costumes stood still in the center of the floor. The music reached my heart desiring a soothing balm. I wanted the melody to charm me as enchanters do snakes. I longed for my spirit to rise to the melody's lulling magic. I tried to leave fear, Maurice, and the ache of Aunt Pepis' departure in the cobra's basket. But instead, as the dancers commenced to slowly move their necks and their beautiful faces came to life, I felt closer to the viper's strike. I made an effort to focus on the ethereal ornate headdresses resembling miniature golden pagodas. Under other circumstances I would have been fascinated by the Thai princesses' gracious undulating of arms and hands while all was still below the waist. As their limbs were brought into the dance, their arms waved and their muscles quivered, I found myself in a forest of fluttering unrest.

The applause and the lights snapped me back to reality and Maurice. He was going to invite me to a private dance anytime now. I suspected he had been orchestrating the steps since Aunt Pepis, with the best intentions, had asked him to look after me. My aunt thought she was leaving me in the hands of a shepherd. But Mr. Wiley was most likely a wolf; a self-assertive one.

"Thank you for a delightful evening Maurice. The meal was delicious and the show, well, I have no words to express how much I enjoyed the dance performance. It set my soul to dancing! But it's late and I need to get back to my hostel."

"I thought we could have a night cap in my room." His voice was honeyed but his smile betrayed his devilish intentions.

"Maurice, I'm afraid it is late, and I really need to return to my place. You promised to take me back."

Still forcing a smile and trying to keep the sweetness in his voice Maurice explained the perils a young lady could encounter alone in the night streets of Bangkok. My heart, though gripped with fear at the end of his alarming discourse, was firmly resolved.

"Are you telling me you're not escorting me back to my place, Maurice?"

"Matter of fact, I am not." His tone was sharp, and the smile was gone.

Fortuitously, the waiter approached our table to ask if we needed anything else.

"Could you please direct me to your concierge?" I asked as I stood up.

"I thank you for dinner and the show Maurice. Good night."

I followed the waiter to the lobby. I was sure Maurice's smile had turned into a grimace of angry disappointment.

## M R Martin

M R Martyn is a two-time Pushcart Nominee, former professional, soul-sucking-content writer, and published print and online fiction author, including a novel and educational children's content.

She lives a nomadic, minimalist lifestyle with her husband and stops to pet random cats and dogs—occasionally, she allows strangers an intimate look at her moondust collection.

M R Martyn finds it hilarious that fiction writers need to make their stories believable to their audience.

# The Importance of Lists

BY M R MARTYN

Loud Muzak played familiar *surfin' music* Rose recognized yet found inappropriate, considering near-blizzard conditions wreaked havoc in the village and made it look like the inside of a snow globe. Rose shouldn't have driven on the icy roads despite only living three minutes away by car; she had made a rash decision. But she needed a packet of vanilla beans, confectioner's sugar, and that irksome something else she was now cruising the aisles for and tried hard to remember.

"You need help?" A lanky store clerk asked Rose as she passed him yet again.

"Yes, it would be great if you could tell me what else is on my list." She laughed. The clerk had heard that same line a hundred times.

She had made a list. On the advice of well-meaning family and friends, her house looked like a Post-It-Note factory exploded.

*Take your thyroid pills.*
*Water the plants.*
*Don't touch the thermostat.*
*Don't leave the stove on.*
*Your keys are in the bowl in the foyer.*
*Eat!*


It was true. Rose had difficulty remembering. It was normal. Everyone said. It was part of the grieving process. She would recover. She was too young for something more serious, like dementia; she wasn't even sixty yet.

Lists. Yes. Rose made lists. She made a list of what she wanted to accomplish and what she had to finish. Her daughter Meghan had bought cute, multi-colored packages of Post-It-Notes, and a litter of neon squares decorated her fridge, kitchen counter, and bedside table.

The little lists helped with the daily tasks but didn't replace the giant void in her heart, and Rose dreaded the thought of her memory vanishing completely.

Yet here she was loitering in the supermarket aisle, looking for that last item on the list that tormented her memory because she hadn't remembered to bring the list.

*How's that for irony? She thought.*

Most of the aisles had thinned out; only a handful of others were desperately looking for that thing they couldn't find. Rose didn't think the man in the produce aisle was really looking for a kumquat or shallots; he was looking for conversation, even if it was meaningless as "some weather!"

Rose had already given him that small token and a smile. It's all she had to offer.

While scanning the shelving in the bakery aisle, she tried to find the clue that would trigger an avalanche of words that may guide her to that singular item she could visualize written on the bottom of her list yet couldn't read. She did a mental checklist: shortbreads, vanilla crescent, Linzer jam cookies, palmier, cannoli, alfajores, kolaches, meringue, and coconut macaroons. She'd been baking this European collection of cookies since she was young.

She had the essential ingredients in the pantry, as any decent baker would. However, without that last elusive ingredient, her foray into her baking endeavor, if the weather forecast held, could end before she started.

She had taken the chance to leave the house when the storm granted the neighborhood a five-minute window. The idea of going came out of nowhere. Perhaps it was the snow and sentimental feeling of Christmas that urged Rose to go. She thrived on giving her home-baked cookies to friends and strangers who would enjoy them. This little gratification went a long way to suppressing her loneliness although that loss had its own agenda.

Since Mike died, the house had become too much. She could manage the inside, but the yard and the long circular sidewalk bending around her house like an elbow was a bitch to shovel. Mr. Chapman helped when he could, but he had other battles. Rose hated that sidewalk; in summer, she hated the sloped lawn.

Standing in the baking aisle, she picked up a few tubes of sprinkles, miniature silver balls, and tiny white snowflakes. She added them to her basket, although the price was ridiculous. And she knew they weren't what she came for.

That elusive item tickled her brain and ran away with the secret in a game of hide-and-seek, and she was losing more often than winning. And for the kicker, her memory played that other game of peekaboo at the most inappropriate moments. Of course, Rose kept that secret under wraps.

The forgetting didn't exactly happen as she always

thought it would happen. It wasn't orderly and how she usually liked to do things. It was random, without rhyme or reason, but always elusive.

Well-meaning people assured her that everyone forgot stuff. Who hadn't scratched their head wondering where they put their keys, where they hid those important papers, people's names, or that convenient lie: oh, I forgot to call, to pay the bill, to send a thank-you note. It was a side effect of living. They suggested she find humor in every situation.

And Rose knew that forgetting always lurked on the other side of remembering.

However, this new forgetting was never as convenient as that. This forgetting habit played tricks. Rose forgot to eat. She forgot what program she was watching a minute ago. She forgot words and names. Common words. The names of family members. She arrived in places and didn't know how she got there. What was worse was that she was aware that these out-of-place moments were becoming a pattern.

It also happened with her dreams. Although Dr. Halat tried to appease her by saying that forgetting her dreams wasn't part of any diagnosis, it bothered Rose more than anything. She'd always been a vivid dreamer, with such dazzling imagery. Within her dreams, she felt so in tune with her world. Sometimes, the images in her dreams were a confusing sequence of pets she once loved and a basket of distorted memories she took comfort in. She resented that forgetting also robbed her of secretly meeting Mike in her dreams and the comfort of grieving and missing him. Yet these dreams also introduced her to people she had never met. Characters whose features she could see down to the moles on their upper lip and recognize the sound of their voices—meeting them in secret rendezvous. After Mike died, sleep eluded her. Missing her husband and grieving disrupted her pattern—her doctor said. It would take time—her doctor said.

One morning a few months ago, she woke with the distinct impression that she had had a powerful dream. But when she transitioned from sleep to waking, the dream vanished but left an imprint. All that day, she felt its residual power, could hear the laughter, and the sensation as if the dream were on the other side of the wall. Only she couldn't pass through the door and the dream lay abandoned on the threshold.

At first, it was a one-off. Like her doctor predicted, dreaming returned, and Rose took comfort in that. Then, the memory lapses happened more frequently, and she googled the symptoms of dementia. Disappointed with her search, the top sites from the leading medical authorities listed cookie-cutter symptoms—a regurgitated list of ten signs.

Her doctor chided her for self-diagnosis, which annoyed Rose. If the NHS, the Cleveland Clinic, the Mayo Clinic, the John Hopkins Clinics all invested in broadcasting medical advice on the internet, didn't that substantiate the facts?

Rose merely twirled her thumbs and said nothing when her doctor told her not to worry. Yet here she was in the grocery store, looking for that thing she couldn't remember. The more Rose strained to see the list she could picture on the kitchen counter, the more convinced she became she had onset dementia.

"You alright then?" A plump check-out girl tidying the front checkout asked with a courteous smile. Rose noticed she was the last customer. The light outside had transitioned into that nebulous white where snow glare and dimness uncomfortably meet and become indistinguishable.

"Are you closing?" Rose suddenly became aware that the piped music had stopped.

Quietude replaced the incessant noise from the cash registers chiming and clacking, or whatever noise a cash register made.

"Yes. The storm. We're closing so everyone can get home safely."

"Okay then. I'll pay for my things." Rose smiled and pushed her cart toward the checkout. Outside, the snow formed soft dunes on top of the cars in the parking lot.

"Sorry. It's really coming down out there. Lost track of time."

"That's alright. We'll get you on your way." The check-out girl faked compassion and put the few items into Rose's cloth bag.

The door silently closed behind her; Rose pulled up her collar and ducked deeper into her coat. She couldn't remember where she had parked, but she concluded the gray Honda was hers since there were only four cars. It had the least amount of snow and was parked closer. She deduced that employees always got shitty parking spots.

She rummaged in her purse for the fob and cut herself on a piece of paper; she should have kept her leather gloves on. A red drop of blood surfaced, and she fished out a tissue to stop the bleeding and walked toward the Honda, clicked the auto start and door locks, and threw her purse and shopping bag onto the passenger seat. She pressed the tissue to her finger—it was a slight cut, but it stung.

The wiper cleaned most of the snow from the windshield, and her breath fogged the interior. Rose shivered in unison with the dropping temperature and pulled ahead. Deep snow grumbled beneath her tires, making it impossible to see where the parking lot ended, and the street began. She relied on instinct. Luckily, she only lived a few blocks away. She looked forward to a piping cup of tea, a blanket draped over her knees while looking through the cookbooks to refresh her memory of which cookies to bake first. And more importantly, figure out how to cope with the missing item on her list.

Her speedometer said she was doing ten miles per hour; she couldn't get much traction because a slippery sheet of ice lay beneath the snow. She remembered the drizzle that this morning had encased every vehicle, tree, and shrub in ice.

A car stuck in a deep drift blocked her street, so she had to keep going straight and backtrack up the laneway that separated the last block she lived on from the small wood but gave everyone on her street access to a garage and stored everyone's whatnots. Mike had imported the habit to park in the garage from Canada, although he had to wiggle himself in and out of the car as the garage was much too narrow for modern cars.

Driving through the storm, she could barely distinguish the houses. Snow dunes formed on people's lawns—people she should have known because they were neighbors, yet she could no longer remember their names. She concentrated on cutting a swath through the deepening snow, her hands knuckling the steering wheel like when she was sixteen and learning to drive while her father yelled instructions and braced himself for impact.

"Eyes on the road!" She could hear his voice and the frustration that he'd rather be at The White Elephant on a Saturday afternoon with his friends than with his teenage daughter, who couldn't tell the clutch from the brake.

Rose awkwardly parked her car in the lane, ten feet away from her garage, because a drift created a natural barrier like a dune in the Mojave Desert. She reached for her belongings, pinched the collar tight, and left deep prints in the snow. The walls of snow collapsed inside her ankle boots and melted against her thin stockings.

Rose used the fence to propel her forward and mistakenly stepped on a shovel buried in the snow. The wood and metal handle sprung upward. The ferocity with which it punched her in the face ignited a spark on impact. If Rose had seen this happen on television, she would have laughed. But the pain was surprising and utterly unexpected.

She lost her balance and fell face-first against the cement fence post; the collision tore her skin on contact with the rough edge. Although she saw a series of sparks like miniature stars in a firework explosion, the intense pain dominated all else, though she wouldn't remember it later.

Rose landed awkwardly on her side, bracing for her fall she snapped her wrist bone in two. On the way down her face smashed against the retaining wall. Speckles of blood from the gash on her nose stained the snow—she might have passed out from the pain momentarily. She felt a slow crawling rivulet of warm blood trickle down her face, over her nose, down along her skin until the collar of her turtleneck absorbed most of it. The rest bled into the snow.

Rose kept her eyes closed and summoned the strength to surmount the fire-like pain in her head when she heard the faint ringing of her shrill telephone. She had one of those old-fashioned phones because she liked how they looked and how she could cradle the receiver into her neck while talking and cooking. She opened her eyes, and a giant fat snowflake landed on her pupil. Instinctively, her eyes blinked.

She tried to sit up, but the movement sent a burning poker of pain through her body. She fought for strength and prayed the pain would cease. Undoubtedly, Rose knew she had to get up or crawl toward the gate, use the lethal post to pull herself up and unfasten the latch—something she could do in her sleep most days.

Rose talked herself into taking three long breaths before trying to rise. She was sure now that it was her phone that kept ringing, though, for a split second, she thought the ringing stemmed from the pain. She grimaced when joyfully, she could hear Rusty, her neighbor's annoying Jack Russell, bark. That meant Mr. Chapman was coming outside to take the dog for a piss. Small bladder. Rusty barked incessantly. She overheard Mr. Chapman say, "Oh, stop it! Just do your thing."

Rose could hear Mr. Chapman's frustration. The family dog should have been their teenage son's responsibility, but the moody child neglected the dog shamefully. She strained to listen, and between Rusty's sharp yaps, she stammered, "Help me! Help!" Only Rusty cut her off with each bark.

Rose brought her legs closer for warmth, and cold snow infiltrated her boots. During the fall, her slacks had risen to mid-calf and her exposed skin burned like fire. Shifting only intensified the cold.

One more minute—Rose bargained with herself, braced herself for the pain, and dug deeper for the strength to rise.

Rusty's bark changed from annoying yaps to frantic barks and intermittent growls. Mr. Chapman reprimanded the dog, "Shut the fuck up!" The words billowed through the snowy quietness.

And then the screen door slammed. The distant phone stopped ringing. Rusty barked through the glass, and only a stillness attributed to heavy snowfall accompanied Rose's breathing. The snowy landscape took on a pale blue hue. A tear rolled over the bridge of her nose and splashed into the snow, burrowing like a worm next to the traces of blood.

The annoying ringing in her ear broke the stillness; she heard her pulse emit like a signal through the snow.

The news would report that it was the worst storm of the century. The snowfall broke records for the accumulated inches and the coldest day on record. Logistics became a nightmare for the number of accidents reported on the highway, injuries related to accidents, insurance claims associated with accidents, and broken water pipes.

Rose opened her eyes; the snow quickly covered her red coat and black slacks. Her teeth chattered until a warmness spread throughout her and she could no longer feel her body. Her blurred vision made everything look like a mirage, and the endless white shimmered like heat set on atmospheric boil. She remembered the item on her list.

When the snow plough came down the alley, the driver cursed the gray Honda parked at what he called: "a fucking stupid angle." The car forced him to pass closer to the opposite fence line than he liked, and the blade sent a stream of dirty snow into an arc that left a tall snowbank that someone would eventually have to clear by hand.

When the dull glare of sun returned for half an hour that late afternoon, Rusty pissed on the mountain of snow. He sniffed the dropped leather glove frozen to the ground. Mr. Chapman lit a cigarette, cupping the flame and checking over his shoulder to ensure spying eyes weren't watching.

He wondered why Rose had parked her car that way until he saw a small mountain of plowed snow covering her garage door. He wondered if he should offer to shovel the snow; then again, he corrected his thought pattern, she could always ask for help. *She has my number.*

He stomped with Rusty down the plowed path toward the street that circled back on the sidewalk to the front door of his house. Using the front door would allow him an excuse to slip into the two-piece bath and wash his hands and face with the potent flowery soap and remove traces of his cigarette. He rarely smoked on his street; he waited to get to the park and hide beyond the row of evergreens before quenching the craving.

When he hung his coat up, he said to himself, "it's getting dark so quickly."

Later that night, he woke at two o'clock to the sound of ringing. At first, he thought he dreamed the sound, but he distinctly heard the soft ringing as he lay in the stillness. He recognized it as being Rose's antiquated phone. He considered closing the window, but not with his sleep apnea. Nah, he just couldn't bother to get out of bed. Instead, he hoped everything was okay—only bad news ever came after midnight.

In the morning, he took his cup of coffee to the den. He'd be working from home today; such was the privilege of being the boss. He fired up his laptop, checked on the latest news. As predicted, the snowstorm had left a swath of destruction in its path. Road closures occupied the newscasts.

When the police cruiser pulled up at Rose's door, he craned his neck. Two officers rang the bell and knocked loudly; one stomped in the deep snow to look inside Rose's living room window. Mr. Chapman shouldn't have been so nosy. He watched the officers shift on their cold feet and wait impatiently.

On second thought, Mr. Chapman rose from his chair and inserted himself into their visit by opening his front door. "Can I help you?" he said while his breath sent plumes of white in their direction.

"Do you know Rose Grimshaw?"

"Of course. She's lived on this street longer than most. Did something happen to her daughter?"

"No. We're looking for Rose. Her daughter said she's been calling all night. No answer, and that her mother wasn't the sort not to pick up."

"Her car's outback. Covered in snow. So, she's got to be home." Mr. Chapman gestured to the north.

The officer stomped through the high snow toward the gate when Mr. Chapman called him back.

"Come through the house. You won't get that gate open without a shovel."

While the officers backtracked through the deep snow, Mr. Chapman slipped on his coat and boots. He waited by the door.

Rusty barked and sniffed the police officers' legs, but as a dog, he had a solid amount of respect for anyone in uniform, and he behaved. Mr. Chapman led the way out the backdoor; he had already shoveled a path for Rusty. Yellow snow marked the way.

"That's hers, I think." Mr. Chapman brushed the snow covering the license plate away and nodded. "Yup. Snow plough really socked her in."

"You think she may have gone someplace with someone?"

Mr. Chapman didn't appreciate how the officer probed and dug in his eyes for an interrogation. Mr. Chapman blinked and looked away.

"Not that I know. She has friends. But for the last year or so, she's been staying home. Lost her husband."

Rusty peed on the high snowbank; he scratched at the glove frozen in the snow, biting the leathery thumb.

"I guess we need to find a way in. We'll try the front again. Maybe she is a sound sleeper."

"She keeps a spare key under the dwarf holding the lantern. In case you need to." Mr. Chapman didn't like to divulge this careless habit and had warned Rose several times to find a better hiding spot. Now he felt guilty for knowing where the key was.

"She have any medical issues? That you know of?" The shovel dug around in Mr. Chapman's eyes again; cops made him uncomfortable.

"No. Never one to complain."

"Thanks for your help. What's your name?"

"Chapman. Fred."

When they entered Mr. Chapman's house again, Mrs. Chapman rolled her eyes, questioning her husband with unspoken words. She nodded at the officers while pinching her fuzzy housecoat.

Mr. Chapman closed the door on the officers and the cold that entered the front door. He explained to his wife that they were concerned about Rose at the behest of Rose's daughter.

"I'm sure the old bird's fine. Probably drank herself to sleep or mixed up her meds. You know how old people are." Mrs. Chapman poured herself a cup of coffee and stared out the window with a blank look on her face.

"When are you going to shovel the driveway?"

"I have work to do. Get your son out of bed. Since he's not going to school, he might as well make himself useful."

"Yeah, like he's gonna listen to me." Mrs. Chapman turned her back on her husband and plopped a piece of bread into the toaster.

Mr. Chapman sat back in his office chair; his coffee had gone tepid. He saw one officer leave the house, get something from the cruiser, and return a few moments later.

Mr. Chapman decided it was only courtesy to get his coat and boots on again and shovel Rose's long sidewalk. There was a fat chance his son would do it for nothing. And he didn't want another confrontation.

He heard the tail-end of the weather forecast; they expected another three inches of snow.

He yanked his woolen snow hat down over his ears and wound the scarf across his lips. Sometimes he resented his son and that lazy attitude.

The patrol car remained parked in the driveway all morning. Mr. Chapman shoveled three times to keep up with the falling snow. He took Rusty for three walks, three smoke breaks, and debated the independent thoughts of what he would say to his son at the dinner table tonight. They couldn't let him continue as he was.

At midnight, the snowplow made another pass. Because the driver had a cousin who lived in the same neighborhood, he also cleared the back laneway again. There was no point in denying that who you knew paid dividends.

The evening news had shown the highlights of the havoc on a loop; every essential service personnel heeded their call of duty. If only his son had such inspirations.

Rose Grimshaw's latest Facebook imprint made the evening news. A quick and breathless interview with Meghan, Rose's daughter, asked about her mother's last whereabouts.

Rusty hadn't stopped barking all day and evening as officers came and went. Nosy onlookers tried to pump Mr. Chapman for details that he couldn't answer. Rose Grimshaw competed the following morning with highway and school closures, weather advisories, and stay-at-home warnings.

"Last seen…" Mr. Chapman's head snapped around, "… at the independent supermarket on Crenshaw Avenue, just before closing. The anchor said, "Rose Grimshaw was last seen wearing a reddish coat, dark slacks, and carrying a cloth shopping bag with flowers on it."

The news anchor also included that Rose, now classified as missing, seemed dazed. A courtesy interview with a checkout girl added a personal detail. "She wasn't out of it, if you know what I mean, but she was oblivious kinda—she was in our store for about an hour. We asked her several times if she needed help, but she just shook her head. I think she bought some baking stuff."

Mr. Chapman was confident they had the right Rose. Rose had always been an avid baker, and with Christmas two weeks away, it only made sense. His family always looked forward to the tin of international cookies. But what made little sense was that Rose vanished. Who would harm that demure old lady? Sadly, Mr. Chapman had suspicions about his son, who wasted hours playing games pretending to kill. However, the police let it slip that nothing appeared disturbed or stolen.

Over the last few days, Rusty had barked himself hoarse and was now barking with a winded rasp. Mrs. Chapman talked on the phone with the vet, who advised her to keep the dog calm and secluded and away from disturbance.

Rusty was now whimpering, scratching, and frantically yipping in the two-piece bath. Mr. Chapman had no doubt that when Rusty ceased with the pathetic behavior, he was unraveling the toilet paper or chewing on the toilet brush during those rare intermissions of quiet.

Although Mr. Chapman kept vigilance, Rose's house remained dark and quiet. As the snow melted on the sidewalk, nosy passersby would point at her house and even dare to look inside the dark window until he shooed them away.

A reward poster made the rounds on Social Media

channels, light standards, bus shelters, and the supermarket's bulletin board. Everyone on the street speculated. Meghan was beside herself. She phoned Mr. Chapman for an update every evening.

Mrs. Chapman noticed the first green shoot of an early crocus under their bay window where the west-facing sun always fooled the flowers into sprouting too soon. Christmas was a distant memory. Winter had been too long and severe. Everyone was sick of snow.

The roads were a mess; there was talk of flooding. The village didn't have it in their budget to remove any significant accumulations of dirty snow on the side streets; they concentrated on major arteries and highways leading in and keeping to their strict budget despite irrational complaints.

Mr. Chapman returned to his routine of going to work, and each time he saw a gray Honda, he wondered what happened to Rose. Rusty recovered his barking voice and was still pissing on the giant heap of ice on the north side of the fence in the alley.

Hundreds of people called the hotline and claimed they had seen Rose in locations that always proved false. Everyone has a look-alike.

Mr. Chapman no longer bothered to hide his smoking from his wife. Although she was often on the cusp of nagging him, he shot her a look that stopped further discussion. He never bothered her about the chocolates and candy she consumed when she thought he wasn't looking.

Rusty discovered the body; in hindsight, Mr. Chapman believed that Rusty had always known. As more of the snow pile melted, the dog became obsessed with tugging on a corner of red wool cloth. It's true what they say about a dog and its bones.

Meghan had sent a tow truck to move the car to storage

weeks earlier since Rose's garage front had become a deposit for excess snow. The cops had dusted the car for suspicious prints and other telltale signs of foul play.

Mr. Chapman cocked his head when Rusty pulled out a leather handle that slowly gave way from under the snow. It looked like a purse. And then it was a purse. He dropped his cigarette butt, and it hissed for a brief second on the wet ground.

He fought Rusty for the purse and when he won, his hand dove into the purse to retrieve the wallet. His gut churning with excitement and trepidation rolled into a nausea-forming ball in his throat.

The wallet came out and dragged a square, orange piece of paper with it and cut his finger with surgical precision. It fluttered like paper flutters before it lands.

The license identified Rose Grimshaw.

The Post-It-Note, which was stained with two drops of blood, was a short shopping list. Two ingredients: vanilla bean, confectioner's sugar.

Beneath the short list it said: "My name is Rose Grimshaw; I live at 2023 Burnham Thorpe."

# The Train Man

## BY M R MARTYN

I couldn't believe it. But there he was, the handsome man I had met on the train in Germany three years earlier. I stood motionless as a still portrait of his attractive face was broadcast on the television. I know I stared; my mouth was surely agape; the mug in my hand crashed unceremoniously to the tile floor sending the dog scampering.

When I met him, he was eating a tomato and cheese sandwich. Such a strange little fact to remember, yet when I thought of him over the last three years, two things stood out for me, and the sandwich was one of them.

I was on my way from Frankfurt to Linz, Austria. My visit to Germany that year taught me Germans keep a rather good secret. I would be foolish and even reckless to share it on such a public forum. Revealing what I learned would change everything.

But that morning, as I stared at the television, the anchor's lip babbling, eager to share the tantalizing tidbits confused and intermingled with opinion and fact, made me relive my German experience.

His name, they said, was Jacob Braun. He was thirty-six, an influential architect from Bonn.

On the train on that June day, I sat in the wrong seat, in the wrong carriage, and potentially at the wrong time. Coming from Canada, I learned all about the importance of the railways that built the country. My grade eight geography teacher bored me to death with RR2 this and the CPR and CNR that, that no teenager would ever find interesting. He didn't teach us how to navigate the system, only the tedious elements that forty years later weren't helping me find my way through the network of train lingo and fast-moving stations.

In Canada, people associate the train with the past. Too bad for those hardworking individuals who devoted their lives to laying track and dying for the economy's advancement and prosperity. In Canada, people drive everywhere. Only those who live in major urban centers rely on some type of train or subway service. Cars and trucks dominate our transport system. A scenic train journey is for people who can afford the opulence of chugging across the vast terrain on a Via Rail vacation.

In Europe, people rely on the train. I envy them the luxury of traveling to their destination in style and never having to find a parking spot; never mind parallel parking which is on the driver's test but infrequently used. Traveling by train is second nature to Europeans. Thinking of the incident, I remember another particularly striking feature of the man. He had beautiful hands. The sort men who play the piano should have. His digits were long and slender. Each nailbed had a distinct lunula showing, and his cuticles were healthy and pink. He wasn't the sort of man who got his fingers dirty. Riding the train can be such an intimate experience because you can't escape the proximity of other patrons regardless of how you try to hide behind the cover of a book, earbuds, or staring rudely out the window.

Because I travel frequently, I speak with many people, sometimes poorly in foreign languages I can't quite grasp. My train partner was highly educated. I sensed that from our short conversation and his mannerism. His impeccable English, even though it was laced with the typical German accent and lyrical lilt, suggested a worldly education.

I had just finished my sojourn to Germany, visiting many villages and cities reachable by efficient train links. In Darmstadt, I toured my first Hundertwasser building and became fascinated by Germany's beautiful and serene parks.

While Germans understand structural elements as is so evident in cities like Wiesbaden, Bremen, and Leipzig, their parks charmed me. Parks in Germany reflect nature. Somehow those landscape architects found the true meaning of balance between serenity and nature. God couldn't have done it better.

Reserved as they seem to strangers, Germans keep the secret of their beautiful country to themselves. Jacob kept his secret as he conversed with me and smiled. Guarding his secret, which the news was spelling out, went unnoticed for nearly a decade.

During the lulls in our conversation that morning, I looked out at the passing scenery, and flashes of lush greenery from perfectly manicured clover, wheat, corn, and beet fields zoomed past my periphery.

I remember being nervous. Shifting anxiously, thinking the train conductor would usher me unceremoniously from the carriage; I must have talked too much.

Although my German has deteriorated, I still understand the basics. Jacob was reading Die Welt, a popular news magazine. The front cover captured a series of photographs of missing women. Grainy images of women loved by family desperately searching for their whereabouts and clinging to that deceitful monster called Hope. I couldn't say for sure, but there were at least twelve squares with portrait faces of young women. *Vermist!* Like people on our Canadian milk cartons, each missing German person had a name and a family desperate for answers. I couldn't help them then.

Jacob, I remember, exited at Regensburg. A beautiful city most tourists have never heard of. Yet, it's so charming with its medieval core, its surviving 12th Century stone bridge, and intersected by the blue Danube that Strauss made famous with his waltz serenade.

Enough already. I knew Jacob had boarded the train in Bonn from my short interlude. He said so. And since it was the weekend, he was making his weekly trip to Regensburg. I didn't know the importance of the statement until I saw Jacob on the news.

Jacob smiled at me as he alighted off the train, his suitcase wheeled behind him. I'm an observer. A bit of advice to my family, friends, or even strangers within my proximity. I see you. I notice intimate details that will eventually give you away.

The newsfeed had switched to a courthouse staircase. Jacob's lawyer faced a hundred microphones and recorders shoved in his direction. *Nicht schuldig. Der falsche Mann.*

Of course, Jacob was innocent. Of course, the police arrested the wrong man. In some lecture halls, the world over, attorneys must practice that phrase, *not guilty*, repeatedly until they sound authentic. I once abhorred defense lawyers. I couldn't grasp their rationale for defending criminals. I've since learned that we wouldn't have rights and laws without them. I believe in justice and truth, though both are not always swift and dutiful. What else would we do instead?

The lawyer was a stout man wearing a fine suit. He had a polished look about him and a seriousness that suggested his client was as innocent as he claimed. He barked into the microphones, *"nicht schuldig!"* to every question and accusation.

I learned many things about train travel in Europe. Train travel is an elegant way to cross from one country to the next. I learned the word alight.

When the automated voice announced the words, "watch your step as you alight from the train," I assumed something got lost in translation. But alight really just means getting off a means of transport. It means get off or come down. A lovely word that doesn't quite capture what happens as a person exits a train dragging an oversized suitcase like Jacob did that morning in Regensburg.

Jacob smiled at me once more before he alighted, and I waved. I wondered what on earth he could be dragging in that cumbersome luggage. I speculated he transported exotic antiques or religious artifacts and architectural salvage to decorate his apartment. As I mused over what sort of apartment a man like Jacob would own in Regensburg, I formed a detailed character sketch. He was a modern man, yet I sensed he'd choose an apartment with floor-to-ceiling windows, the shutters spread open, and a breeze billowing in the sheer drapes. The apartment would have to be renovated but with the original charm intact. It would be just off the downtown core, in a warren of narrow passages and cobblestone streets. There'd be an antique elevator, and Jacob would manhandle the luggage to the top floor.

I pictured an exposed wall, the original brick, and beams setting the theme. The kitchen would be ultra-modern and small. The washing machine built into the bank of cabinets as Europeans do and which always horrifies American and

Canadian tourists on all those international travel shows. A washing machine in the kitchen is where audacity and practicality meet ignorance.

As the train pulled from the station, I saw Jacob weaving his luggage through the crowd and terminal. A few pigeons scattered and parted the way for him. I'm quite sure he no longer thought about me.

For the next hour, I created a life for Jacob. I made assumptions and was right on one account. Jacob was notoriously meticulous. While I pictured him in his make-believe apartment, I assumed Jacob decorated tastefully with high-ticket items, like the marble bust of Beethoven or Mozart, a crystal glass bowl in liquid shades of blue. A landscape painted by an acquaintance with talent. Jacob wasn't the sort who decorated with trash bought off the internet.

He'd keep his shoes in a row, polished as leather should be, the warm scent wafting in the room whenever he opened the antique armoire that housed his wool jackets, his leather shoes, and the umbrella with the carved handle. Every detail about Jacob was exactly like the knit in his merino wool socks and cashmere sweater he wore that day.

His girlfriend would be tall, lanky, and athletic. She'd have poker-straight hair like she had grown and styled since she was young. She'd gather her blonde strands into a ponytail whenever she got down and dirty to sprint in the park. It would bounce with each stride. I think I called her Giselle, or Gaby, then changed her name to Nina. She had the sort of complexion that tanned easily; she had a permanent healthful glow and no wrinkles in sight, although she was a year or two older than Jacob.

Nina would joke about having children. Secretly she didn't want any because, like Jacob, she preferred order over chaos. She had a shrill authoritarian laugh and a direct way of speaking to people, making them feel vulnerable with no place to hide. She worked in finance. Numbers were her thing, and she could understand and debate complex topics.

On her nightstand, she kept a few copies of the works by Schiller, Nietzsche, and Goethe. She didn't read modern fiction and deplored romance novels and films.

If Nina had a weakness, it was her inability to resist chocolate. She hid bite-sized bits of Suchard and Lindt in the kitchen and her coat pockets. Although there is no shame in liking chocolate, Nina thought it was her Achilles Heel. She didn't want anyone to know, especially Jacob.

Jacob knew about Nina's secret addiction. He found it intriguing that she would go to such lengths to hide this secret. Nina didn't live at the apartment; she only came for weekends. She owned an ultramodern home her parents built for her. It was all glass, steel, and white with sharp corners, hygienic tiles, and futuristic furniture imported from Sweden.

I didn't like Nina. She was the sort of woman who made me insecure with her stallion-like beauty. We had nothing in common. I didn't like math at all. But I wanted Jacob to be happy.

Jacob wanted to have children eventually. A boy or girl. It didn't matter to him as long as they were healthy and miniature replicas of himself and Nina. Jacob found Nina fascinating. He'd never met a woman who was as intelligent and confident. Nina knew it all and believed that knowledge was a permanent condition. Jacob would watch her over the rim of a book and mused secretly that Nina, though seemingly perfect, had a giant flaw. She was blind. Blind to her ignorance and impeded vision of life. It's why he kept her around. He wasn't so much in love with her beauty, but with that giant fissure that exposed her for what she was once you got up close and personal. She was a snob.

When the train reached Passau, I had to show my credentials to the border security who boarded the train. He wasn't interested in my Canadian passport. He seemed to be looking for someone. A refugee or illegal.

I slowly stored Jacob away in my memory bank for safekeeping. The last time I saw Jacob, he opened the door to his apartment and felt content to have reached his destination. He slipped off his shoes, stripped his garments, and folded them neatly into the hamper. He wanted a hot shower before Nina arrived. He left the suitcase in the hallway. He poured himself a glass of merlot and sat barefoot on the Bauhaus chair facing the street and sinking sun. His stomach rumbled, thinking about dinner.

As the news ticker spun across the bottom below the anchor, a series of faces populated the screen. It's when I recognized Nina. Every single face had a classic symmetry. Pale skin, long blonde hair, and startling eyes lined to accentuate their irises and keenness in their brows.

Those women in the picture had something else in common. They were missing. They had vanished from their ordinary lives without a hint of where they were hiding. Their missing date ranged from six years ago to one month ago. I dug into the information about the case available on the internet.

With trepidation, I returned to my travel log and confirmed the date. The day Sabine Hofer didn't show up for work, missed her lunch date with her girlfriends, and hadn't been seen since coincided with the date on my ticket stub.

In my pathetic German, I explained what I witnessed on

the day to the agent taking my call on the tipline. It's circumstantial, he told me.

The police released a few details, like the remnants of a tomato and cheese sandwich and track marks on the carpet from a large suitcase. There was no DNA.

None of the women came from the same city. Their last whereabouts became pin marks on a map that followed the train line in a country that is breathtaking and, perhaps, the tourist industry's biggest secret.

Despite my keen sense of observation, I had sat across from a serial killer, and I found him charming.

# This Little Piggy Mystery

BY M R MARTYN

Theo couldn't help himself, and even as his arms pumped with the athletic fury of a seven-year-old, running away from the scene on juvenile adrenaline, away from the toes protruding from the hedge, keeping track of the number 10 on Noah's jersey, the childish nursery rhyme overtook him.

**This little piggy went, wee, wee, wee, all the way home.**

When Theo's mind recognized the blood-red polish on the longer second toe, it was too late to wish that **this little piggy stayed home.**

That sunny afternoon, two weeks before graduating from grade one, Theo and Noah's childhood abruptly ended. Noah would develop an endless quest for thirst even before he reached his teens, and Theo became a sophisticated long-distance runner without ever putting on sneakers.

On most nights after, Theo would hear the echo of his voice. Most often, the echoes were the tail end of his screams interrupting his sleep; he'd awaken with his pjs stuck to his damp skin and be startled by the surreal technicolor images of toes and bluish skin, knowing he couldn't un-see what he had seen.

His parents handled the situation as delicately as possible from the outset of that June day.

"Mom, Mom!" Theo huffed and ran into his mother's arms. Donna had set her gin and tonic on the picnic table. An internal monitor told her something was wrong when she saw the two boys dart through the park toward the revered old oak where she was sitting in the shade. She was keeping Theo's brother entertained; this **little piggy had roast beef,** so he wouldn't be a nuisance to the two boys about to unlock the mysteries of adulthood.

Theo buried his face in his mother's summer dress, for he was entirely out of breath—literally, and he gestured with his slightly pudgy finger toward the hedge at the end of the park.

Theo was Noah's junior by a few months; although they shared the same height, the age difference caught up to Theo and was perceptible to those who knew both boys. It's also how Noah outran Theo, and he didn't waste a second on a foolish nursery rhyme when **this little piggy had none**. Noah was mature for his age.

"What?" His mother tried to shake the fright from Theo as she listened in on Beth and Mark and what Noah was saying about toes. Something about Sally—none of it made sense. Mark glanced at Richard, and they set off on a trot toward the hedge. Donna didn't think it was a good idea and called out. "Where are you going? What did Noah say?"

Beth hoisted Noah up, who was now sobbing into her arms; the realization of what he had seen had caught up with him while Theo was still working his way through **this little piggy went to market.**

Both boys would develop habits that shaped the rest of their lives. They'd outgrow the bedwetting—but never the nightmares. One would openly discuss the event with anyone and never let it go. The other learned from his parents what's past is past and only allowed his dream state access to the memory. Of course, the incident also shaped Theo's phobia about toes—he would never go to the beach, and he disliked summer—the sight of open shoes and nail polish.

Mark and Richard came back solemnly. Mark went to the house on Mango Street to call the police. There were whispers and knowing glances; Beth shifted Noah in her arms and grew impatient for Mark. Richard shook his head and raked his curls into a frenzy while Donna tried to flatten Theo's by petting his head while feeling the tears wetting the thin material of her summer dress. She rocked to a rhythm and shushed Theo, who wanted nothing more than to remember the rhyme about happy piggies as they were before he made the connection.

The boys recognized the toes. They had seen the toes make footprints in their sandbox. Sally said it was called Morton's toe and giggled when she wiggled her extra-long second toe—she always painted hers blood red. Theo had a crush on Sally. Noah said he'd marry her one day.

Sally was the most enigmatic of adults in their life, although their mothers didn't share their enthusiasm but said it wasn't Sally's fault. Theo never understood what exactly wasn't Sally's fault. Sally's biggest problem was bringing a moment of imperceptible silence like a come-along whenever she entered a room. Men would smile wider and adjust their posture. Women would purse their lips and send silent missiles toward their husbands. However, the proof was in the pudding—the messages seldom translated correctly, as ensuing arguments would attest. Even liberal-minded people like Donna, Richard, Mark, and Beth fell victim to Sally's allure. On many nights, the falsely decoded messages needed redirecting behind closed bedroom doors and angry voices. But—it wasn't Sally's fault.

Everyone living on Mango Street was either born there or had lived within a five-mile radius. Mark, Donna, Beth, and Richard had known each other since grade school and returned to the street when new houses popped up like mushrooms on wide suburban plots that you couldn't buy in the inner city.

Sally came into their midst when the Dennisons rented out a room that Mr. Dennison had refurbished into a studio for his photography business; and then the economy turned sour. At first, the setback embarrassed Mr. Dennison.

Mrs. Dennison didn't allow pride to stand in the way of surviving a downside in the economy caused by the idiot running the country, and she did all the work. She posted the classified ad, turned the studio into a cute apartment, and even put flowers in the vase when the new tenant moved in. She had spoken to the prospective tenant from Georgia on the phone and even called the restaurant that had also hired Sally sight unseen. On the phone, Sally exuded southern charm; that slow drawl reminded Mrs. Dennison of *Gone With the Wind*—funny that it would come to bite her in the ass. Sally's references checked out, and her last employer said she was the best he had ever had.

Everyone on Mango Street was prepared for Sally's arrival. Sally was making the long trip from McCaysville, Georgia, in her secondhand Ford. Mrs. Dennison tried to overcome her shock by wearing a sweetness-personified appearance and proudly showing off the jaw-dropping beauty to the neighborhood.

Mr. Dennison received the missile message, though

everyone would later find out that he didn't follow the instructions his wife intended for him to follow. And Mr. Dennison unintentionally started a club—men only—because no man is an island. Sally was an excellent swimmer, as everyone found out on the afternoon of her arrival when the community christened the opening of their swimming pool. Sally accidentally slipped into the pool and came out of the water with the frilly dress clinging to all the wrong places.

That afternoon, Sally drew the short straw and became **this little piggy who went to the market to get slaughtered.**

Robert Radmer was born and raised in a small town on the shore of a great lake. He has spent the past few decades balanced on that edge between the local and the worldly, viewing each from the perspective of the other, and being confounded by both. He hopes that clarity will arise from the crafting of short stories.

# "So, One Night"

### BY ROB RADMER

Jimmy and me get together about once a month for a few drinks and some shooting-the-breeze. Nothing too important gets said. We just do it out of habit, mostly, maybe hoping for a few laughs and an excuse not to drink alone. Last time we met we're watching some ball game on the bar TV and playing peek dice in a half-assed way, and Jimmy wants to tell me some story about one of his girlfriends, and I fight him off pretending I hate all these secret stories of his supposed harem. I give him the usual shit about his fantasy life, but deep down, I love it when he does this, cause truth be told, my love life hasn't been too productive of stories late. Even my fantasy world is beginning to let me down in the interesting story department, and it pleases me to listen to him tell his yarns that, shit, might even be true. So, I calm down, and he begins.

"So, one night, she comes up with this wild idea that death should be a regular part of her life."

After another beer ordered, another cigarette lit, another moment of silence, he launches into his tale.

"I mean, here is this kid, everything's going her way, I mean, she's struggling, but she just got the new job, bought the house, she's paying bills, she's getting lots of sexual attention from friends, acquaintances, and even strangers—you should hear some of the stories she tells me—and now she wants to add a touch of death to her day. What the hell does that mean? And what am I supposed to say? I mean, what I want to say, but you know, I gotta hold back because ya can't just blurt out every damn fool idea that jumps into your head, people will think you're nuts, or worse, boring. So what I wanna say is something like, "Hold on kid, you'll have plenty of death in your life all too soon. Let's not rush this thing,' but I mean I can't say that kind of thing, I mean it's cruel and sort of a downer, but shit, it's true even if it can't be said."

We were in one of those places that leave bowls of free peanuts lying around everywhere so that you get a sense that you are doing something interesting while you are really just working up a good thirst. Jimmy and I loved places like this. I actually hated peanuts, and especially hated that sort of rough-but-flakey, sort of dusty texture that peanut shells had. Normally my fingertips revolted at that blackboard-chalk feeling. It's amazing what a fellow will put up with for a bit of talk to go with his beer.

"So what I did say was something like, 'Yeah, death can be a real friend, helps you focus on what might be important, maybe helps to pick and choose, gives you some guidance on stuff to avoid.'

"Of course, this sounds like the bullshit it is the moment

it's out of my mouth, only I can't take it back, and I can't really fix the damn words now that are out there, I mean, I realize that saying any more will only make things worse and make me look more of a jerk.

"So I just stay quiet, maybe ask her if she needs another beer or something, offer her a cigarette, spend some time finding the pack and lighting us each one. But all the time the idea of death is just hanging there between us, both of us knowing it, and both of us can't quite get a handle on the death-as-a-part-of-life thing.

"I mean, this kid is smart. She sees bullshit a mile off and runs away if you're lucky or calls you out in public and humiliates the shit out of you if you're not."


I love this guy's stories. They always involve women, and they are always cute and always smart. I don't know where he finds them, and I don't know where they've always gone by the time I get on the scene. Does he invent all these situations? I'm not sure that I want to find out one way or the other. I reach for another fistful of peanuts and listen to him go on.


"So now we've got the big concept, a change-your-life-kind of thought, and it's just hanging, and neither of us knows what to do or say next.

"The thought crosses my mind to just suggest going back to her place to fool around some, but something in the back of my mind seems to tell me that getting laid is not in my immediate future, I mean if I don't handle this goddamn death thing I may never get in the sack with her again, and I have a real sick feeling that it's not just with her that I won't be getting laid."

Jimmy's story is getting more and more depressing, and to top it off he is getting his usual incredible run with the dice. I am never certain about the truth of his stories, but it is clear from his skill at calling liar's dice that he can fling the bullshit with the best of the con men. I am beginning to think that the money going steadily from me to him is just some sort of payment for the entertainment he provides. I slide another round over to him and it seems to provide the fuel to continue.

"Now, I'm totally spooked, and I can hardly look at her, and my bar room chit-chat skills have left out the back door, jumped on their horses and ridden out of town. I mean, the silence is so thick at these two barstools that other conversations have begun to kinda slow down, people are beginning to look around, and the owner of the place has begun to stare at us as if we smell bad, or we got the plague or something.

"I'm dragging on my smoke to beat the band, but she is sitting quiet, not drinking, not smiling, not fucking breathing as far as I can tell, and I realize I gotta take a leak, but I get the feeling that right now is not a good time to excuse myself, only I'm thinking that leaving the room might be the only acceptable response to this godforsaken idea of hers, like maybe leaving and coming back might be a good way to restart this conversation, and Jesus, I realize now that I really do have to take a leak, real bad, like when did all this come on, I've only had a couple of beers, the night's young, I'm usually good for a couple hours, at least, but man, I am suddenly really needing a visit to the pisser.

"But you know, I can't get up the nerve to leave, can't handle saying "Excuse me," or "Hang on just a minute, I'll be right back," or even the lame "I gotta get some more smokes." Nothing will come out of my mouth, my brain and my mouth are locked up, I'm beginning to think I'm lucky that my lungs and heart are not affected by this fucking autopilot fuckup, and how the fuck do I start my brain again, and do I have a chance in hell of ever getting another date with this chick—when all of a sudden she says, 'I've gotta go to the girl's room.'

"Simple as that. She doesn't wait for me to say anything, good thing too, cause I don't think my vocal cords were unlocked yet, she just slides off the stool away from the bar."


Jimmy takes a break as he comes to the realization that all of this talk of pissing has driven him to the knowledge that he has to relieve himself. It's funny that this basic need can be ignored for a while if you are having a good enough time. It's comforting to know that you are in charge of your life for at least the occasional moment. I ponder this business of eating, drinking, and pissing, and realize I am having a good time. Jimmy returns, all jovial and all 'cause he has just completed one more successful urination, and he starts in.

"Well, you know, chicks always for some reason take their purse when they go to the can. I don't know, makeup, or something, some sort of shield to protect them from guys staring or something, so of course I don't think anything of it when she grabs that little leatherette bag and heads away from the bar. I'm so goddamn relieved that one of us has done something or other to release the tension that I practically feel like I've taken a leak right there—you know that great relaxed feeling you get? And I actually have to kind of sneaky-like check my crotch to see if I have pissed my pants, and I'm so concerned and worried about this that I don't even notice her heading out the front door until it's just the back of her head and that cute little ass that I'm never gonna get to see again."

So I call the bartender over to order another round, and while we wait I settle up with Jimmy for the last (for now) of the peek dice losses. Quiet overtakes our talking, and we just stare at the game on TV, gathering up a few more peanuts, shucking and remembering, chewing and imagining, recalling the old times, and maybe getting just a tiny little glimpse into the future.

# Commencement

BY ROB RADMER

The field of marshmallows around my feet looked strange, illuminated, and revealed solely by the motorcycle's low beam. The high-school-graduation-night prank was a beauty, full of wit without malice. Dozens of bags of the stuff had been cast upon the heretofore untroubled confederation of Bermuda, Blue, Rye, and other motley strains of grass that confabulated to produce our mutt of a lawn. The butt of the joke, my English-teacher mother, cheerily appreciated in the early June evening the snowy look of our front yard. She in her wisdom saw it simply as a benign manifestation of creativity driven by hormones and leavened with commencement joy. Her response (and command) was a simple, "Get raking."

As I in the dark raked the white spew from the black-green tangle I could think only of the non-commencement aspect of my own life. Junior year finished, senior year looming like a Great Plains thunderhead on a hot August afternoon. I was anxious to finish school, get out of the house, begin to live a life unfettered by parental preoccupations with their zany misperceptions; but too aware of the swift-passing year, weirdly longing for the earlier, simpler days when I was twelve. The seeming sea of creamy-white roiling around my ankles appeared as a silent yet powerful reminder that I faced an endlessly scrolling blank page, and this I was somehow in charge of lining, texturing, and coloring my life upon it. I had no idea that an outline was being etched at that moment with each sibilant, susurrant rake-stroke.

My buddy with the assertive little Honda had spotted me TV-bluelight-backlit in the dark and had pulled headfirst up to the small-town concrete curbing which sharply delineated the public sphere of the city from the private domain of my parents. The bike's roving beam swept over our violated terrain, illuminating the now-bare patches, small, raked pile, and the remaining carpet of sugar, flour, and air which constitute the childhood delight that is the marshmallow. Disbelief turning to easy pleasure, he shut the bike down, hiked it onto its kickstand, and participated in the normalification, the de-prankizing, the simple tidying-up of my front yard. We worked swiftly and giddily, drawing pleasure from having even a small role in the prank. We savored the tactile pleasure of handling the candy, shuddering in delight as its dry powdery surface shooshed against youthful skin on a summer night, the firmness wonderfully balanced by the sensual giving and reshaping of the fluff as we raked and stuffed goofy handfuls into paper bags, all the while aware of the aura of magic that seemed parcel with the prank. Finished, and foregoing the usual Question-and-Lack-of-Response routine of teenage leave-taking, we climbed aboard the motorcycle and started off into the still-magical night, headed for the Lake, the beach, the edge of the visible world, the regions where adventure, possibility, and the unknown were generally agreed to reside.

Freshly commenced was my flirting partner Katy, and as we approached the beach behind the headlight-flash of the little Honda I could see the eyes and smile of the person with whom I had grown so comfortable during five years of public school. We had been and still were bantering fools, laughing and exploring life and friendship, but nothing more, nothing deeper, the one year age difference having been an unconquerable barrier to real intimacy in the tightly stratified public-school setting replete with unconquerable barriers—age, geography, heritage, social standing were as the Himalayas, the Hindu Kush, the Andes…

Once, when I was in seventh grade and she was in eighth, in my first year undergoing those exquisite torments that are the chief characteristics of junior high school, I had caught her eye across the Sahara Desert of the school orchestra, and we had begun a light-hearted but sturdy ritual of randily calling out each other's names upon chance meetings in the hallways. That year too I had the lottery-winning good fortune to have her assigned to be my accompanist in the district music festival, which had conferred upon me the potential bonanza of a late-night bus ride with its semi-private close quarters after a long day from home. But all of this came to nothing, having fallen victim to social stratification powered by the alternating currents of pubescent awe and childish fear.

Commencement night, marshmallowed and motorcycled, no wiser, no more worldly, and still so perpetually girlfriendless that I had begun to compose odes glorifying celibacy, I see her walking toward me in the dim yet theatrical headlamp light, and suddenly the roaring in my head was not emanating from the illegally open-pipe mufflers of the Honda but from the resonating of the blood in my head crashing in waves against the riprap of my suddenly addled brain, with the added cacophony of a three-way shouting match among id, ego and superego joined further by the dawn-song of the new-wakened bantam cock-fighter within, challenging every man-jack in this-here place to battle, all this in addition to a distant and echo-y public-address-systemed voice calling claiming-stakes race between two horses named Incubus and Succubus, both of them running yet somehow simultaneously tearing at the flapping rags of my now-worthless immortal soul, all of this raging fully and intolerably inside my failing consciousness; yet even more confusingly all of this sensory overload was being violently overridden and obliterated again and again by the explosive ka-ROOM, ka-ROOM of my heart as it kept stopping, then comically restarting itself like a 1951 Ford bread truck on a damp-cold October morning: ka-ROOM - vaporlock - Damn! zg-zg-zg-zg - ka_ROOM - ah, there she catches - oops, death silence, grab the key, OK, she's turning over zg-zg-zg-zg-zg- ka-ROOM, -Whoa! shutdown! -don't flood her -maybe just a tap on the gas pedal -once more, baby, you can do it, we're not dead yet -zg-zg-zg-zg- kaROIFF Christ, a backfire, that can't be good (is there any gas in this thing?) Damn! (This ignition has never worked right) - try once more (jamming this screwdriver into the busted ignition might work?) That's it, twist - zg- zg- zg kaRROOOOORRRR! HOLY SHIT! The carburetor's caught fire!, this is it she's gonna blow, abandon ship, save yourself....

Each successive explosive heartbeat now carried an intensifying meaning like late-inning pitches in a World Series game, time slowing down yet each moment a full-fledged adventure in living and dying both; and yet among all of this crazed disorder, amongst this breakdown of the data stream, in spite of the imminent collapse of cognition, I could clearly register and appreciate the gentle sway of her soft outline as she approached and enveloped me like a breath of warm-sweet-June-Lake Michigan-beach-breeze, and through the din both real and imagined I heard her say my name softly, in the very same two-beat song of the randy-bantering early days; but now, this time, she spoke with a held-back, lingering-leisure, with a promise of sweetness held near an open flame, warm and cozy, cinnamon toast on a winter morning, breathtaking, mind-blowing, awe-inducing; the quick-frozen memory of my name on her lips had an audio-score background accompaniment that seemed to emanate from my upper eyelids banging noisily in the lower, sounding lonely, lost and forlorn like a flagpole rope slapping in a November gale … Time, the wind, the waves, the motorcycle engine, my heart, time time time, all stopped, all poised motionless, balanced, weightless, eternal until all the known world (the world as embodied in me), my consciousness, all tipped now over the edge of the life-abyss, and capitulated fully, totally, completely, emptyingly...I was in love. Startling then to realize (and even now the thought causes me to tremble) that she, too, had been struck by that same thunderbolt of adolescent love, engendering full-throated roaring lust, primal, and easily described: She was 18, commencement was over, so LET'S COMMENCE, DAMMIT! Background music'd by Tommy James and the Shondells, Crystal Blue Persuasion'd into an awestruck but fully committed grabbing for the stuff of life, she possessed an unconscious but sure knowledge that life starts exactly NOW!, and every second wasted was a second lost, and that all of the disparate meanings, varieties, and shadings of the word "life" were just equivalent to, merely synonyms of, only stand-ins for, the word "love," which, of course, was just another word for "sex."

"Richie," she said.

The summer was a blur, progressing from a non-stop and unstoppable torrent of words, both of us talking at the same time, starting finishing each other's sentences, no topic untouched, no thought taboo; communicating ideas, stories, passions, panics, histories, dreams, fantasies, truths and more truths; words spoken at what seemed the speed of light, words that were responded to, commented upon, returned, refuted, rejoined, rebutted, rejected, accepted, appreciated, incorporated, built upon, expanded, developed, smiled at, thanked for; the next phase was quiet, still, breathholding, watching sunset-drenched river bottoms, expectantly waiting for the unthought; then to first touch, hand-hold, arm-rub, cheek-caress; the delicate exploration of a new world, the discovery of how impoverished a thing imagination is when presented with the marvel of simple reality; then on to double-date, country-lane full-body groping, sweat and mucus blending into primordial ooze, steamy and fecund like a Jurassic swamp, becoming further lost in each other's body and soul, both of us now converted to a profound and utter paganism like reverse-Sauls on the road to Damascus, knocked from the ground of our unknowing childhood premises up onto our new-found existential horses by the white light and whirlwind power of cosmically ancient DNA, the billion-year-old cellular forces gathered and spread in their rainbowed glory through the prism of procreation, while the blazing summer sun was tight-focused on she and me, melting and melding two spirits into one soul under the concave glass of a clear Wisconsin sky.

First intercourse—I remember so little, driven by primal forces beyond my ken, cognition subsumed into simply acting, being, doing, performing. Two virgins becoming one something-else, two spiritual and emotional realms conjoining, but in that moment transforming in an ancient alchemy the spiritual and emotional into a new-old form, turning not lead into gold but in some hyper-transmutation turning lust into God. We worshipped at an altar constructed not of earthly marble and jewel, but of heavenly flesh and spirit, and as we reunited those falsely-separated concepts we communed and rejoiced.

We became fleshly again. Two-ness returned. The magical summer was running its course, and our ardor cooled with the sinking, day-shortening late-August sun. Passionate energy was still abundant, but the hard facts of bloodied sheets provided room for doubt, and real-world consequences allowed humdrum teenage angst to reappear, raising the old spectre of that unscrolling page and those questions of my ability, my desire, my will to inscribe a life-story upon it. But something had become clear in those warm summer days—I had been given something, a gift given by an unknowable benefactor and accepted readily by me without discomfort, dismay, or false humility. This present that I now held firmly with my mind's grasp was the gift itself; the present, the fundamental now. The awareness of and the meaning of the present was itself the gift. And this, this present, like a child's toy furtively assembled on Christmas Eve, came with a set of directions, instructions written in an incomprehensibly parsed translation— "Your shiny new gift must be clutched tightly while loosing it completely. Incorporate it as a constant aspect of the day, and it will provide for many years the flavor of a life lived between grace and joy."

I look back, and I recall the simple command that led to this flavoring, this spicing of my life and I am thankful to that woman who I can only imagine once had a summer as the one I have described, and who was still connected in memory to that bright, golden flash of her fresh, supple, innocence-leaving youth. She commanded, and I obeyed, in a simple, ancient pattern of dominance and submission, but here coupled to giving and receiving—

"Get raking," indeed.

*C. Marshall Rea*

Marshall Rea was born in Oklahoma City in May, 1944. In mid-1949 his family moved to Houston, Texas. In 1968 he graduated with honors from Sam Houston High School in Houston and won a full tuition scholarship to Baylor University, where he majored in biology and chemistry in pursuit of his dream to be a doctor. By his junior year at Baylor, after 6 years of debating going back to his freshman year in high school, he decided he wanted to be a lawyer.

Marshall met the love of his life (Jean Thompson) at Baylor and they married in April, 1966. They brought three sons into this world (Douglas, Brian and Kevin) who are grown, married, and have brought six wonderful grandchildren into their extended family.

After graduation from Baylor in 1965 Marshall enrolled at the University of Texas Law School in Austin, graduating in 1968 with a law degree. His first job was with a trial firm in Beaumont, Texas. By his third year (1971) he decided to work for a law firm in Houston, Texas. He returned to solo practice in the late 70's. He finally found his "niche" in the area of real estate (selling, buying, leasing, clearing title issues, etc). In 2006 he and Jean bought and moved into a home in San Antonio, Texas. Marshall started phasing out of his law practice after 2010, and they remain in San Antonio to this date.

Pressured by his sister, Libby Belle, he has this to say about his personal experience in writing. "When I start writing I am usually in a fog. The fun part is when the fog starts to clear. At that point I don't just want to write ... I HAVE to. The challenge is knowing when to stop."

# *Buck Day in 1956*

## BY C. MARSHALL REA

**B**ack in 1956 when I was 12 years old and lived on the north side of Houston, Texas, I had a 13 year old buddy nicknamed "CR". During the summer of 1956 CR and I had a little tradition we called "Buck Day" when we took a bus ride from our homes in north Houston to James Coney Island and the Majestic Theater in downtown Houston.

**Here's what a dollar covered back in 1956 for one person:**

- Bus ride from N. Houston to downtown…..15 cents
- Chilidog (25cts), Fritos (5cts), Coke (5cts)

at James Coney Island in downtown Houston…..35 cents

- Matinee movie Majestic Theater (12 and older) …..25 cents

(Ticket price for child <u>under</u> 12…10 cents)

- Ice cream donut OR comic book (each 10cts) …..10 cents
- Bus ride back to N. Houston…..<u>15 cents</u>

**Total: For one person $1.00**

Thus we needed 2 dollars for Buck Day to be possible … and now to the dark side. One Saturday we were short on cash, with only a buck fifty between us. **The challenge was, how do we cover the missing 50 cents.** Undaunted, we took the bus downtown, figuring we'd each have to skip the 25 cent chili dogs, in order to spend only $1.50, instead of 2 bucks.

By the time we got downtown, the craving for a chili dog evolved into an obsession. In desperation I came up with a bold idea and laid it out for CR. He was "all in". We thrashed out a game plan while eating our usual meal at James Coney Island. When the hunger subsided, I began to have doubts about our plan, but pride would not let me back out.

The first step in our plan was to buy only one of the 10 cent items (the donut) at James Coney Island and to share it, instead of buying two. **This saved us 10 cents.**

The second step was more challenging. After our lunch at James Coney Island we walked several blocks to the Majestic Theatre. According to our plan, CR turned into the alley next to the theater, and I went to the pay booth at the front entrance. I lied to the attendant, telling him I was under 12, and gave him **10 cents** for one under-12 ticket, thus **saving us 40 cents off the usual 50 cent ticket cost for two 12 and over tickets**. I was a small, scrawny kid. CR would not have passed for under 12. The bored attendant gave me a quick glance, yawned, and handed me a ticket. I grabbed it and walked quickly into the theater, my heart beating like I had just finished a hundred yard dash. **With 50 cents in savings, we reached our $1.50 budget.**

The third step was the greatest challenge: once I got into the theater, how would CR make it in? I casually (but nervously) entered a narrow room along the edge of the theater, directly below the balcony seating area. On the exterior wall of that room was a door designated as an emergency exit. This door opened to the alley where CR was waiting. **The door was locked on the outside, but on the inside it could be opened by pushing a wide horizontal bar on the door**. Back in 1956 there was not an alarm to warn the door was being opened from the inside. I slowly pushed the door open, and CR quietly slipped into the theater.

At this point my heart felt like it was going to explode. We made our way up the balcony stairs and found seats to watch the matinee. Any time I saw an usher near our area, I figured the game was over, and we'd be arrested, escorted to jail in a police car, bound hand and foot, gagged and blindfolded. We would probably spend many years in jail.

The movie ended without drama, and we took our bus home. I told CR I just couldn't go through this again. He agreed. But then, the following Saturday we came up short on the two bucks … you know the rest of the story.

**PS:** CR and his family moved out of Houston after the

summer of '56. I was sad to see my best friend move away, but deep down I realized that together we were probably headed for a life of deception and crime and would spend most of our lives in penal institutions. Fortunately, the statute of limitations has run on our misdeeds described above.

# Especially You: A Soldier's Choice

BY C. MARSHALL REA

I dread these long and sad good-byes,
the sorrow in your lonely eyes.
I wish I didn't have to make you blue.
But the path I chose in life to take
and the solemn vow I chose to make
can hurt the ones I love … including you,
can hurt the ones I love … especially you.

Oh when they made those towers fall
my shattered country still stood tall
I knew one day I had to take a stand,
to finally step up to the plate,
to pledge my heart, my life, my fate …
It's the price I pay to live in this great land.
It's the price WE pay to live in our great land.

Can't you hear it in my voice
that I'm committed to my choice
but it hurts inside to know I caused you pain.
Even though we'll be apart,
please don't take me from your heart.
One day I'll come back to your arms again.
One day you'll be back in my arms again.

Please just try to understand
I can't be who I really am
if I turn my back when my country needs me too.
I hope someday you'll come to learn
that I have got to take my turn
Defending this great land … including you,
Defending those I love … especially you.

# Crumbs: On the road of life

BY C. MARSHALL REA

## STORY IDEAS

"The Unreal McCoy"—secrets of a self-made misfit.

"The Road Least Traveled"—a do-it-to-yourself guide to places and situations you really shouldn't be in.

"Confessions of a Mad House-Husband"—the inner struggles of a troubled man who challenged traditional male stereotypes, then sought direction in life from a neurotic, man-hating fortune teller.

## NO BUDDY

A Beagle's Tale

Insights on life inspired by the antics of a free spirited, lovable, often annoying little Beagle named "Buddy" ...and his relentless search for a home to relax in.

The following section reflects a philosophy of life generally known as BuddyThink, gleaned from a scholarly study of events in the life of Buddy the Beagle. Except for Buddy, any resemblance to real people, animals, places, products or events is entirely accidental, unintentional, or, at worst, the result of innocent subliminal influence with no intent to appropriate the intellectual property of another. Furthermore, the Statute of Limitations has probably run on most claims, or the matters are considered under copyright law to be in the "public domain" and thus free for shameless exploitation. So back off!

Notwithstanding the foregoing, I will sue your butt if you attempt to illegally publish, distribute or use all or any part of this copyrighted material for your personal profit or hygiene. Further inquiries should be directed to my attorneys, Dewy, Cheatum & Howe. They operate out of a vintage Winnebago that patrols a five county area in the "Hill Country" area of Central Texas. On Tuesdays and Thursdays, between 11:00 Am and 2:00 PM you can usually find the lawyers, at Billy Gene's Restaurant on the Junction Highway, just outside of Kerrville.

For further help call 800-GIT-HELP and ask for Sissy. If she's gone, ask for Bubba. Listen close, 'cause he chews, and the spittoon is a good 10' from the phone. He's good, real good. You won't believe it until you see it ... but that's another story.

With that little matter behind us, please sit back and learn about life based on the incredible journey of Buddy the Beagle, the Zen-like school of thought he inspired known as

"BuddyThink" and the wisdom filled insights we have come to know as "Buddyisms".

It may change your life. Then again, it may not.

There is no intent here to make a disparaging reference or comparison to the ancient and venerable belief system known as "Buddhism" and its followers, known as "Buddhists". Indeed, my intense studies reveal that Buddy's revered ancestor, the Great Beagle goes back to an era that preceded the Buddha, and those Beagles who came after the Great Beagle served as powerful role models for the very traits the Buddha mistakenly attributed to human origin: vanity, self-indulgence, greed, sloth and the unquenched lust for food, drink, comfort and pleasure.

Go ahead, remain in your state of ignorance and doubt. But someday, when you open your eyes and your heart to the Truth, you will "see" a disturbing parallel between the path we walk as Humans today, and the path begun in antiquity by the Great Beagle and still traveled by his descendants, including Buddy the Beagle.

## BUDDYISMS

Never waste an opportunity to do nothing.
If it doesn't have to be done right now, it is simply not important.
When in doubt ... sleep.
If it's comfortable, shaded and not moving ... sleep on it.
The best place to relax is where they sit ... or sleep.

My sacred duty is first to protect my domain and the humans

I allow into my pack, unless, of course, that interferes with my playtime, my sleeping, my eating, or exposes me to unacceptable levels of pain or discomfort.

If you're happy, yelp. If you want to chase something, yelp. If you lose it, yelp. If you catch it, yelp. If you're upset, yelp. If you want to go outside, yelp. If you're hungry, yelp. If you want to play, yelp. If you're scared, yelp. Got the picture? Thank you very much.

So you don't like my yelping? Just look at all my other, more lovable qualities and live with it.

Avoid moderation ... especially when eating.

If it looks remotely like food ... eat it.

The pain of being sat on or stepped on is far outweighed by the rewards flowing from the offender's guilt.

If you eat something weird or nasty and get sick, the incredible attention you receive almost compensates for the stupidity of your action. So why change?

If it looks dead, slimy, or disgusting ... roll in it, unless you can eat it.

If it runs ... chase it.

If it fights ... back off. Even a little bird could put your eye out.
If it dies ... drag it to the back door as a trophy, after you roll in it or try eating it, of course.

Except for eating and sleeping, nothing is more satisfying than chasing a cat up a tree, unless it has an attitude (the cat, not the tree). Ditto for squirrels.

He wants to pet me, his lap is soft and warm, and his shirt is full of crumbs and food stains. It just doesn't get any better than this.

When it comes to people, there is no hatred, prejudice or bigotry in me. I will ignore the faults and deficiencies of anyone who feeds me, pets me, or plays with me ... even if they are only human.

This does not apply to cats, squirrels, birds, butterflies, or any other creatures I find useless or annoying.

Anyone who wants to play with me, pet me or feed me, earns my devotion ... until they stop.

What is all this business about "intruders"? If they talk nice, pet me, or feed me they can't be all that bad. And if they try to hurt me, I'm outta there! There's nothin' in my contract about risking pain!

When they are lookin' right at ya, behave.

If they look away, go for it.

If you have to ask who "they" are, you are clueless.

What they don't know can't hurt me.

I never met a cat I didn't hate. Ditto on squirrels.

I don't have any particular interest in females. Is it something in the water?

I keep hearing about being "fixed." So what exactly was wrong with me that needed fixing? Why didn't they ask me first? Hey, it's America. I got rights! Where were PETA and the ACLU? Bet they'd listen to me if I had the money to hire a lawyer or could do that "voting" thing.

Don't take too seriously anything said by that "Dog Whisperer" fella. Do you honestly think I will let some human be leader of my pack? Fugeddaboudit! Now scratch my tummy ... oooh, a little more to the right, hmmmmm.

You can't write about Beagles without some kind of tribute to the incredible George Schulz (may he rest in peace) his Peanuts family, and his immortal Beagle character, Snoopy. Okay, got that out of the way....

## CRUMBS
Food for Thought.

Random insights (crumbs) on life from a senior citizen who still doesn't know what he wants to be when he grows up.

Stories, myths, and truisms to inform, entertain and inspire, balanced with anecdotal evidence that the human race just may be in serious trouble.

A relationship with a woman can be like a visit to the Grand Canyon: beautiful, mysterious and inspirational from a distance, but complex, challenging, and dangerous when you get too close.

They say the road to Hell is paved with good intentions. I say the road to Heaven is lined with dangerous side roads. Exit at your own risk.

It has been said that "those who fail to study their history are condemned to repeat it". This implies that the study of history will have a profound and positive impact on the actions of a person, or a people, and positively change the course of their lives. Really?

From my own experience, the following may be closer to the truth: "it is important to study your history so that you will recognize your mistakes each time you repeat them." Sadly, self-knowledge does not always guide us in our self-governance.

When I turned 40 I got one of those catchy birthday cards that said: Well, there's one good thing about being "over the hill" ... at least the rest of the journey is downhill.

Funny ... until you actually start that "downhill run" and learn, too late, that your engine is out of tune, the suspension is shot, the brakes are weak, visibility is poor and you forgot to pack a good map and reliable memory. Unfortunately, the Rules won't let you start over. With dedication, hard work, sacrifice and drastic changes in life style, you can back up maybe a mile or two ... so what's the point? Just get back in, and let'r rip! A siren would add a little flair.

Why do people love to pick on lawyers, politicians and used

car salesmen? Why not pick on the real problem makers we face in this complex world of manic change and rampant "improvement" covering just about everything affecting our daily lives, such as:

## Cell Phone Makers ...

who offer sexy "smart" cell phones that no one ... okay, no one like me ... can figure out how to operate before the next "improved" or "updated" model or operating system arrives, that consistently work only in major metropolitan areas ... in Japan, that expose you to the hazard of violent "phone snatchers" who prowl in public venues like hungry techno-predators.

These marvelous devices serve primarily as a target for spammers, and your Aunt Ethel or Uncle Fred who overload you with tweets, texts, photos, videos, emails and Facebook alerts about family history and medical remedies, as well as human interest stories, rumors, hoaxes, warnings, public service messages and jokes that were lame 10 years ago. Welcome to the "Information Age".

Were things really that bad in the days of portable "brick" phones, pagers, answering machines, phone-line faxes and modems, DOS, and Western Union? How did we manage to make it to the moon in the late 60s without the miracle devices we now take for granted? Or was that moon thing just another hoax, as I learned in a shocking video on You Tube. It went viral, so it must be true. Guess I won't know till it's fully covered in a cable news investigative report, then spelled out in ponderous detail in Wikipedia.

## Blender Makers ...

the creators of blenders that have 40 speeds, toasters with 30 settings, TV remotes more complex than the control panel on an F-16 fighter jet, microwaves with a dozen cooking modes, clothes and dish washers with 25 cleaning options, flashlights with focus rings, adjustable intensity and swiveling heads. Face it, few people (especially men) use more than two settings, and even they usually max out at three.

## Razor Manufacturers ...

who market razors that have more than one blade. I used to have a great single blade razor. It gave me an excellent, close shave (okay, an occasional razor cut, and only a handful of those incidents required a trip to the ER. Why do I need three to five blades now? Have pollutants in our water and air somehow altered our genetic code, resulting in facial hair stronger than Kevlar strands, that will yield only to multiple rows of titanium coated, super sharp surgical steel blades? When they finally max out at 10 blades, will someone come up with a daring new concept: a light, disposable razor that requires only one blade?

Better yet, will they offer a more revolutionary product: a compact, handheld, electric, battery operated device with spinning, concealed blades that smoothly cut those pesky facial hairs and eliminate the need for those sharp, dangerous, wound-inflicting, germ laden, temporary blades that require expensive replacement blades, exotic creams and foams laced with chemical additives bearing scary names, and the wasting of our precious drinking water. We'll give this device a fancy, high-tech name like ... electric shaver.

As an added bonus, these miracle shaving devices will be made in some country on the other side of the World, sparing our local environment from the blight of the manufacturing processes, and freeing our workers for more productive and meaningful jobs in the fast food industry.

## Car Manufacturers ...

that boast how a sleek, sexy, aerodynamic new low profile car design is the greatest design advance in the last 50 years ... despite the small tradeoff that it blocks your view of the traffic behind you and next to you. As a bonus, for a mere $900, you can add an amazing new remote viewing accessory that enables you to actually see on a little 5 to 7 inch screen the "traffic behind you and next to you". Sadly, you still have to watch out for those reckless, unenlightened, greedy tightwads on the highway who did not buy the option ... and thus cannot see the traffic behind them and next to them (which includes you).

## and finally, Huge Auto Insurance Companies ...

that all claim, if you switch to them, your annual premium will average $500 less than what you can get from the other "major carriers" ... even if you have 3 convictions for drunk driving, 4 at-fault wrecks and 12 moving violations over the last 3 years. And just who are those "major carriers" they use for comparison of rates? My intensive research (on Google, of course) revealed three obscure insurance companies whose names curiously begin with "Major Carrier ..." They were all formed in offshore tax havens that have iron clad secrecy laws, and they are all licensed to provide auto insurance in your state.

Curiously, these "Major Carriers" insure only an elite group of drivers who must provide unimpeachable proof that they meet or exceed all the following underwriting guidelines:

1. a flawless driving record with no accidents or moving violations over a continuous 40 year period,
2. no record of treatment for any injury or known medical or mental conditions over the last 20 years,
3. credit scores above 750 for each of the last 10 years,
4. proof the applicant has never smoked, breathed, absorbed, mainlined, bathed in or ingested any substance deemed by their medical staff to be additive, harmful non-beneficial or annoying, followed by a series of rigorous drug tests,
5. and, finally, proof the Applicant has never used or needed corrective lens, hearing aids, antacids, laxatives, and over the counter meds for athlete's foot, jock itch, heartburn or flatulence. Dang! This part was clearly directed at me!

These Major Carriers quote auto insurance premiums that (surprise!) average at least $500 per year more than premiums charged by the other big insurers in your state, thus giving credibility to the claim "we can save you an average of $500 or more a year on your premium, compared to the major carriers."

Unfortunately it is almost impossible to find out if these major carriers have any actual policy holders in your state due to layers of complex laws and regulations at the state and federal level, and the vagaries of international laws and treaties protecting the foreign entities.

I tried to get CNN, NBC, CBS, MSNBC and FOX to

investigate this, but encountered a strange indifference …
until I learned a significant part of their ad revenue comes
from those large auto, business, home, health and life
insurance companies. The only media outlet that expressed a
real interest was a small community paper in West Texas
called the Buford Clarion. Coincidentally, they were bought
out by some unknown offshore investment company just a
week after I made my inquiry, and they no longer take my
calls. It sorta makes you wonder ….

I experienced a similar lack of enthusiasm when I took my
case to various state and federal consumer protection
agencies … until I discovered most were staffed with former
executives from those major insurance companies.

I appealed to my congressman, only to learn that a major
source of his campaign funding came through a PAC formed
by the large insurance carriers. Undeterred, I asked for a
meeting and was amazed when his assistant set me up for a
face to face meeting with the congressman right in his office
for three uninterrupted minutes out of his incredibly busy
schedule.

When we met, he actually shook my hand and called me by
my first name, without even looking at any notes! He listened
patiently and compassionately to my 2-minute pitch, never
losing eye contact and nodding sympathetically along the
way. When I finished, he flashed his famous grin, patted me
on the back and said (and I will never forget this) "I'll look
into this partner, and you can take that to the bank!" He
actually called me "partner"!

I felt like I made a new friend. The man had looked straight into my soul. [A chill is going up and down my leg as I write this.] A staff photographer with a fancy digital camera took several pictures of me shaking the congressman's hand. In less than a week I received in the mail a disc with several beautiful, professionally enhanced digital photos of the event that made me look 30 pounds lighter, 15 years younger, and 5 inches taller … what a class act! I am having a photography shop transfer those to photo quality paper so they can be properly framed and hung in a place of honor.

My interest in this whole matter sort of cooled after that. I did briefly consider the possibility of consumer litigation, but a wise and seasoned trial attorney friend (who made me swear to protect his identity) confided to me that trial and appellate judges in Texas are elected, and their campaigns are largely funded by … you got the picture.

Finally, I just learned from my broker at BubbaTrade that, by sheer coincidence, these big insurance companies now constitute a significant part of my modest, diversified stock portfolio, that a recent hot tip (not insider info, he assured me) correctly anticipated an upcoming stock split in one of those companies, and they skillfully handled the split in a way that almost doubled the value of my 401K overnight. What a country!

This matter is not really worthy of our continued attention, so let's just let it go. There are other, more pressing issues to focus on, like the inexplicable rise in the price of hazel nuts over the last decade. My people are on it … and you will hear from me soon.

## MISCELLANEOUS

If a Man of Leisure
Meets a Woman of Pleasure
In a Moment of Silent Sublime,
Will the Lack of Communion
Cause Loss of a Union,
with only a Meeting of Minds?

I have always wanted to breed dogs. In a strange way, it seems like something close to playing God. I would take a magnificent Rottweiler, cross breed it with a pure bred Dachshund, and end up with a delightful breed called Rottwieners.

Mix a nomadic dog with a Shitzu, and get a … No-Sh… well, you get the point.

## PET NAMES

I never really understood why some people put so much energy and worry into naming their pets … as if the name will either alter the pet's behavior or change other people's perception of the pet. Take it from me, this thinking is wrong. A couple of simple examples should clear this up:

You climb over a neighbor's fence to fetch your kid's baseball. You look up and see a snarling Great Dane the size of a small horse charging at you, fangs bared, ears and tongue flapping in the wind. You hear a woman's desperate cries in the background, "Stop, Freckles, I said, Stop! Bad dog, Freckles, Bad, Baaaaad Dog!! Be honest, would that name make you stand up, look Freckles in the eyes, and laugh?

You take your kid to a neighbor's house, because your kid has to sell 5,000 candy bars by Friday to support his little league team, and you are deeply concerned you'll end up having to buy them yourself ... like you did last year ... and the year before. Suddenly, from out of nowhere a frenzied, snarling Chihuahua, not much bigger than two Twinkies, attacks your shoe laces. A large man comes to the door and shouts, "Down, Godzilla, Down!" He has in his right hand a 10 oz bottle filled with water (it's larger than Godzilla). As he sprays Godzilla, soaking your pant leg and shoe, he apologizes effusively for the dogs uncontrollable, inexcusable behavior. At that point are you in a state of shock, pondering what horrible injuries would have been inflicted if this brave man had not stopped the savage Godzilla from mauling you?

No, to my way of thinking we should name dogs the way we named people back in the old days ... when names said something about you, names like Baker, Carpenter, Smith, Farmer, Hunter, Groper and so on.

Yep, we'd finally see dogs with real names that actually make sense, like Slacker, Belch, Sluggish, Puddles, Shed, Stinky, Gorge, Yap, Slobber, Scratch, Dozer, Tic, Bother, Crotch, Tooter, Hump, and my favorite ... Apathy.

*Yes, I could have expanded this message to talk about naming cats but face it, I'm just not a "cat-person". The day you see signs that say "Security Cat on Guard" or "Beware of Cat", a special training center for "Seeing Eye Cats," or a circus that features Clowns with "Stunt Cats", I will become more open to accepting them. I keep hearing how "smart" cats are. Maybe that's why they're so independent. Given the choice, at this stage of life I'll settle for my nervous, neurotic, co-dependent, anxious to please little poodle named "Pookie". By the way, Pookie is afraid of cats, so that ends the discussion for me.

*My editor warned me about this kind of candor and said it could cost me 5 ... maybe 10 ... sales from that great market of cat lovers out there. If I receive at least three strong responses from the cat crowd, I will do some serious soul-searching on this issue. It's not that I will "flip-flop" on the matter ... I may simply "evolve" into a viewpoint that just happens to please a large segment of my rather small audience.

You know, maybe I am ready to enter politics!

# *Kenneth Robbins*

Kenneth Robbins is the author of seven published novels, over forty published plays, two volumes of poetry, and numerous essays, stories, and memoirs on-line and in peer-reviewed journals. With his wife, Dorothy Dodge Robbins, he has co-edited four literary collections, including "Christmas on the Great Plains," UP Iowa. His fiction has received the Toni Morrison Prize and the Associated Writing Programs Novel Award. His plays have been recognized by receiving the Charles Getchell Award, the Festival of Southern Theatre Award, and the Gabrielle Society Humanitarian Award along with productions throughout the US, Canada, Japan, Denmark, and the United Kingdom.

His radio play, "Dynamite Hill," has been aired over National Public Radio and BBC Radio 3 and is a recipient of the Corporation for Public Broadcasting Program Award.

He is a former Fulbright Scholar to North Macedonia, the recipient of an Artists Fellowship from the Japan Foundation, a Malone Fellowship through the National Council on US/Arab Relations, a Louisiana Division of the Arts Fellowship in Playwriting, and a writing fellowship from the Fundacion Valparaiso, Mojacar, Spain.

# The Galena Burn

BY KENNETH ROBBINS

The pig-tail bridges were still there and in use. We parked our rented Celebrity under the third one and my dad sat on the concrete slab that supported the creosote-coated pine timbers. I wandered up the side of the hill, walked through the rudely carved tunnel, and admired how perfectly the hole through the mountainside framed distant Mount Rushmore. "Impressive!" I yelled down to him. He didn't respond. He seemed bored.

I admired the size of the timbers supporting the bridge and the fact that such timbers would still be in use some fifty years after their installation. I remarked on the number of two-by-fours set on edge covering the trestle from one end to the other. "Six hundred," Dad said. "They were untreated, so it took six hundred." He had counted them.

Cars, trucks, and massive campers made the wood flooring creak. I ducked, though I knew after fifty years the expanse wasn't going to collapse.

He sat. I couldn't tell if he was pleased by being where

we were or not. He hadn't complained, so I assumed his thoughts were pleasant enough. I wanted to be privileged to them, but he kept me out.

The drive through Keystone getting to the pigtails had been a letdown for him. "Look at this junk," he said over and over. "Back in our time, this was a nice little village. A grocery store, a couple of churches and a few bars. Look at all this. Worse than Gatlinburg." Gatlinburg was my father's measure for cheapness.

We had lunch at Rosie's. The food wasn't very good. "This is all show," he said, referring to the bordello-style decorations in the multi-level restaurant. "There wasn't any place like this back when I was here. All show."

Mount Rushmore pleased him I suppose. We strolled the Avenue of Flags and found Georgia's. "I didn't know we were the thirteenth state," he said, reading the plaque.

He bought Mom a small brass replica of the four presidents in the large, crowded gift shop. "The mountain looks pretty much the same," he said. "But all this —" The sweep of his hand took in the flags, sidewalks, visitor's center, cafeteria and gift shop. "— this you can take and flush."

"Let's come back tonight and watch the lighting ceremony," I said.

He just grunted. He wasn't about to come back, and I knew it.

After an hour at the pigtails, we continued up the side of Iron Mountain. The ponderosa pines were straight as pins. I marveled at the various rock outcroppings. "Different from the Appalachians," I said. Again, he merely grunted.

In spite of his persistent grouchiness, I was having a grand time. Afterall, this return to the Black Hills was for him, not me. He had talked about the place often as I was growing up, his salad days in the Corps, how he and his

CCC buddies had carved this road out of the granite cliffs, built the pigtails, blasted through the stone. All that was missing on this trip was Mom, but she had decided to stay home, leave the happy feet to us.

We reached the top of the mountain and pulled off into the Norbeck Overlook and parked. He sat there, not moving. "Well?" I said.

"The camp was on the other side of the mountain," he said.

"Don't you want to get out?"

"What for?"

"Well, to see."

"I've already seen it."

"Yeah, but that was fifty years ago. It might have changed a little since then."

"I can see. It's the same."

"Well, I plan to see." I left him in the car. The overlook was built on top of a large boulder. Climb the wooden and stone steps and you can see forever and a day across the expanse of the Black Hills. In all directions, dark almost black forests stretched into the horizon. The blackness was broken here and there with spires of rock and massive outcroppings of granite. So, this was the Sioux's magic land. Paha Sapa. Holy land. Dad sat in the car. The trip may not be working for him, but it was doing wonders for me. I was standing in the spot he had told me about on so many occasions. I was breathing the pine scent he had called the most wonderful in the world. I could sense what it was that had excited him so about those days fifty years ago. I was beginning to envy the youth he had spent in such a place. There had been no Civilian Conservation Corps when I was a kid.

"I don't know," he said as I slid behind the wheel.

"About what?"

"If we go on down the highway, we'll come to the camp," he whispered. "Or what's left of it."

"Right. That's why we're here."

"I don't know if I'm up to it." He got out of the car and wandered along the asphalt path to the overlook. He climbed the stairs using the handrail to pull himself up. I followed. Probably when he was here as a young man, he scoffed at the idea of handrails and stone steps, but not today, not since his prognosis. We were atop fabled Iron Mountain. The Iron Mountain of all the stories he had told me.

"Ain't changed much," he said. "Fact, it ain't changed at all." He pointed. "That way's Custer. Over there's Harney Peak. There's a lookout tower atop Harney some of us boys visited once. Wonder if it's still there. I did some work on Sylvan Lake Lodge and the Visitor's Center in Custer State Park. Rock work. I never saw it finished. Wonder if they still use them? There's this rock over at Sylvan Lake, real unique. It has five sides to it. You hit the stone a certain way and the thing splits perfectly smooth. Five sides. I did some of that rock work. The Needles are over that way, too." He flipped a pine cone at a chipmunk. "Use to catch those things," he said, "and use their guts as fish bait. They was fish back then in Squaw Creek, fish you could eat." He leaned against the railing for a long while. I didn't bother him. I could stay there for an age and not grow tired of the vista. After a bit, he sighed and said, "I'm tired. Where we staying tonight?"

I didn't have the vaguest idea.

We drove back down Iron Mountain the way we had come, up Mount Rushmore once again, and down the backside. We passed Horse Thief Lake and my dad said, "Used to be a camp down there, logging camp and CCC.

Bet it's still there, underneath the water." He sighed. "Nothing's ever the same."

We reached Hill City and took a left. Custer, straight ahead.

"Would you look at that?" Howie said.

"What?"

"They're carving up another mountain. Jesus, why don't they leave these Hills alone? Crazy Horse," he scorned. "Who the hell wants to see a mountain carved like an Indian!"

Our room was comfortable, but it was too early in the afternoon. There were too many things to see. I hadn't come all this way from my home in Georgia to spend time in a motel room.

"This is my trip, remember?" Dad said as he sprawled across one of the beds. "Wonder what your mother's up to? You know she and Jamie never get along after a time."

"She's probably relishing being free of you."

"Probably crying her heart out being left alone like this."

"Dad, I couldn't afford three tickets."

"I know, I know. How much time difference is there did you say?"

"Two hours. They're two hours later back home. They're probably all outside, enjoying the late afternoon."

He dialed. No one answered. He lay back on the bed and closed his eyes. "God, I'm tired, son."

"You're not enjoying yourself very much are you?"

"Sure. More fun than getting tarred and feathered."

"Dad."

"It makes me feel old, Winston. Older than the Hills themselves. You'll understand one of these days."

I hope not, I thought.

"I have memories of all these places we've been, and the memories don't coincide with what I'm seeing. I miss your mother. I've not been this lonesome for her in forty-five years." His voice trailed off. That much, his missing Mom, I could understand.

He was sleeping soundly as I slipped out the door and walked down Custer's main street, wide, lined by numerous stores selling Black Hills gold, trinkets, hardware, and pizzas.

I found the dance hall Dad had told me about. The Custer Community Building, dedicated August 11, 1927, by Mrs. Grace Coolidge. The largest all-log building in the United States. I wanted to see inside, but it was padlocked. On the lawn outside the log building was a small stone structure: the city's first jail. It was all too quaint.

He was at the writing desk when I walked into the room. "Well, hey," I said, a bit surprised to see him up. "Have a good nap?"

"No. Your mother sends her love."

"You reached her?"

"She and the kids went shopping in Atlanta today."

"Well, how about some supper. There's a pizza place…."

"Sure, sure. Winston, I figure I helped a minimum of 10,394,400 people see the faces on Mount Rushmore."

"How do you figure that?"

"Well, we were at the pig-tail bridge an hour today."

"There abouts."

"No, exactly an hour. I kept track. In that hour 71 vehicles drove over the bridge. Now, counting a twelve-hour day seven days a week from June 1 through September 30 with 71 cars as a mean average, I figure 5,197,200 cars have used the bridge I helped build over the past fifty years. If there's an average of two people per car, that makes 10,394,400 persons. Now, that should make you feel a little useful, don't you think?"

The next morning, we got an early start. We spent the entire day clamoring around Jewel and Wind Caves. On the way out of Wind, Dad pointed to a rock building and said, "Look at that. That's C work. Nice going, fellas."

The next day we drove up to Deadwood. When in the Hills before, he told me, they hadn't made it north to Deadwood, and he wanted to see Calamity Jane's gravestone and the place where Buffalo Bill got shot. It was Wild Bill Hickok I tried to tell him. But he wouldn't listen to me.

The third day he wanted to drive to Hot Springs and see the Mammoth site. "Look, Dad, we didn't come here to be tourists."

"We didn't?"

"We're gonna visit your old camp site sooner or later. Well, it's getting later every day you postpone it. How're you feeling anyway?"

"Will you leave me alone?"

We drove down to Hot Springs.

The next day I insisted. Today's the day, I told him.

"Let's drive through the Needles Eye," he said.

"Now, Dad--"

"It's on the way. Don't get all in a huff, son."

Sylvan Lake has to be the prettiest little pond in the entire world. Nothing like it in the Blue Ridge back home. The water was ice blue. Giant slabs of granite poked out of the lake like God had placed them there purposefully to create an artistic vista. The Lodge was where we should have been staying, not in a motel in Custer. It's a romantic place, perched atop a ridge, overlooking both the Lake and Harney Peak. Up the road we passed through the Needle's Eye, the most unusual tunnel I'd ever seen. I was thankful we had the Celebrity. If we'd had a camper like some we'd seen, we'd probably still be stuck in the crack they call the Eye. I gawked at the Cathedral Spires that stood like guardians beside the road. All the while, Dad sat there, silent. How was he taking all this?

"Stop," he said. "Back up."

"What is it?" I asked. We sat in the middle of a three-way intersection. Then I saw the sign: "Center Lake."

"Pull over for a minute."

He sat in the car staring down the road that crossed the stream of water we'd been following for the past five miles. His hands were shaking a little. Maybe he needed a smoke. He had been good about not smoking in the car during our drives. "You want to get out?" I asked.

He sat for a full minute, staring down the road. "They paved it," he said, finally. He got out of the car, leaned for a moment on the hood, then crossed the highway, past the Center Lake sign, and stopped in the middle of the small log bridge that spanned the creek.

I followed. I noticed that there was only a trickle of water in the streambed. "When I was here before," he said, "the water was knee-deep and full of trout. We used to keep Meatloaf's skillet popping with fish out of this stream."

He moved to the end of the bridge and squatted so he could gaze beneath it. Then he edged down the bank through the waist-high growth of brush and disappeared under the creosote-coated timbers. I followed to the edge of the bank and waited. He didn't come back.

"Dad," I called.

"Come here," he said. "I want to show you something."

I wasn't dressed for this. Tennis shorts aren't much good when you push through brambly undergrowth. I found him sitting on a stone, worn round by years of spring runoff. "Look at that," he said, and pointed to a spot under the bridge. I craned my neck. There, etched into the wood of a crossbeam, faint but still readable, were the letters: "HMC + MLC," surrounded by a large, off-centered heart. "My sweetheart bridge," he whispered.

"Who is MLC?" I asked.

"I don't remember."

As we walked back to the car, I noticed his step was a little lighter. "Let's see if the Visitor's Center ever got finished," he said.

It had. The rock work had the CCC stamp all over it. I had come to recognize the work, having seen it now at Wind Cave, Devil's Tower, and Sylvan Lodge. "How did you move such large stones, Dad?" I asked.

"Wasn't easy," he said. He wandered around the back of the building. "I want to see something," he said.

He ran his hand over a stone at the base of the building. "This is it," he said. The stone was mostly granite with some rose quartz mixed in. "We were working on this corner when I went AWOL. Here, put your hand here."

The stone felt almost cold. It was rough and clear, a mixture of granite and quartz.

"I chipped a piece of quartz from this rock," he said. "I've never told you this, but look." He took a key ring from his pocket and dropped it into my hand. It had the same cold feel as the rough stone. The end of the ring was a piece of rose quartz, clear as glass but far more delicate and sturdy. "When I got home, I had a friend make this key ring for me from the quartz I took from this rock. It's my lucky charm. I've heard that if you chip away from a rock, you weaken the entire stone. Not so. This stone has done pretty good the past fifty years." He thought for a second before he added, "Better than me."

Inside the Visitor's Center were numerous displays dedicated to the Hills. "I remember a couple of our boys were working on these when I left," he said. There were stuffed elk, buffalo, and coyotes on display. There were information booths on lumbering, Indian life, and gold mining. Then we found the display honoring the C's. There was a monthly report from Camp Lodge, several old photographs, one of a swim team from Camp Custer, another of a baseball team from the Narrows ("Worse team in the Hills," Dad said), and one of the interior of a camp barracks. There was a baseball bat, a pick, and a double-bladed axe. There was a map of the hills with the various camps marked on it. Camp Lodge was no more than three miles away up Squaw Creek.

"You want to go?" I asked.

"Guess so."

As we signed the guest book near the exit, a park ranger came in from outside and up to the desk. He asked to use the phone in the office near the entrance. The receptionist asked how things were going. The ranger replied, "Damn things jumped our lines," and disappeared into the office.

"Anything wrong?" I asked.

The receptionist smiled. "Not at all," she said. "Summer fires are routine around here."

As we turned onto Center Lake Road, we noticed the smell of smoke for the first time. "Awfully dry to be having forest fires," Dad said.

"Nothing to worry about," I said.

We turned the bend, topped the hill, and stopped. Dad's mouth fell open. His breathing quickened. His knuckles turned white from where he clenched the door handle. There, in front of us, were the barracks, the commissary, the rec hall, all still there. Some of it was gone, but "My God," he said, "look at this."

Instead of Camp Lodge, the sign read "The Black Hills Playhouse." He looked at me. "You knew about this. This is a set-up, right?"

"I swear, I didn't know anything about it."

"You and your damn theAYter," he barked. "Get me away from here."

We turned around in the drive and returned the way we had come. We drove in silence until he said, "I'm ready to go home, Winston."

"Our plane tickets are for five days from now," I told him.

"I don't care. I'm ready to go home. I'll walk if I have to."

I packed. He watched an old movie on television. I called the airline about rebooking our flight home. Our original tickets were special fares; it was going to cost us an extra five hundred dollars apiece to get home the next day. I told him that; he didn't seem to care. He would take the extra money out of his savings. He wanted to go home.

This trip had been my idea. I didn't know what to do except drive to the airport in the morning, return our rental car, exchange our tickets at the United counter, and return to Georgia. We would call Mom from the airport and have her meet our flight in Atlanta. In a way, I felt relieved. The trip hadn't turned out to be what I had hoped. The longer we stayed and the more things we saw, the more depressed Dad became. He was smoking more. It didn't matter, he said, the damage was already done. He had developed a deep raspy cough. And as far as I could tell, he had lost more weight. His cancer was eating him alive, and I wasn't helping by forcing him to face a past that was just as well left alone.

When I came back to the motel room with a sack of hamburgers, fries, and soft drinks from the Chief Restaurant next door, he was watching the news broadcast from Rapid City. There were images of helicopters, men dressed in yellow slickers hosing down trees, smoke-filled air, flames leaping amid deep green foliage, and wild animals darting through haze. The commentator was saying, "The fire which began three days ago in the deep forests of Custer State Park has now been declared out of control and is threatening personnel at the Black Hills Boys' Camp and several outlying campgrounds. Officials at the site indicate that more than 1,000 acres of forest have been destroyed in the past five hours. What began as a routine localized blaze is now on the verge of becoming the worst fire in the Black Hills in fifty years. More tonight on Eyewitness News."

"This could be something," Dad said, his eyes taking on more life than they had had in days.

"Is it close to us?" I asked.

"Well, it's in the park."

We ate our hamburgers and fries. The weather forecast called for sun. In sports, the Atlanta Braves had lost again, and Dad moaned. "Damn incompetents," he said under his breath. "Any team that loses three games in a row to the Cubs should be shot."

We slept well that night. The prospect of going home made the motel bed softer.

"This is bad," Dad said. He was watching the morning

news as I showered. We needed to be at the airport in two hours. His dawdling made me uneasy about making our flight. But he insisted on keeping up with the fire. "Come here, Winston," he called.

I dripped water on the carpet as the report continued. The fire had grown significantly over night from a thousand-acre blaze to a ten thousand-acre one. The fire had crowned and was racing with the wind through a forest made vulnerable by one of the longest and most severe droughts in Black Hills history. Evacuation proceedings had begun the night before at numerous park sites including the Game Lodge, Sylvan Lake, Blue Bell, various outlying resorts, all the campgrounds, and the Black Hills Playhouse. "Jesus," Dad whispered. "The damn fire's gonna eat my camp." The Galena Burn (it already had a name) was being compared to the McVey Fire of 1939.

"Do you remember the McVey Fire?" I asked.

"It came along after I left," Dad said. "I missed it." He listened to more details as I dressed for the journey home. "I didn't miss the Blackwater Burn, though. That's when I got baptized, son." He pulled on his pants. "You know, it could be a lot of fun."

"What could?"

"Fighting a fire again."

"Ah, now, come on, Dad."

"I know how. Hell, I'm a Pulaski Medalist."

"That was fifty years ago," I insisted. And you're fifty years older."

"So? I can't sit by and let this fire eat my camp, Winston."

He was serious. That's why I laughed.

"I'm not joking."

"You heard the man. All the roads into the Park have been closed. Besides, we have a plane to catch."

"I know all the back roads," he said.

I'd not seen him this alive since the doctor had sat down and explained to everybody just what having inoperable lung cancer really means. He looked ten years younger. He stood erect, as if the adrenaline flowing through him had an impact on his posture. He motioned to me with his right hand, like a young boy motions to his collie dog. Come on, he seemed to say, do this for me, boy, just this little thing.

I've always had a soft place in my heart for collie dogs.

The Custer entrance into the Park was barricaded by a temporary wooden fence. Several park rangers, college-age girls with tanned faces were on guard to prevent sightseers like us from getting through. Smoke was thick, creating a haze that partially blocked the sun. The girls tried to be pleasant, but I could see the worry in their faces. Obviously, nobody knew which way or how fast the fire was moving. I noticed that their vehicle was parked on our side of the barricade, just in case.

"But we're volunteering to help," Dad said.

The ranger looked at him and shook her head. I could see she wanted to be cheerful but was hampered by the task she was ordered to do. "We need younger men than you on the fire line, sir," she said. "I'm sorry."

"Where do you go to volunteer?" he asked.

"The U.S. Forestry Station in Custer, I think. It's on the Hill City highway, on the left."

"Why don't you just look the other way for a minute. My

son and me will be through here, and you'll never know the difference."

"Sorry, sir. It just isn't safe."

"Which way's the fire heading?" I asked.

"The last word we had they were evacuating Keystone. That's scary, isn't it?"

All of us nodded. "What about Camp Lodge?" Dad asked.

"Sir?"

"He means, the summer theatre. We heard it had been evacuated last night."

"The Playhouse was one of the hot spots. And that was such a nice place to go, too. God, Valerie," she said, turning to her comrade, "I'm gonna miss the Playhouse, aren't you?"

"I know a way," Dad whispered as I backed away from the barricade.

"Come on, Dad," I tried to reason with him. "We'll only get in trouble."

"That's your problem, boy, afraid of a little trouble. I said I know a way."

Through Custer, toward Hill City, past Mount Rushmore, up the Iron Mountain Highway (for some reason, it all looked different this time around), past a few resorts that were in the process of packing up, to a small dirt road, dusty and rutted. There was a barricade across the road, but it had been moved to one side. No rangers stood guard here.

"The Camp is just a few miles on," Dad said.

The smoke was much thicker. We passed several work crews. Men were working feverishly with heavy machinery, plowing a firebreak a few yards in from the road. They were too busy to pay any attention to us. We drove on. The smoke was thick as fog. I had to turn on the headlamps to see but they didn't do any good. I slammed on the brakes as three frantic mule deer bounded across the road. Occasionally, through the dense haze, we caught a glimpse of yellow fire tongues licking away at a decades-worth of accumulated undergrowth.

"This is bad, Dad," I said as I braked again, this time for two long horn sheep. "We could get killed in here."

"I'm half a corpse already, son. Keep going."

The road turned to pavement. "Black Hills Playhouse, 1/4 mile," I could barely read the sign. We were squeezed to the side of the road by a convoy of army trucks, speeding up the road the way we had come. A jeep pulled beside our car. A man, wearing a gas mask, banged on our hood. I held a handkerchief to my face as I rolled down my window.

"What the hell you doing in here!" he yelled.

"We're volunteers," I answered. I could feel the incredible heat generated by the fire.

"It's your funeral. Report in on the left. Here." He tossed two gas masks into the car and continued up the road. Dad and I quickly put on the masks. We pulled into the entrance of what once was Camp Lodge. Now it was the staging area for the war against the Galena Burn.

Dad and I joined the twenty or so other men working against the blaze. A handful of small buildings that served as dormitories for actors and technicians were in danger from the approaching fire. We picked out our tools, doused our clothing in water, and moved into the line of men who were clearing a firebreak around the dorms. The heat was severe even though the fire was on the other side of Center Lake. I marveled at the precision of the men and how easy it was to fall in with them and work like I had never worked before. There was no talking. There was no need to talk. No one was in charge, yet everyone seemed to know not only what to do but how to do it. Dad was right with them. He manned a small chain saw, clearing the hillside near the dorms. I helped dig a trench in the clearing.

A beehive of helicopters crisscrossed the skies. Each carried a huge bucket of water. Center Lake must be nearly dry by now, I thought. A water truck pulled up to the dorms. I dropped my shovel and helped hose down the buildings. The spray cleared the air. I took off my mask and leaned against the wet wall, catching my breath. One of the workers joined me and lit a cigarette. He offered me one. I almost laughed at the absurdity of his gesture.

"You from Custer?" he asked.

"From Georgia."

"No shit!"

And we went back to work. I was near exhaustion already, but we didn't stop. There was no time to stop. The heat was growing more intense by the minute. I looked around for Dad. He was far up the hill, chain saw still in action. Directly behind him came a huge tractor, plowing a path through the trees six feet wide. Sparks were falling around us, hailing down on the roof of the dorms but none took hold.

Word came through. The fire had crowned again and was moving like a locomotive through the forest just beyond the lake. Then the order was issued. Fall back to the center of the theatre compound. Focus efforts on saving the larger buildings. Fall back, fall back now.

Some of the workers were taking a break. I found Dad sitting on the steps of one of the original CCC buildings. He was tired but invigorated. He had color in his face again. He had a can of Coke in his hand. He sipped at it occasionally and offered me some.

"Having fun?" I asked.

"This was the Brown Palace," he said. "Now it's some sort of clothing place. Sewing machines, clothes racks, I don't know."

"Costume shop," I suggested.

"Yeah, you'd know about that. It smells different from when I was a kid." He nodded his head. "Kenningston Place ain't there anymore."

"I'm sorry."

"Nothing left of old KP except the back steps. I helped build those back steps. They're still there. That building," he nodded again, "was the commissary, and that one was the rec hall. They got food in there now, some sort of canteen it looks like. We played ball over there across the creek. They've let it grow up. Where the theatre building is now used to be the mess hall. The corner stone for the theatre says '1956.' I suppose they tore the old mess hall down. Well, I don't guess it matters much, not once this fire gets done with what it's gonna do."

A bell rang out.

"What's that?" I asked.

"Chow. Would you believe it? They serve their meals in the old hospital. Damnedest thing."

We worked through the day. We could see a red glow on three sides of us. Dad had joined a squad of men headed for Center Lake. More water was needed, and the Lake was the only source we had.

I took a break and wandered into the theatre. It was a

beautiful building with a high cathedral ceiling in an auditorium that invited relaxation. A balcony ran along the rear and sides of the auditorium. The stage setting had been abandoned untouched. The image it created was of a warm inviting room, one that I would like to have in my own home. I found a playbill lying on the floor: *You Can't Take It With You*, a show I had done several times as an actor and director. I wish we had taken time to see the production, but that wasn't why we had come to the Hills. Now there was a distinct possibility no one would ever see another show in this building. I left the theatre by way of the main entrance. There in the center of the lobby was a large, framed color photograph of an elderly gentleman, kindly greeting all with a half-smile and knowing eyes. He wore a cowboy hat and held a pipe in his hand.

"That's Doc," a voice said.

I turned. A massive man, too large for his plaid shirt, lounged in the doorway.

"Yeah," he continued. "Old Doc was quite a character. He knew about fires. It was Doc who kept his head on back in the fifties when the old mess hall burned down."

"You knew this man?" I asked.

"Sure. I've been going to plays here since I was a kid. Old Doc started this place right after the War. It's been going strong ever since. Be a shame to see it lost to a damn forest fire."

"Is he still living?"

"Naw. He's probably sitting next to The Big Man right now, asking for rain. Wouldn't be surprised if he don't get it, too." He nodded his head in farewell and moved past me into the auditorium, across the stage and out the back.

The bell was ringing again. I rushed outside and around the corner of the theatre. I didn't need to be told. I could see. The fire had reached our break on the hillside near the dorms. Men were rushing up the hill toward the fire line. The heat was searing, but I didn't notice it at the time. I found Dad. He was working a hose attached to a water truck and was again watering down the sides of the fiber-board buildings. A pile of blankets had been pulled from inside the dorms and left for anyone to use. I grabbed one and Dad soaked it for me. Then I beat the flames with all the strength I had left. He turned his hose on me and gave me a drenching. The water was manna. The men worked as one. We lost track of time. It didn't matter. Nothing mattered except the fire, the blanket, and the water that sloshed inside my all-court shoes.

I felt wetter than I needed to be. I turned to Dad to say, "Hey, spray somebody else," only to find him, standing with face turned toward the sky, his hose emptying wastefully onto the ground. The men were cheering. I cheered, too. I threw my blanket into the dying fire and sat down in the beginnings of a mud puddle. Huge drops of rain pelted down on us all. We could hear the sputter of dying flames all around us. Never had I enjoyed a summer shower so much. I sat like a turkey, head back, mouth open, drinking in the water from heaven.


There was the nasty smell of ash in the air. Dad and I had spent a restful night in one of the dorm rooms, eaten a grand breakfast of bacon and pancakes with the twenty-five or so fire fighters who had become like family to us, and were now strolling through the charred forest down toward Center Lake with three of the men. One was from Sturgis, the other two from Hot Springs. The rain had soaked the earth and turned the fire into smoldering beds. I looked a sight. My beard on the left side was singed close to the skin; the right side was its normal inch of growth. Dad gave me a hard time about that.

I tried giving him a difficult time about his limp. It had come up suddenly that morning.

Center Lake was a jewel in a black mist. Smoking piles of coal surrounded the water. Somehow, the campground and support buildings had survived, but not the trail up the side of the mountain. Or the boat ramp used mostly by fishermen. It, along with everything around it, had been reduced to ash.

Dad took everything in. What I saw meant very little to me. I could only guess at what he, a survivor of the great Blackwater Burn of fifty years before, saw in our surroundings.

We sat on a boulder at the lake. Dad took off his shoes and dangled his feet in the water. Feet wasn't enough for me. I stripped to my underwear and leapt into the lake. The icy water shot sparklers through my body for an instant and then was gone. I swam out ten or so yards and lay on my back, staring up into the clear blue sky. I couldn't see the black sticks that a few days before had been ponderosa pines; I couldn't smell the ash; I couldn't see the smoldering haze. It was just me, the cold water, and the sky. I wanted to be on the way home, but I didn't want to think about all the rest: Dad's illness and what that meant, his little cough I could hear even now, his new limp. I wanted it to be just me, the water, the sky, and my dad, healthy.

"Hey, Winston," he called after his coughing spasm had past.

"Yeah?"

"I'm not AWOL anymore." And he laughed. He lobbed a large stone in my direction. It hit the water and splashed me with a welcome chill. "I guess I have you to thank for that." I swam to the boulder and climbed out. Why hadn't it been like this all along?

We sat without speaking. The breeze turned my skin to chill-bumps, and it felt good. At that moment, it seemed to me as if the world was as close to being perfect as any of us could ever expect it to be. Dad leaned against me as he said, "We can go home now, don't you think?"

I nodded. "Yeah," I said.

# How Mitchell Gillette Lost and Found His Laugh

BY KENNETH ROBBINS

Mitchell Gillette could remember the precise day, hour, and minute that he lost his laugh. He would have known the second, but the digital clock on his bedroom dresser did not display seconds. It was five-thirty-two a.m. on Saturday, October 18. It was at that fateful moment when his wife, Claire, shook him from a deep but fretful sleep. After that, he had no reason to laugh. Nothing was funny about the elbow she planted in his side.

"You're snoring," Claire said.

"Huh?" At first, he thought it was a joke. He might have laughed if it had been a joke.

"I can't sleep. Would you turn over on your side?"

"I'm sorry," he said, and did as she bid. He was too groggy to argue.

A few minutes later, the elbow was back, jabbing harder this time. "Mitchell, you're snoring again."

"Really?"

"This isn't funny, you know." He could hear the vinegar in her voice.

"What time is it?" He didn't need to ask. The clock on the dresser across from his wife did not lie.

"Time for you to let me get some sleep, okay?"

"I'm real sorry, sweetpots," he said.

She moaned and pulled the covers over her ears.

He snuggled against her, feeling her warm buttocks pressed against his crotch. Only there was no joy in touching her ample bottom, not this time. Instead, there was her whine, high pitched and bitchy, "I'm hot, Mitchell."

"Sorry," he said. He did not sleep the rest of that night.

The following evening, there were two pillows on his side of the bed where before there had been one. "What's this?" he asked.

"I read if you sleep with your head elevated, you won't snore."

"Where did you read this?"

"*People Magazine.*"

"Oh," he said and crawled into bed beside his wife. The extra pillow gave him a crick in his neck. So, when he was certain Claire was asleep, he dropped it to the floor.

The clock read four eighteen when the jabbing elbow arrived.

"What!" he barked.

"Can't sleep," his wife said.

"I was dead to the world."

"Me," she said. "*I* can't sleep."

"Why not?"

"You know why not." She slipped from the bed.

"Where're you going?"

"To the sofa."

"No, you're not."

"Yes, I am."

"No! I'll go."

"I have to get some sleep, Bumpkins." She had an edge to her voice. Her endearment was one he detested. He knew there was no endearment in it at all.

"I said I'll go to the couch. I'll go to the couch." This he said with more than an edge to his voice. He was pissed royally now. He, too, needed sleep. What was wrong with his wife anyway.

The sofa was hard and covered with cat fur. He sneezed himself to sleep.

The next morning at breakfast, he asked, "Is it really that bad?"

"What?" she asked.

"My snoring."

"I said I'd go to the sofa."

"I mean, describe it to me."

"How could I?"

"Does it sound like this?" And he tested a sound on her.

"No. Leave me alone."

"How about this?" He gave his best shot at what he imagined his snoring to sound like.

"I said, leave me alone!" In a moment, she said, trying to find some sweetness in her voice, "It's not that bad anyway."

"Not that bad? Sweetpots, you can't sleep. That means I can't sleep. I don't know what to do."

"Stick with the second pillow." She thought a moment, then said, "And don't sleep on your back."

He took both suggestions. Problem solved.

A week later, Mitchell did not wake as Claire slipped from bed. He was not aware that she had left until four fifty that morning when he turned over to find her side of the bed empty. "Claire?" he whispered.

No answer.

He looked for her in the bathroom. Empty. In the office. Also, empty. Down stairs in the kitchen. No Claire. The den: Claire was asleep on the sofa with all three cats curled up beside her.

"Sweetpots?" he said as he touched her shoulder.

"Huh?"

"You okay?"

"I just got to sleep."

"Sorry. Is something wrong?"

"I can't sleep, Mitchell. How many ways do I need to say it?"

"I'm using the two pillows."

"Well, it's not working."

"Come back to bed."

"I just got comfortable here."

"Will you, please." He jerked the covers off her and waited for her to get up.

"It's cold!"

"Then go back to bed."

She did, reluctantly. The cats glared at Mitchell as they trailed behind her. They had been disturbed as well and did not like it. They recognized the enemy.

"Try these," Claire said, placing a small package on the dinner table.

"Band-Aids?"

"Sort of. 'Breathe Right.' They cross the bridge of your nose. Supposed to correct snoring."

"So does dying."

"Will you just give them a try? There's another product, a nose drop …"

"No!" When he was a kid, he had almost drowned when his mother had poured nose drops down his nose. "I'll try the Band-Aids." He would try anything short of nose drops.

At three thirteen a.m., Mitchell was jarred awake. "What!"

"The 'Breathe Right' isn't working."

"I took it off."

"What for? You know I can't sleep."

"And I couldn't breathe."

"I'll go downstairs."

"No, you won't. I'm the one with the damn problem."

He was too groggy. He missed the third step and crashed to the landing below. The fall woke him up.

"Honey, you okay?"

"Hell no!" he shouted.

"Do you need anything?"

"Hell no!"

An hour later (he guessed at the time since there was no digital clock in the den), he was awakened by somebody snoring. Now he was disturbing himself! Be damned. He turned his face to the back of the sofa and covered his ears with the pillow. He was too tired to argue even with himself.

"It's really a simple operation," Claire said.

"What is?"

"To have your nose fixed."

"I'm not having my nose fixed. It's fine."

"That's a matter of perspective. You won't go?"

"No. Thank you."

They were not sleeping together any more. Mitchell missed his soft comfortable bed and he learned to despise the God forsaken sofa. They had picked out the bed together. Queen size, extra soft to accommodate his lower back. Sleeping on the sofa was bringing his lower backache back. He walked with a slight stoop. It hurt too much to stand up straight.

"Why don't you visit your mother this Christmas without me," Claire announced over Thanksgiving dinner.

"How come? We always go together."

"I have work to do."

"What sort of work?"

"Things have been busy at the office and I'm behind."

"What about Christmas together?"

"Bumpkins, at your mother's, we have to sleep together. It's expected. . ."

He left the dinner table. He left the house. He left the yard. He left the town. He did not know where he was going until he got there. Once there, he did not know where he was. He slept in a motel that night and did not call home. The next day, the day after Thanksgiving, he did not have anything to be thankful for. He became aware that he had lost his laugh. Not that he had laughed a great deal before. But at least he had had a laugh which was available to him.

He had not been aware of having a laugh until it had left him.

When he returned home the following morning, Claire was not there. She left no note. He did not know where she might be. He did not care. He kicked the cats off his bed and slept the best sleep he had had in over a month.

The next morning, Claire showed up, looking brighter and chipper than he could remember.

"Where have you been?" he asked.

"Where have you been?"

"I asked first."

"I was afraid of staying in this big old house by myself," Claire said, "so I went to a friend's."

"Which friend."

"You're supposed to answer my question next."

"I drove to Monroe and took in a movie."

"Why didn't you call?"

"There wasn't a phone at the movie house."

"What did you see?"

"My turn. Which friend?"

"Somebody from the office. Has a guest room. You don't know them."

"Them?"

"Okay, him. We're going to be married."

"But you're already—"

"That's being taken care of."

"—married, to me."

"You'll receive the papers sometime today."

"Papers?"

"For the divorce."

". . . why?"

"Bumpkins, I've got to sleep."

That's how Mitchell Gillette found his tears. He wept as he packed his things into his Volkswagen bug.

Then he got angry.

Then he got drunk.

Then he got divorced.

Then he got laid.

Then he got angry again.

Then he decided to get even. After all, he needed sleep, too.

His name was Harvey Lee. He, Mitchell, wondered if Claire called him, this Harvey fellow, "Bumpkins." Secretly he hoped so. A just punishment.

Harvey was a lawyer, specializing in divorce proceedings. He had three ex-wives and three neutered female cats. That made six cats altogether, all neutered, all female. The thought of six cats following Claire from room to room in what had once-upon-a-time been his house made him long to laugh. All he could manage was a smirk.

At first, Mitchell parked his car in the vacant lot across the street from his former home. He had been amazed at how easily he had lost not only his wife but his house, his den, his bedroom, his bed. The judge had said that snoring could be considered when broadly defined as cruel and unusual punishment, and that since he, Mitchell Gillette, refused to have a nose job, he lost his house. No appeal. Harvey Lee proved to be a better lawyer than Mitchell a husband.

Later, he ventured into the front yard. How many times

had he cut that grass or trimmed that hedge or picked up empty beer cans left over from the raunchy parties next door?

Still later, he worked his way over the back fence and stood on the wet grass outside the window to the den. The fence had been easy to scale, even for someone like him: overweight, out of shape, aging, sleepless. He could hear someone inside the house, snoring. Did Harvey Lee have the same problem? Was he asleep on the sofa? Had he already been banished from the sanctity of the bedroom?

He raised his nerve. Or: he overcame his hesitations. Or: his desire for revenge overwhelmed his sense of restraint. Or: he wanted to discover if his snoring problem had merely been an excuse. Whatever. He still had a key to the back door. They had not changed the locks. Stupid people.

The snoring was coming from the dark bedroom. It was louder than a chain saw taking out a fallen tree. It was so loud it made the flooring throughout the house vibrate. This new guy, this lawyer named Harvey Lee, had a major problem!

Then he stood there, a shadow in the dark bedroom with only the red glow from the digital clock giving light. He realized: the snore did not belong to Harvey Lee at all. Not at all!

So that was how he got his laugh back.

He laughed all the way to the county jail where he spent a month for breaking and entering.

He did not care. He had his laugh back and it felt too good not having to quibble over where he lay his head.

# Creeping Charlie

BY KENNETH ROBBINS

"The thing that bugs me most is the randomness of life." Willis sits with his tennis racket between his knees. He is trying to balance a tennis ball on the end of his racket, but it refuses to oblige.

"Random life," I say. "That's an oxymoron, isn't it?"

"No," he says. He gives me his usual condescending glare. "It's a redundancy. I read in the paper about this professional tennis player who dropped dead in the middle of his serve. Heart attack."

"I read that. Congenital. He was born with it. Same as Pistol Pete. He was lucky to last as long as he did."

"Lucky. Is optimism congenital with you?" He smirks the same as when he aces me to my backhand, the same pleasant, irritating smirk.

"Look," I say. Do I smirk too? I wish I knew. "Letting life's randomness bug you is the same as saying: The thing I cannot tolerate is intolerance."

"Or how about this one: I hate bigots." He is actually smiling.

"Me, too."

"You, too what?"

"Hate bigots."

"Then you're redundant by nature."

"Aren't we all?" I *am* smirking. I can't help myself. "Here today, gone tomorrow. Like your tennis game," I say. "One of these days I'm going to beat you, buddy, you know that."

"Are you certain?"

"Absolutely. I have ten years on you. Time is on my side."

Ellin is in our front yard when I drag my beaten bones home. She is bent over from the waist, knees locked, fiddling with the grass. She is forever bending over like that. How she can bend from the waist without giving at the knee baffles my brain. When I work in the yard, I sit.

"Did you win?" she asks.

"Are you still a virgin?" I reply.

She kisses me and smacks her lips. "Salty."

"Willis is depressed."

"Why? Did you take more than two games off him?"

"You're so funny. No. The random nature of living has him despondent." I sit on the front step and watch her pull at weeds. "I tried cheering him up, but you know Willis. Once a sour thought enters his head, it's there to stay."

"He hasn't been looking well."

"Willis?"

"He walked by here yesterday. You would think his last friend in the world had died."

She pulls on a weed that seems attached to a string. A foot or so from the ground, it snaps. "What are you doing?" I ask.

She holds the weed for me to see. "That's why it's spreading," she says. "It's a runner."

"What is it?" I ask. She shrugs and bends again.

I sit beside her and pick at the weed. It has round leaves, usually three in a bunch. It doesn't grow tall enough for the mower to cut. It has covered over half our front lawn, squeezing out the grass Ellin and I had planted five years ago. This yard is more her toy than mine, but when something begins eating the fruits of our collective labor, I sit up and take note. I pull at a weed. It snaps. I work my fingers under its web of runners and pull. I feel the roots slipping out of the soil as fibers in ten directions come free of the earth. "Jesus," I whisper. "We've got to stop this mother, El. Pretty soon it'll be climbing up the side of the house."

We form a small pile of pulled weeds between us.

"Did you finish your essay?" I ask.

"Are you still a virgin?" She is smirking with the rest of us. "I'm on break."

"What's the hang up?"

"I don't know. It feels so simplistic. Why condemn a writer for reflecting the fundamental view of life that prevailed while he was living? It doesn't seem quite fair."

"Well, nobody's making you do it."

Ellin and I take samples of the weed to the Garden Spot. The ageless woman who sits at the cash register and emits an aura of omniscience takes the plant in her palm and fondles it like she might a day-old kitten. She turns it deliberately this way and that and says, "Hm."

"What is it?" I ask.

She says, "It's a runner."

"We know that."

"Some sort of broadleaf."

"So?"

"Never seen anything like it," she says. "Must be a hybrid."

We have a new specimen of evolution in our front yard. Toxic waste has mutated a perfectly normal and usually lovable weed into this beast intent upon devouring our lawn. I envision aliens in space vehicles hovering over our yard dropping tiny little seeds that take root and thrive off inert and lovable grass. Alien weeds are making an earthly debut in our yard. If not alien, if not a mutant, if not an evolution in weed genealogy, what might the blasted thing be?

"Be hanged if I know," the ageless wonder says.

"Any idea what we can do to kill it?"

"A broadleaf herbicide, maybe."

Ellin looks at me and shakes her head. No poison on her premises. I understand. Death by poison is not within our marital decree. We keep mousetraps in the house. D-con is not for us.

"Anything else?" I ask.

"That depends on how eager you are to get rid of it."

"So? What do we do?"

"Well . . . you might pull the suckers out one at a time." She grins like she's told a joke.

"Do you know how large our yard is?"

Ellen punches me in the ribs. "It's not that large."

"Pulling them will take all summer."

"So?"

I give in and say, "Sounds like a good idea to me."

Willis calls. He begs out of our tennis match tomorrow. It's his back, he says. It's been throbbing since our game yesterday. Maybe a day off from physical exertion will help. Besides, he has an appointment with a chiropractor at four and he is certain he won't be up for our tennis date.

"Told you time is my ally," I say.

"Back spasms aren't much fun," he replies.

"My back's killing me, too," I tell him, hoping for some sympathy. "We've got some mutant garbage growing in our yard."

"You should try a herbicide," he says.

"Ellin and I don't believe in high-tech solutions to natural problems."

There is a pause on his end of the line before he says, "Me, neither. Can you believe I'm going to a chiropractor? On my doctor's recommendation, too!"

"Hey, it's better than a spine transplant."

I hear Willis groan. It must have slipped out of him. In all the time I've known him, Willis has never admitted to any feeling, much less pain. "Got to go," he says in a curt manner.

"You okay?"

"Got to go."

"Take care of yourself."

I don't know what else to do with myself. Tennis canceled, I attack the front lawn with renewed vigor.

"This is going to take forever," I say as I pour a can of Diet Coke over some ice.

"You can try an herbicide if you insist. It might be faster."

"We don't know what the sucker is, much less what kind of poison it'll take to kill it. Besides, herbicides kill earthworms."

"Well. . ." She returns to her keyboard and forgets my petty problem. She is deep into a feminist evaluation of the short works of John Steinbeck, and even the future health of our beloved lawn cannot lure her away from her attack on a Nobel Laureate, who, she claims, must finally, once and for all, be put in his rightful and well-earned misogynistic place.

Willis walks by, obviously out for his constitutional, a poor replacement for our usual game of tennis. He is deep in thought and does not hear my greeting of "Yo, Buddy." I try again: "Hey, Willis!"

"Huh?" He stops. His usual sharp, clear vision of things is missing. Instead, there is a vacancy. No, that's not right. Something is there, something more akin to horror than fear. I can see that at first he doesn't recognize me. Then he raises a limp-wristed hand in my direction though he is only ten feet away, stands for a moment or two as if confused by his surroundings, and then comes into the yard and stands over the pile of pulled weeds I've collected.

"What's the chiropractor have to say?" I ask.

"That it's not muscular," he says.

"Is that good news or not?"

"If it's not muscular, then what?"

I shake my head. "My dad slipped a disc once."

"Be damned. The whole world doesn't spin around you and your dad, you know."

"Listen. I'm sorry."

He starts away. "Gotta go."

"Come inside, I'll fix us a Diet Coke." I know he hates soda, especially those filled with fake sugar, but I don't know what else to offer him.

"No. . . no. . ." He returns to the sidewalk.

I follow. "What do you do next? About your back."

"My doctor wants me to see a specialist in Omaha."

"Omaha! Jeez."

"Gotta go, okay?"

"What kind?"

He doesn't answer.

"When?"

"Next Monday. No tennis for a while. Call somebody else."

He is half a block away. I yell: "If you need somebody to drive you — call, okay?"

I pull weeds the rest of the afternoon. My back feels fine. When finished, I look at my handiwork. A full eight hours and I've made no headway. All I'm doing is making bald spots in my lawn. Empty spaces where I'll need to sow new seed.

"Creeping Charlie." This is the assessment of Harry Laurgaard, our county agent. I called him. I didn't have to say much more than a runner's taking over my yard before he knew precisely what the alien is. "You're not doing any good, pulling at it. Creeping Charlie's like a disease. You've got to poison the son of a bitch, else he'll be all you have as a lawn. Bitching weed. Creeping Charlie's taking over the whole town," he says. "You're the third person this morning to give me a call."

"I've had this stuff in the yard for three years," I tell him. "Till now it's stayed in one place, under the fur trees and seemed content. Now it's all over the place. Why is that?"

"Too much rain. The last three years have been drought. Now this summer, you know, rain, rain, rain. Sorry, but there you are."

"So, pulling it won't help?"

"Sure, if you get it all. If you don't, it'll come right back next spring."

"What else can I do?"

"Herbicide."

I attack the weeds. At least I can call the beast by its rightful name.

No herbicide.

No, by God. I'll do this my way, by the sweat of my brow. I will not abide some random weed eating up my lawn. Nor will I condone the use of chemical warfare in my front yard. There are enough pollutants in our waterways without my adding yet another.

I'll get it all, I know I will.

Ellin finishes her feminist essay and gives it to me to edit. It is immaculately written in perfect MLA style. You could study the piece as a model for technical achievement. I put it aside, no red marks on it.

"Well?" she says.

I have no notion how to respond. It is so fine, so brilliantly done. Not a flaw anywhere. . . except. . . "I like it, El."

"Like?" I know what she is thinking: this thing has been too much work to be classified under "like." "Like" is the word that you use when no other word fits; it functions in the same fashion as the ubiquitous "interesting." I know that, but I have no other word available at the moment.

"It's a definitive work, El. You know that."

"Definitive of what?"

"Well. . . style."

"Not content?"

"Ah, come on, Ellin."

"No. I'm a big girl. I can take it. What's wrong with it?" Her eyes are glazing. She has a two-by-four up her backbone. I wish at this moment that I was still single, living in a college dorm with an asshole named Ronald.

"I don't agree with your conclusion, sweetheart, that's all."

"Which one?"

"That Steinbeck should be considered the author of dick literature."

"That's not a conclusion, dear," she says, eyes melting glass. "That's a fundamental point from which to draw my conclusions, namely that dick literature is by its very nature demeaning to women and that John Steinbeck is a prime source for female literary subjugation."

"You don't really believe that, do you?"

"Yes!" She laughs a little, swipes at her bangs, and repeats, "Yes. . ."

"Maybe I should re-read *Grapes of Wrath*."

"I hate it when you make fun of me."

"Isn't it Rose of Sharon who suckles the dying man with her mother's milk? It seems to me that's a fundamental mother earth image which defies any gender-oriented re-definition."

"You just made my point, Gray. There is nothing whatsoever mother earthly about suckling a dying man. In fact ..." She kills me with her eyes and refuses to continue. "It's disgusting how men can be such dickheads."

I'm glad Willis and I have a match. It has been over a month. I didn't realize how much I had come to depend on him as a partner in my fight against a middle-aged spread. In the month since our last encounter on the tennis courts, I have put on ten pounds, all balanced around my midsection: my "Uni-Royal," as Ellin calls it. My spare tire.

We swat the ball back and forth with no pace to speak of. Willis is as out of shape as I am. His serve has so zip. It piddles over the net and sits up for a flat forehand. I am pounding the man. At five-one, I yell out, "I told you time was on my side!"

He sits on the concrete bench between sets, hunkered over his racket. I join him. It has been too long since we last squared off. He is having difficulty catching his breath. "Mind if we rest a minute?" he says without looking up.

"No problem."

"You've been practicing," he says.

"No amount of practice would change my game, man. What I've been doing is growing fat."

"Me, too, obviously."

"I miss our visits, you know. Tennis isn't just a game. It's our social hour. I'm weeks behind in gossip. So, what's new?"

"Nothing. Same old shit. I hate this damnable life. There's no reason to it. Never has been, never will be."

"You're right. Nothing new. Me, I've got a new name. Dickhead. Ellin dubbed me this morning."

"You and Ellin make me wish I'd married."

"You'd want that? Dickhead? Before today, the only time she used the word was in reference to the president. That's because he can't stop himself pussy-grabbing everything in sight. I'm not sure I like the company."

Willis coughs. The spasm shakes him to his white socks. When it passes, he sits, drained of energy.

"Pretty lousy cold," I say.

"Yeah." He drapes a towel over his head.

"You don't look so good, buddy," I say. "Maybe we should call it a day."

"Maybe."

"Are you sure you're okay?"

"No," he says. "I'm not sure."

"Did you win?" Ellin asks as I prance into the den.

"Sure did!" I say.

"Willis must really be sick."

"Or perhaps yours truly is improving in his old age?" She laughs as I pour myself a Diet Coke. She is at her computer again, making a few minor changes in her masterwork.

"Should I submit this? What do you think?"

"I think. . . it's too valuable not to submit. If it's published, expect to be clobbered by Steinbeck scholars, though."

"Male Steinbeck scholars."

"Are there any other kind? You'll probably be deified by female chauvinist pigs."

"That's possible, too."

I settle on the floor beside her and put my feet in her lap. She unlaces my shoes, removes them along with my white socks and caresses my pink toes. She does this without notice as her mind is thousands of miles away, seeing her essay emblazoned on the pages of *Tulsa Studies in Women's Literature* or *Steinbeck Quarterly*. I take the chance and disturb her train of thought. "I'm worried about Willis," I say.

"Why?"

"He's losing weight. The doctors can't find the source of his back problem. He's so damn despondent."

"Do you remember that character from Dogpatch?

Everywhere he went a thunderhead followed and threw lightning bolts at his hat. Well, that's Willis. Only Willis isn't quite so adept at dodging lightning bolts."

"That's not very kind. He envies us, you know."

"I think Willis is a whiner," she says.

"No. That was the Willis at the start of summer. Now, I wish that that Willis was back. These days, he's so quiet. It bothers me."

Her attention is back on her computer screen. "Maybe I'm being too hard on Steinbeck. Maybe he's merely a bi-product, a zero looking for a number to follow. It's a dilemma, not knowing where to put the blame."

"Our new grass is doing well. Have you noticed?"

"He'll be back."

"Who?" I ask.

"Charlie."

I know she's right.

Willis is more silent today than before. He called, asking me over. I don't remember being in his apartment before. Funny. I consider Willis my best friend, but this is my first time to visit him, and he's never really visited me. He has stood in my yard and sat on the front porch, but I don't believe he's ever ventured inside the house. It's a funny thing, being a friend these days. It all feels so random, so disconnected. It's as if aside from tennis, we have no relationship. The idea saddens me.

I admire his place. It is not at all the way I envisioned it. Somehow, Willis struck me as a housekeeping slob who eats off plastic dishes so as not to need dishwashing liquid or who uses the floor as a shelf, the dining table as a garbage heap, and the bathtub as a natural clothes dryer. So, I am surprised. Willis' place is far more organized than mine, and he's a bachelor. The only time our place is as neat is when my mother or Ellin's mom or both, God forbid, are coming for a visit.

He sits staring at his TV. The Irish of Notre Dame are playing somebody. The only constant thing in our lives is the Irish playing football in the fall. Willis stares, even though before today he degraded the game and all who worship it. The last truly great athlete, in his opinion, was Bjorn Borg. It's an opinion we share.

I say: "When are they going to devise a more equitable national championship tournament for football? Like March Madness. Seems like it's time."

He says nothing.

"I wish someone would write effectively about football. Give Ellin a legitimate target for her dick literature theory."

Again, he says nothing.

"You do know what dick literature is, don't you?"

Still, nothing.

"Okay, I give," I say. "What's going on?"

He hands me a file folder. "I can't talk about it," he says. "So, read."

In the folder is Willis' medical report, dated three days ago. The doctor's handwriting reminds me of my own. I can decipher only an occasional word, but that is enough.

I lean forward and place the folder on the coffee table. I run both hands through my thinning hair. I can't look at him. I can't not look at him. There is one word in the folder that I can read. I can't not read it. One word. Just one word. "Jesus Christ," I say, "I hate the randomness of this life."

The TV screen is a blur of human flesh as the Irish fail to hold in a desperate goal-line stand.

Born and raised in the Texas heat, molded and carved and chiseled by a creator that's still chipping away. I like writing and appreciate when people take the time to read it.

# Saint, Sadist, Savior

BY JACOB SURLES

It was chaos, there was blood and shrapnel and screaming. The fumes of some strange material stinging his nostrils. A cacophony of sounds scraped their way across his ears— screams, crashing, and yellow, twisting metal.

Dr. Thaddeus Soros Sr. was an incredibly kind and compassionate man, well respected in the small community nestled in the Appalachian Mountains of Pennsylvania. His jovial and caring nature was so well known that the residents of his town nicknamed him "Saint Thad." One night, while Thad sat in his modest and simple home, he received a call from a close friend who lived a few blocks away.

"My son," the man gasped desperately, "something's wrong ... he needs help ... he won't wake up ... he's barely breathing."

"I'm on my way right now," Thad assured him.

Thad Sr. hung up the phone and quickly snatched up his

shoes and jacket. As he grabbed his keys, the phone rang again. He almost didn't answer, but, thinking it may have been his friend with a vital piece of information, he picked up the phone.

"Dr. Soros?" A dry, trembling voice said.

"Yes," Thad Sr. answered. "I'm in a hurry to see a patient, please be brief."

The man cleared his throat, "Dr. Soros, this is Officer Pickney with the Pennsylvania State Police. I'm sorry to call you so late, Dr., but I have some unfortunate news. Your son, Thomas was killed in an automobile accident a few hours ago. He was driving on Highway 93 and a Greyhound bus lost control and slammed into him head on. He was killed instantly. We apologize it took us so long to contact you. We had trouble identifying both the car and the body."

Thaddeus took a long, deep breath. "Thank you, Officer Pickney. Was anyone else hurt? Is there anything I can do to help?"

"No, Dr. Soros, the bus righted itself after striking Thomas' car. I appreciate your offer to help as well but it is unnecessary." The trooper said this cordially.

Thaddeus now cleared his own throat, "Thank you, Officer Pickney. Have a good night and be safe getting home." He hung up the phone and took a few deeper breaths, contemplating the gravity of the news. Thomas had just turned 16 and gotten his license. Thaddeus Sr. had given him an old, beat-up car for his birthday last month. Thad Sr. closed his eyes and sighed, allowing a few moments to pass by. He opened them to the shoes he held in his hand. Remembering where he must go, Dr. Soros finished dressing and headed out the door to help his patient.

Dr. Thaddeus Soros Jr. was an incredibly cold and callous man, despised and generally avoided by most people in his professional circle. His cruel and heartless nature was so well known that other people in his industry nicknamed him "The Sadist". While Thad Jr. sat in his large, ornately decorated office in New York City staring into space, the phone rang. Thad Jr. let it ring, looking around the room at his extravagant mahogany desk with a platinum picture frame placed on the corner. On the frame, "Triumph" was engraved in gold lettering. Inside it sat a picture of his brand-new Ferrari, with him posing in front of it.

The phone stopped ringing.

Thad Jr. stared at the picture and tried to smile, almost completely forgetting that behind it was a picture of his deceased father and younger brother, Thomas standing together at Bushkill Falls in the Appalachian Mountains of Pennsylvania.

The phone rang again.

Thad Jr. slapped the speaker, "WHAT!?" he demanded.

"Dr. Soros, this is Emily," the woman announced. Emily was his personal assistant for 10 years. She retired the summer before to take care of her husband after he'd been diagnosed with brain cancer.

"Hello, Emily. Be brief, I'm very busy," he said with an irritated tone while doodling on a piece of stationary.

"I'm sorry to bother you, Doctor, but it's about my husband, Terry. His cancer has progressed to the point he needs surgery."

Thad Jr. rolled his eyes, only half listening. He interrupted what seemed to him to be a much too long explanation. "Emily," he said flatly, "please, I'm very busy. Get to the point." Thad Jr. clicked his pen closed, looking curiously at the stick figure he'd just drawn with a knife sticking out of its skull.

"Yes sir, sorry, I ramble when I'm stressed. Terry's surgery is more than we can afford, and I was wondering … well, you're the best brain surgeon I know, so I was wondering if maybe you could perform the surgery, and we could pay you over time. I was very reluctant to ask but I'm desperate to save my Terry."

Thad Jr. clicked his pen back open and started doodling again. "Emily, listen, I would like to help you, but my surgery schedule is booked solid for the next twelve months. I don't even have a free hour during the day. My new secretary has been nonstop scheduling since I hired her. It wouldn't be fair to the other patients who are waiting and paying the full amount up front to push them back or cancel their surgeries. Plus, I don't have a payment plan option, I never have, you know that. If I offered it to you and someone found out, every charity case in the country would be beating down my door. Finally, let's say I perform the surgery on Terry *and* accepted a payment plan, he still couldn't work. Frankly, neither could you because you'd have to take care of him during recovery, so how would you even pay me?" His voice was so cold and dry that it could give arctic winds frostbite.

Emily held back her anger, but tears streamed down her face. "OK, Dr. Soros. Thank you for your time."

"You got it," he said, quickly hanging up before he had to hear any more of the sob story.

The intercom beeped and his secretary's voice meekly stated, "Dr. Soros, just reminding you of your massage at two today and your barber appointment at 11:00 am tomorrow.

"Ok," he said dryly, turning the intercom off.

Thad Jr. looked across the office at his son, Thaddeus III. "All right, call your mother to pick you up. Oh, and tell her to pick up a bottle of Angels Envy on the way home. But don't tell her until you're in the car. I don't want her taking too long to get here."

The ten-year-old looked at his father, trying to muster up the courage to say something other than, "Yes sir", but fear won that internal battle.

"CONTACT!" Ramon screamed as the battle erupted, opening fire on the enemy soldiers trying to surround the position of the Para-rescue Jumpers.

Bullets riddled the walls and windows as the PJ's scrambled to cover the wounded and take defensive positions.

Teddy reached the window next to Ramon just in time to see the enemy soldier take aim. Positioning himself to shoot, Teddy couldn't bring himself to pull the trigger.

The sound of automatic gunfire muffled Ramon's gasp as the bullet slipped through the side of his vest, puncturing his lung.

"He's got a punctured lung," Thad Sr. said stoically, pulling out his portable medical kit. He reached in and grabbed a long, coiled up plastic tube that very much resembled a thin garden hose.

Just then a large, scruffy man burst through the door, a look of rage painted across his ruddy face.

"Is this the son of a bitch who attacked my son!?" he yelled, storming toward the man lying in a pool of blood on the floor under Thad Sr.

Thad Sr. jumped to his feet immediately and met the man in the middle of the room, jabbing the blunt end of a scalpel into his ribs. "It is," he growled, "and if you want to live to see justice done, you'll turn around and let me help my patient or so help me, I'll skewer you like a shish kabob."

The man turned pale and slowly backed away, never turning around until he reached the door.

Thad Sr. turned back to his patient and got to work. A few minutes later, the desperate gasping stopped, and the man could breathe.

"HE CAN'T BREATHE!" the woman screamed as the man under Thad Jr. gasped desperately.

Thad Jr.'s hands gripped the man's throat, holding him against the cold pavement as the angry screaming shattered the night air.

"YOU CUT ME OFF! Thad Jr. growled. "YOU COULD'VE KILLED ME!"

There was no one around strong enough to break up the fight.

Teddy sat quietly reading his new comic in the backseat of the sedan, oblivious to the violence happening on the frigid street just behind the car next to him.

Ramon sat quietly engrossed, reading his new comic, oblivious to the violence happening just across the room.

The captain burst through the door, immediately breaking up the fight.

Teddy jumped, startled out of his nap.

"What the hell!?" he snapped, instinctively. As he wiped his eyes he looked over at Ramon who was still engrossed in his comic.

"You still reading that comic book?" Teddy asked, jokingly.

"Graphic novel." Ramon replied, his tone very indicative of his desire to be left alone.

Teddy cocked his head sideways to look at the title.

"Promethea."

On the cover was a woman holding a caduceus.

Thad Sr. reached back into his portable medical kit with a caduceus on the cover.

The man was still lying on the floor in a pool of his own blood. Still alive, he looked up at Thad Sr., regret pouring from his eyes and down his cheeks.

"You'll regret this!" The woman screamed as Thad Jr. drove away, leaving the man lying unconscious on the concrete in a pool of his own blood.

Teddy looked down from his bunk to see the man lying in a pool of his own blood.

"You ok?" he asked.

"You're ok," Thad Sr. said calmly.

"He's ok," Thad Jr. reassured himself.

Thad Sr., his son and grandson hiked deliberately through the woods toward Bushkill Falls. At eight years old, Thad III struggled to keep up.

"Come on, pick up the pace," his father growled, "if we don't make it before dusk then we'll be setting up camp in the dark."

Thaddeus Sr. stopped on the trail, pretending to have something in his boot. "The boy is going as fast as he can, Thad, cut him some slack. We've set up camp in the dark plenty of times. It won't hurt us to do it again."

Thad Jr. gritted his teeth at his father's interjection. "Just because we can doesn't mean we have to."

"Oh hush, you used to push your brother to hurry too, and it never did any good. Everyone is doing their best, all the time." Thaddeus Sr. said matter-of-factly, putting his boot back on.

Thad Jr. snapped, "Do we have to talk about my brother Tommy every time we come up here? Can't we just talk about something pleasant?"

Thaddeus Sr. turned slowly and stared his son in the eye. "Son, we should remember the loved ones we lost as a way to honor their memory. It won't do you any good trying to shove the loss of Thomas down in your boots. When the dead are forgotten, they truly cease to exist, and you'll excuse me if I'm not in a hurry to forget my son."

Thad III listened intently, trying to capture every word of his grandfather's wisdom.

"I don't need you to tell me how best to handle my own emotions," an indignant Thad Jr. replied. "We all deal with things differently and for me it's just easier to try and forget that Tommy ever existed."

Thaddeus Sr. took a deep breath, holding back the tears that desperately wanted to escape his eyes. He thought of a great many terrible things to say to his obstinate son, but, instead resigned himself to simply replying, "Okay, son." He tied his boot and looked over at his grandson, giving the boy a wink and a smile.

Thad Jr. winced, knowing full well that his own father liked his son better.

Teddy winced as the military judge read out the sentence.

"Thaddeus Soros III, you are hereby given a Dishonorable Discharge for neglect to adequately perform your sworn duty to protect your fellow servicemen. I would add that you should thank your lawyer, for were you not so well represented I would have gladly given you a harsher sentence. I believe the inaction that led to the death of your teammate, Ramon Hereford, should have resulted in jail time. Though you are granted a sentence that does not require incarceration, I believe your heart will pay the ultimate penalty, as you know full well that Ramon's death is due directly to your unwillingness to protect him. May God have mercy on your soul."

"And may God keep and cherish his soul," the Reverend said solemnly at the end of his prayer.

Thad III wept as his grandfather's casket was lowered into the ground. He looked up and saw his father, hardly paying attention, and Thad III was filled with rage. Suddenly he blurted out at his father, "YOU AREN'T EVEN PAYING ATTENTION, YOU MISERABLE PIECE OF SHIT. YOU LET HIM DIE BECAUSE YOU WEREN'T PAYING ATTENTION AND NOW YOU'RE JUST IGNORING HIM AGAIN! HE'S DEAD BECAUSE OF YOU!"

Thad Jr. reared back and struck his son with the back of his hand, knocking Thad III to the ground. He snarled at his son, "You're dead to me as well. Never contact me again!" Thad Jr. stormed over the graves in his path, across the cemetery, and got into his car.

From his car Thad III could see the cemetery, and he decided at the last minute to pull off and visit. He walked slowly and deliberately across the grass, being careful not to step on the graves of those laid to rest. He stopped at the gravestone of his grandfather and knelt down, digging his fingers into the dirt.

"Papa," he whispered, "I leave for boot camp today. I wasn't sure if I should stop by before I left, but I couldn't help myself." Thad III took a deep breath and could almost hear his grandfather's reply. "Of course, you should have stopped by!"

Thad III looked down and started to cry. "I miss you so much, Papa, I think about you all the time. I wish you were here to see how far I've come."

The breeze gently rocked Thad III, and he closed his eyes and listened, hoping to catch his grandfather's voice in the wind.

The wind was getting stronger as Thaddeus Sr., Jr., and Thad III hiked up the side of a rocky incline. Thaddeus Sr.'s foot caught a patch of loose gravel and he slipped, barely catching himself on a root growing out of a rock next to him.

"Oooooo-hohoho … that was a close one!" Thaddeus Sr. laughed nervously.

Thad III was nervous as he drove off the base and headed back to civilian life. He knew Ramon's death was his fault, and he could hear the shadowed echo of his father's criticism in his mind. "Coward."

"Don't be a coward," Thad Jr. said impassively as he watched his son maneuver across the ledge. "Your grandfather is waiting for you right there, and I'm right here, just pay attention."

"You're not paying attention," Thaddeus Sr. said to Thad Jr. as they headed to the funeral service for Thomas. "I asked you to make sure that you remember Thomas positively at the service and speak positively about him to the family."

Thad Jr. rolled his eyes in the passenger seat and said, "He's dead, father. What does it matter how I speak about or remember someone who is dead?"

"He's dead," the doctor said, regretfully. "I'm sorry but your father's injuries were…." Thad Jr. stood for a moment, scowling at the news as Thad III broke down completely, curling up in a ball and weeping in his chair. The tears slipped from his eyes and tumbled down his young face.

Thaddeus Sr. was crossing the last ledge before they reached the campsite when he lost his footing, scrambling to reach out to his son for help. Thad Jr. was surprised at his father reaching out and instead of helping, he reflexively recoiled his hand.

Thad III reached his hand out and grabbed his grandfather's arm. As his grandfather pulled him over the stream, he asked poignantly, "Papa, why do we come such a long and dangerous way just to go camping?"

Thaddeus Sr. chuckled, "That's a *good* question!" He sat down on a rock and pulled a canteen out of his pack. "We come to this spot because it was your uncle's favorite place to camp. The three of us — me, your uncle and your father would come up here in the summer and camp. As the years got on, your Uncle Thomas wanted to keep exploring further and further into the woods. One day we all set out to hike as far as we could, and Thomas led the way. We ended up so far in the mountains that it took us a full day to travel. So, for the four years after, we kept coming to this spot, led by Thomas, who managed to memorize the route in his head on the first trip. As we kept coming, the route kept getting harder and harder due to erosion, but Thomas never gave up. After he passed, I decided to bring your father out here every year as a way to honor Thomas' memory. Your father never liked it, but I made him keep coming. It's important that we remember the dead, son, because those who pass aren't truly gone until we stop speaking their names. Do you understand now?"

Thad III nodded. "Yes sir. I like coming out here with you, too. Thank you for bringing me."

Thaddeus Sr. smiled, hugging his grandson tightly. "You're a good boy, Thad, and very sweet. Never compromise that sweetness. You're meant to love, not to hurt, always remember that."

Thad Jr. watched with terror as his father slid off the side of the ledge and tumbled down the steep slope. "NO!" he screamed, immediately angry that he had recoiled his hand instead of reaching out to grab his father.

Without hesitation, Thad III looked back and saw a steep, gravel rockslide heading down toward his grandfather. He bolted back across the ledge and leapt onto the gravel, sliding on his side down the path.

"Thad! Wait!" His father yelled, overcome by panic.

"WHY didn't you defend your teammate?" the lawyer grilled.

"I was overcome by panic," Teddy stated dryly.

"WHY DIDN'T YOU REACH OUT YOUR HAND!?" Thad III screamed at his father from the bottom of the ravine where his grandfather lay, unconscious and hardly breathing.

"TAKE MY HAND!" Thad III screamed at the soldier on the gurney. "WE'RE GONNA BE OUT OF HERE IN LESS THAN FIVE MINUTES!"

It was chaos, there was blood and shrapnel and screaming. The fumes of some foreign material stinging his nostrils. A cacophony of familiar sounds scraped their way across his ears — screams, an explosion, and gray, twisting metal.

The sound of gunfire was deafening, blistering the ear drums of the PJ's as they tended to the wounded behind the small, makeshift barricade shielding them from enemy fire.

The captain yelled, "TEDDY! AFTER YOU LOAD, PROVIDE COVER FIRE FOR ROGER!" Everyone called Thaddeus III, "Teddy". It was short for "Teddy Bear" because of his soft, gentle persona.

Teddy and Ramon loaded the wounded soldier onto the

helicopter and Teddy unslung his rifle, returning to the barricade. He could see a swarm of soldiers all firing from various positions about one hundred yards out. Teddy took aim, then lowered his sight and began firing into the dirt. Then he aimed high and began firing over the heads of the enemy. Ramon looked back from the helicopter as he finished securing the wounded soldier and saw Teddy intentionally missing, squinting, and shaking his head.

After a few minutes, all the wounded were loaded, and the unity of PJ's were back on the helicopter. They unloaded a savage barrage of fire on the enemy as the helicopter lifted off, escaping into the night.

"Anyone injured?" the captain asked.

In unison the other four PJs held their thumbs up, indicating they were unscathed.

Teddy looked at the jump seat across from him to see Ramon smirking at him. Ramon knew Teddy intentionally didn't aim at the enemy he was supposed to be shooting, but Ramon also knew Teddy was the bravest and most adept field medic in the entire Army. Ramon knew Teddy was not only brave, but intelligent, fearless, and most of all compassionate. Teddy and Ramon arrived in the unit at the same time and over the last two years they had developed a bond that transcended soldierly brotherhood—they were kindred spirits.

Teddy smiled and shrugged his shoulders in response to Ramon's smirk. They shared a brief glance and then Teddy went back to watching his patients.

They saved four Navy Seals that day. It was one of Teddy's proudest moments.

The proudest moments sometimes erupt from the darkest events in a person's life. For Teddy, the darkest moment was the day his grandfather passed.

Time passed slowly as Thad Jr. stood frozen on the ledge, staring down into the ravine where his son, Thad III stood over his grandfather. The echo of Thad's scream had just finished its last repeat through the ravine, "… HAND, HAND, hand, hand, hand…." Dr. Thad Jr. couldn't catch his breath as the feeling of loss savagely overran his mind. He could see his son at the bottom, desperately trying to revive his grandfather but Thad Jr. couldn't act. Darkness fell on him, and suddenly, he felt nothing at all.

"I understand that you felt angry that I left in the middle of the night, son," Thad Sr. calmly spoke as he tried to coerce Thad Jr. from the bathroom. "But Thomas' death couldn't supersede my duty to care for a patient. Thomas was already gone and there was nothing I could do to get him back or help, but I *could* help Jim's son. It was the greater good. Not only that, but I am bound by an oath I took as a doctor to help those in need." Thad Sr. leaned his head against the door, tears building in his eyes. "Please, son, open the door. I love you very much and want to be there for you."

"YOU JUST LEFT IN THE MIDDLE OF THE NIGHT! TOMMY'S DEAD AND YOU DIDN'T EVEN TELL ME!" Thad Jr. sobbed through the door.

Thad Sr. sighed deeply, holding back his emotions, "I had to, son. I had to help my patient. I can't sacrifice the living for the sake of the dead, it's just not the moral thing to do."

Thad Jr. slammed his fist against the door. "GO TO HELL!"

"I hope you rot in hell," Ramon's father snarled through the screen door at Teddy. "You let my boy die because you couldn't do what you signed up to do."

Teddy and Ramon laid in their bunks talking after their successful operation. "I didn't sign up to kill people," Teddy said. He was slightly embarrassed that Ramon had caught him intentionally not killing the enemy soldiers. "I signed up to save as many people as I could, and that's exactly what I intend to do. I have two goals; be a great doctor like my grandfather, and avoid ever having to kill anyone, ever."

Ramon chuckled, "Well, I hope you reach both those goals. Do me a favor, though … if you see someone trying to shoot me, at least try to stop them. Shoot 'em in the leg, the arm or some shit."

Teddy smiled, "Deal."

"What's the deal?" Thad Jr. asked, his voice void of emotion or urgency.

"It's not looking good," replied the doctor, "he's got a dozen broken bones, a punctured lung, and blood on his brain. He hasn't regained consciousness since the fall, which also doesn't give us much hope. We're doing everything we can to save your father, but, coming from a friend, he's going to need a miracle."

Thad Jr. turned around and walked out into the waiting room, where his son sat anxiously.

"Well? He's gonna be ok, right, Dad? He was still breathing when the helicopter …."

Thad Jr. stuck his hand out, signaling his son to stop. "He's not going to make it. There are too many different injuries, all of which are fatal on their own." Thad Jr.'s voice was icy and dry, almost inhuman.

Thad III could still hear his grandfather's voice saying, "You're meant to love, not to hurt, always remember that." He prevented himself from saying the terrible things he wanted to say to his father in that moment.

In that moment, Thad Jr. couldn't believe what he was hearing. Tommy was not just his brother, he was his only friend, his confidant, his motivator, his everything. Thad Jr. felt the blood drain from his face, leaving it pale and cold. His emotions were chaotic, like Confederate surgery at night. He remembered a year back when he and Tommy snuck out and went around the town throwing toilet paper over trees. He let out a small smile when he remembered that no one ever figured out it was the two of them. Because Tommy was such a good kid, no one would ever believe he did it. Tommy covered for Thad Jr. the next morning when their father confronted the two of them, swearing up and down that he and Thad Jr. had played cards until bedtime. Thad Jr. trusted his brother so deeply that Tommy was the only one with whom he would share his deepest emotions. Now that Tommy was gone, he felt empty, as if his emotions had died on that same highway where his brother was killed. Thad Jr. heard his father coming up the stairs and bolted for the bathroom. As he locked the door, he felt only one emotion—rage, and it coursed through his veins, fueling his heart like a sports car speeding through the night.

Teddy's sports car sped through the night, slicing the wind with surgical precision. His thoughts also raced, careening around his mind recklessly, sliding and skidding through the corners. He flew past a sign that said "Speed Limit 35" with a giant, black "S" underneath. Teddy slammed the gas pedal down and the engine surged, pushing the speedometer past the 70mph mark. Teddy gripped the wheel and gritted his teeth.

Ramon gritted his teeth as he turned and fired his rifle, instantly killing the man who had shot him. Teddy rushed to catch Ramon before he hit the ground.

"Fuck man, where are you hit?" Teddy asked, his face feeling flush from guilt.

"Under the ribs," Ramon rasped, trying to catch his breath, "and you broke our deal, fucker."

Teddy started to pull Ramon's jacket off as the gunfire increased from inside the house. Teddy knew this meant his unit was preparing to exit the building for an escape.

Ramon laughed, "I knew you wouldn't be able to though, you big softy, killing just isn't in your blood."

Teddy smiled, "I'm so sorry, brother. I promise I'll make it up to you."

Ramon closed his eyes and gasped, trying to catch his breath.

Teddy scrambled to cut away Ramon's uniform to stop the bleeding. He reached the hole, and a feeling of dread overwhelmed him. The bullet had not only punctured Ramon's lung but had hit his liver; black blood flowed from the wound.

"Hold on tight and don't die," Teddy pleaded to Ramon. "I'm gonna drag you out the back to the chopper."

"Deal." Ramon said, sarcastically, letting out a gurgling chuckle.

Teddy dragged his friend through the house and out the back door where the rest of his unit had already gathered, firing madly at their attackers.

"TEDDY! WHAT THE HELL HAPPENED?" his captain demanded.

"He's hit in the upper stomach, and I think it went through his lung as well!" Teddy reported.

They loaded Ramon up on the helicopter and escaped with two other rescued soldiers who were also seriously wounded.

From his jump-seat Teddy looked across the helicopter to see another member of the unit, Roger, glaring and shaking his head. Roger mouthed "I saw," at Teddy and suddenly he felt a sinking feeling in his stomach.

The driver of the yellow VW Beetle felt a weird, sinking feeling in his stomach as he made his way through the mountains and approached the sign that said, "Speed Limit-35" with a giant, black "S" underneath. He was certain he heard screeching tires and slowed down just in case, as he lit a cigarette.

Teddy tried to light a cigarette while speeding through the winding mountain highway. He didn't even smoke, but he'd bought a pack at the gas station because his hands wouldn't stop shaking, thinking a cigarette might help. He fumbled the lighter and stared at the tip of the flame, trying to line it up with the cigarette. Suddenly, he realized he was coming downhill to the next corner too fast. He dropped the lighter and slammed on the brakes, cutting the wheel in hopes of avoiding driving off the side of the mountain.

Less than a second after the tires started to screech, he saw a yellow Volkswagen Beetle coming around the corner toward him. Teddy gritted his teeth as his sports car slammed into the side of the Beetle, driving it toward the guard rail. The Beetle rolled from the force of the impact and both cars smashed through the guard rail and down the side of a steep incline. The cars rolled and tumbled together down the hill.

It was chaos, there was blood and shrapnel and screaming. The fumes of some strange material stinging his nostrils. A cacophony of sounds scraped their way across his ears—screams, crashing, and yellow, twisting metal.

What was left of the two cars smashed into the rocky basin with a loud bang that sounded like a cannon going off.

Teddy's head was spinning as he opened his eyes. He looked around and could see that the passenger side of his car was completely collapsed. He looked down at himself and saw blood on his hands, and his legs were crushed by the dash. He shook his head and tried to get free from his seatbelt, but it was covered by sharp, twisted metal and shattered plastic. He quickly started to look around, trying to find a way to pry himself loose, but he was trapped. As he looked out the window, he noticed the body of the driver of the other car lying just a couple feet from his window. It was lying on its back, a disfigured lump of broken limbs and bones protruding from the skin. The face was cut and bloody, and the lifeless eyes were staring at him through the darkness.

# The Perfect Gardner

## BY JACOB SURLES

I t was July in the deep south, so even at 8:00 a.m. the judges stood in unending heat that radiated from both the unforgiving sun and the asphalt covered concrete. The sweat was beading on their foreheads, dripping down their backs, and soaking their crevices, but for the moment, all that went unnoticed as they stared intently at the most perfect, blood-red rose they had ever seen.

"Ms. Mary, how do you do it?" Petunia asked in an excited tone tinged with anxiety. "Every year you grow a perfect rose; you really must be the perfect gardener. Honestly, it's so unbelievable. I would *kill* to have your skill and know your secret."

Ms. Mary smiled slyly, her sharp, bright blue eyes squinting from under her wide-brim hat. "You're too kind, Petunia, really. I'll tell you my secret ingredient," she said, leaning forward.

Petunia and the other two judges leaned in excitedly, eyes wide with anticipation. Ms. Mary simply whispered, "Love."

The judges laughed heartily, and Ms. Mary smiled

sweetly, slightly chuckling. Everyone loved Ms. Mary. She was a beacon of joy in the local community and a maternal figure in the small neighborhood that had been engulfed by a seemingly endless, sprawling city. She regularly helped troubled youths, paying them a fair wage to help her tend her prize-winning garden. Eventually the workers would migrate on, as youth do. The neighborhood always spoke of the loving way that Ms. Mary sent them off by cooking a large feast for the teens the evening before their departure and giving them a batch of warm muffins the next morning when they left for their next adventure.

"Well," remarked Tom, the head judge, "we're happy you have so much love to give, Ms. Mary. Everyone in the community enjoys seeing and smelling your beautiful garden. Just the other morning my little Abigail was saying how her walk to and from school was made so much more enjoyable because she passed by and smelled your amazing flowers."

Ms. Mary let loose a beaming smile and replied, "Aw, Tom, such a sweet thing to say, and hearing that made my day!" As she said that she leaned forward and whispered, "As would winning this competition." Her grin was as cunning as it was cheerful.

Tom felt his heart flutter and a surge of heat come over his cheeks. Ms. Mary was in the latter part of her 70's yet there was something undeniable about her attraction. Her piercing blue eyes were a stark contrast to the wrinkles that had overtaken her face. And though her frame and figure had been consumed by time, they still showed a glimmer of the beauty of her youth.

Good God, thought Tom, I bet that woman was more than most men could handle in her younger years. Tom giggled and looked down. "We still have a few more contestants to judge, Ms. Mary, but I get the feeling that history might repeat itself for the eleventh time."

Ms. Mary reached out her slender, worn hand to the judges, and Tom jumped to be the first one to shake it.

"Thank you, Ms. Mary." said Petunia. "We will see you shortly at the announcement ceremony." She jabbed Tom lightly in the ribs to shake him from his daze, rolling her eyes as she commented dryly, "Come Tom, we must give our attention to the last few contestants now."

He didn't know where he was. Furthermore, he didn't know where he came from. He was an orphan named Ronin, which may have been ironic for the first decade of his life. The last few years, however, it was more akin to standing in front of a convex funhouse mirror when you have an already large mole on your cheek—the discolored figure ends up encompassing the bulk of your reflection, consuming your image. Every time it stares back at you, you find it more and more difficult to smile at the caricature-like size of your flaw.

He often thought to himself he should have changed his name, but why bother when no one knows who the hell you are, anyway. By this time, he had been in six different foster homes, three different orphanages, and two juvenile halfway houses as the result of his two stints in juvey. This was his first time in a major city, surprisingly. Well, it was the first time he could remember. He was told he was born in the Bronx, in New York City and spent the first two years of his life there, raised by a single mother addicted to heroin. He was told she overdosed six months after his second birthday. He didn't remember that, or her, or why he came to this city.

He was still high on some glue he'd been huffing earlier in the day.

"Shit, where the hell am I?" he muttered, completely oblivious to the giant green sign with white letters just three feet behind him that read, "Welcome to...."

"Damnit!" he cursed, "What the hell am I doing here?"

He'd been walking most of the day and his legs were tired and his high was wearing off and somewhere along the way he'd dropped his paper bag sprayed with glue so right now he had to pick between scrounging for food or getting more glue and another bag. He took out his water bottle and gulped down a large swig, which instantly got his appetite going. The decision was made. He slung his bag over his shoulders and treaded on toward what he assumed was the downtown area.

Ms. Mary stood in the foyer of her moderate home and stared at the trophy in her hands. The shining plaque that read," First Place, 10$^{th}$ Annual Gardening Competition" reflected her smile, and she took a deep sigh of relief as she placed her prize on the highest shelf to the right of nine other trophies that all shared the same inscription. She stood for a moment, staring at nothing, lost in a tired daze. A minute or twenty later, she snapped out of it and realized she'd been staring directly at a picture of her late husband, Gerald, the entire time. She picked up the picture, behind it a stick of deodorant and a bottle of aftershave. She smiled at the picture first and then picked up the deodorant and then the aftershave, inhaling each deeply, allowing herself to be momentarily overcome by the nostalgia. She imagined him walking into the foyer and embracing her from behind, whispering, "Oh, hello, my love," as his coarse hands slid up the back of her forearms to the back of her hands, their fingers lacing together and his arms wrapping hers around her own waist. They would hug and sway this way almost daily and occasionally he would sing softly in her ear, "Those fingers in my hair/that sly 'come hither stare/that strips my conscience bare/it's witchcraft." Goosebumps formed on her skin and her eyes began to water. She took another breath of those familiar scents and kissed the picture before putting her keepsakes back on the shelf.

"I miss you so much, Gerald," she sighed, reaching out and grabbing her car keys. She and Gerald used to take weekend drives. Most days they just cruised slowly without purpose around the city, talking about how much it had changed around them over fifty years of marriage. These days Ms. Mary drove around with a purpose—hunting for someone to help and for someone to help her.

It was July in the deep south and even at 9:30 a.m. Ronin opened his eyes to unending heat that radiated from both the unforgiving sun and the asphalt covered concrete. The distinct smell of piss and rotting food slapped him in the face. A loud metal door clanging and the sound of rustling plastic and feet jostled him completely awake.

A deep, strong voice boomed, "Hey, shithead, you can't sleep here. Move on or I'll get the hose and start washing the dumpster, maybe accidentally soaking you in the process." The man sneered, holding a huge bag of garbage in his hand.

Ronin snarled, "Been forever since I had a shower. Maybe I'll just lay here a bit longer."

The man scowled and raised his tone, "Maybe I'll just beat you to death here in this alley. World probably wouldn't even notice one less bum." Finishing his threat he tossed the trash bag at Ronin. The bag slammed against the concrete next to him and burst, splashing him with fresh restaurant garbage. "Oops," the man said sarcastically, "it slipped."

As the man walked back into the restaurant, Ronin spit at him and cursed under his breath. The metal door clanged shut, leaving Ronin alone again in the hot alley.

Ronin pulled himself to his feet, brushing leftover food off his clothes. The sun beat down on his face and he blew his nose in an attempt to expel the stench of the dumpster that had saturated his nostrils throughout the night. A throbbing pain started working its way through his head, and almost instantly Ronin felt a craving for some kind of high. He knelt down and opened his backpack, searching for the paper bag sprayed with glue he had dropped the day before.

"Damnit!" he screamed, frustrated. He frantically started to pull everything from his bag, dropping all his belongings in the alley. Reaching the bottom and realizing that his search was fruitless, Ronin slumped his head down and began to cry, overwhelmed by the hopelessness of the situation.

"I'm in a damn alley next to a damn dumpster searching for a damn paper bag filled with glue!" Ronin whined. "I'm so pathetic and alone and miserable and hungry!" The moment of hopelessness seemed to stretch on for eternity, consuming the time around the boy until he was abruptly startled by the sound of a siren. Immediately, Ronin jumped to his feet and bolted toward the opposite end of the alley, leaving the only items he possessed scattered behind a dirty dumpster in an unfamiliar city. An ambulance passed at the opposite end of the alley behind him as he ran.

As soon as his feet hit the sidewalk, Ronin's survival instincts kicked back in and he stepped up to the first person he saw and asked, "Spare some change, mister?"

Ms. Mary walked into the garage and paused, staring at the large, shiny sedan. This was Gerald's favorite possession besides his garden, and she held it with a reverence that was matched only by her desire to maintain the amazing, prize-winning nursery. She muttered a short prayer before moving to the car and getting in. The summer sun poured in as the garage opened, and Ms. Mary pulled slowly out into the driveway. Before starting her hunt, she always stopped for breakfast—it helped keep her spirit and her energy level up. Her favorite place was called Grady's, one of the few family-owned restaurants left in the neighborhood. It wasn't fancy, but it was close and had good food, and she adored the way Grady Patrick always treated people with respect.

"Hey there, Ms. Mary!" Grady's voice boomed across the dining room, overwhelming the sound of chaotic chatter and clanking dishes in the busy restaurant. Ms. Mary felt so much comfort hearing Grady's voice; it was strong, deep and simultaneously resonated with confidence and kindness. She smiled and made her way toward the empty table near the edge of the kitchen, close to the back door.

As she approached, Grady stepped up and pulled out her chair, bowing deep at the waist as he gestured to her to sit. "Madam," he smiled, "your table is ready."

Ms. Mary giggled," Oh, Grady, bless your heart! How are you, dear? How's Georgia and the boys?"

"They're fantastic!" Grady beamed. Ms. Mary was the only person who asked him about his family. He loved her deeply as a son would love a mother, even though they shared no relation. "As you know, Greg finished his master's program last month, and he has a big interview next week.

George is taking summer classes to get ahead and looks to finish his bachelor's degree by the end of fall, which is a full semester early. Georgia is doing good as well. She came by this morning right after the competition and told me you won first place again, by a landslide. She wanted me to tell you she's sorry she wasn't able to come by the booth and say hello, but she was so busy working that there was barely time for her to breathe. You can imagine how hectic it is trying to organize and run an event of that size. Seems like it's grown so big over the last few years that she can barely keep up with all the new people."

"It's no problem at all, really," Ms. Mary replied kindly. "I'm just happy it's still her that's in charge. I know what you mean about new faces. When I go to the Neighborhood Association meetings these days it seems like the front half of the room is all the older folk who've been living here for decades, and the back half is full of people I've never even seen in the neighborhood."

They both laughed for a moment, then sighed in unison.

"I suppose that's just the way of things," Grady remarked, "out with the old and in with the new. Time just keeps herding us all toward oblivion."

Ms. Mary sat for a moment and smiled at Grady, trying to forget his statement. She shook her head slightly and replied, "I'm just glad I keep getting younger."

Grady smirked, "Me too, Ma'am. You give us all hope that we can be as beautiful as you are when we ..." as he spoke, the dishwasher came around the corner holding a huge trash bag and slipped. Immediately and unconsciously, Grady threw his arm out and grabbed the man's shirt, catching him before he fully lost his footing.

Ms. Mary and the dishwasher froze in wide-eyed awe of how fast Grady had reacted. It was as though his instincts of compassion were so rooted that his movements were reflexive machinations guided by a higher power.

"That was an incredible save!" exclaimed Ms. Mary.

"It really was, boss!" the dishwasher added, his voice cracked and shaking from both the close call and the sheer speed of Grady's movement.

"Wasn't nothing," Grady reacted. "You see a man falling and your instinct is to catch him. Plus," he smirked, "I didn't want to have to clean all this fresh trash off my floor."

The three of them chuckled heartily and then Grady excused himself.

"Sir," he nodded to the dishwasher, "why don't you let me take this trash out? You head back in the kitchen and help Carl wrangle those pots."

"Yes sir, and thank you again," the dishwasher responded with a shake of Grady's hand before heading back to the dish pit.

Grady turned to Ms. Mary. "All right, ma'am, I should get back to work. "

Ms. Mary smiled at Grady. "It's always good to see you, Grady. I'll make sure I say goodbye before I head out. And you tell Georgia I hope to see her soon."

Delighted, Grady said, "I will. It's good to see you as well, Ms. Mary."

He walked past her with the trash bag and headed out the back door. As he stepped out into the hot alley, the distinct smell of piss and rotten food slapped him in the face and the metal door slammed shut behind him with a loud clang.

Within minutes, Ms. Mary's food arrived. She began to pray over her meal. As she neared the end of her prayer, she heard Grady come in from the alley ordering the dishwasher to get back outside and clean up spilled garbage. A moment later she heard an ambulance pass. "Dear Lord, please help guide those who need help and protect them from evil," she added at the end, hoping whoever was in that ambulance was okay.

The guy ignored Ronin's plea for money and didn't even look up from his phone. It didn't bother Ronin, though, he was very used to it.

"People would rather ignore the parts of life they don't like than look those inconvenient truths in the eye," he repeated. One of the orphanage teachers had told him that once when Ronin asked why the orphanage and the landfill were so close to one another but so far away from the rest of the nearby town.

"Spare some change?" he asked repeatedly as he passed people on the crowded sidewalk, but everyone simply pretended he didn't exist. To see him was simply inconvenient.

Ronin turned left at the next block, unaware he was circling back around to the front of the restaurant where he had just been assaulted. He stopped short of the front windows of Grady's Place and slumped down against the wall of the computer hardware shop next door. He curled up, pulling his knees toward him and resting his mouth on his left knee. He bit hard onto his joint, sinking his teeth into the dirty jeans and squeezing the numb flesh with his jaw. Tears of starvation started pouring down his face, and he began to hum to himself, trying to relieve his heart of the despair that had corralled him in a pen of frustration and hopelessness.

"God, put me out of my misery," he prayed. "Just let me be tossed into the landfill to be forgotten by time."

He stole that last part of the prayer from the guy who brought the books around at the last detention facility where he stayed. He remembered the older boy's face, a giant scar streaking down from his forehead over his eye and ending on his cheek.

"Step dad tried to kill me," the older boy remarked one day when he saw Ronin staring at his scar. "He woke me up one night when he was drunk, straddling and rubbing on me. I fought back and bit him and he got mad, dragged me into the kitchen and went after me with a chef knife. Stabbed me five times in the arms and shoulders, then slashed my face. After he was done he left me bleeding on the kitchen floor and passed out on the couch. I crawled to my mom and woke her up from her drunken slumber, but instead of taking me to the hospital she told me to keep quiet and never tell anyone. She gave me a fistful of dish towels and a bottle of rubbing alcohol and locked me in a closet. I waited for a while then broke the door to escape. Once I escaped I went to the kitchen and grabbed the same knife my stepdad used on me. I went into my mom's room and stabbed her right in the throat while she slept. Then, I went into the living room and stabbed my stepdad in the back of the head five times, same number as he stabbed me. State said I was justified in killing him, but not her, which don't make much sense to me. Standing by and doing nothing seems just as bad as doing the thing yourself. My grandparents wouldn't even look at me during the trial. I was still covered in stitches and fresh wounds, but they didn't want to believe that their daughter would let something like that happen. I spit at them as I walked by after the Judge sentenced me—they still wouldn't look at me. They'd rather save themselves from the angst of seeing the damage than face the horrible truth. Ignorance is bliss, I guess. Doesn't bother me much now, though, seeing as how I'm still alive and they're dead, rotting in the dirt to be forgotten by time."

Ronin snapped back from the memory and wiped his eyes. His hunger was raging at this point, driving him to his feet like a machine with no operator. He reached out and touched the arm of a passerby.

"Buddy, please, I'm starving. Can you spare any change to help me?"

The man stopped and reached into his pocket, pulling out a decent number of coins and handing it to Ronin before walking off without ever making eye-contact.

Ronin quickly counted the change: ninety-five cents.

"Jackpot!" he whispered. He scanned the block, looking for a store. Across the street he noticed a bodega. They'll have glue and bags, he thought to himself, and started heading over, determined to escape from the prison of his reality.

Ms. Mary finished her breakfast and sat quietly sipping her coffee while contemplating where she would go next to find the person she was looking for. It had been twelve years since Gerald died, and a year later when she began to search for a means of catharsis. She would venture out and find a suffering young man in need of aid and offer him a special helping hand. Once a year she would bring a troubled teen into her home, feed him, provide him with some new clothes, and in exchange he would help her tend her garden for three months. Her means of finding them was fairly simple—she would drive around the city near areas with homeless shelters and look for young men who looked desperate.

The first year she struggled with trust, and bought herself a taser and an emergency siren, placing them in an easily accessible pocket of her loose-fitting gardening pants. As the years had gone on, however, she realized that even on the far side of seventy years old, she was stronger than a starving, addict teenager. Most years the boys would spend the first month acclimating themselves to manual labor. Often times they were slow and deliberate with their motions and most of them struggled with crippling withdrawals. So far, they had all broken down at some point during their stay and escaped into the night to acquire more drugs. She didn't mind, as long as they still managed to help with the work. Each one would leave, get high, then get hungry in the next twelve hours and return for a guaranteed hot meal. Ms. Mary paid them as well, so the steady source of drug money was another way for her to keep them shackled to the debt of helping her.

She remembered the first year vividly, as though it were yesterday. The result of its conclusion ended up being the catalyst that drove Ms. Mary to continue on, avoiding the daily suffering she had experienced the first year after Gerald passed. The boy's name was Roger, he was thirteen and addicted to methamphetamines. She found him lying on the concrete, a block from the homeless shelter, his clothes soaked in sweat and so dirty that the blue denim of his jeans looked black. She took him in and for eighty-nine days he worked in her garden, sleeping in the guest room that she would lock from the outside whenever it was time for bed. She knew it was cruel, but she couldn't stand the thought of him stealing something that had no real monetary value but was sentimentally important to her. On the 89th day she walked out to the backyard and found Roger sitting next to a pile of mulch, avoiding his work. As she walked up, she picked up a small garden pick to help him with the trench he had been digging. When Ms. Mary approached him, she noticed something in the dirt beside him. The boy heard her walk up and quickly started working. In the dirt next to him lay a broken pocket watch. It had fallen out of his pocket, and he hadn't noticed.

Ms. Mary stared silently, her eyes glaring down at the broken watch covered in dirt. It was Gerald's military watch he bought while abroad during the war. He had sent the watch back with a note promising Ms. Mary that he would return safely. She held it every day he was gone and when he returned home, he carried that watch until the day he died.

Rage climbed her, gripping her mind like the claws of a demonic horseman grabbing the reigns of a stallion that had ridden out of hell. Without thinking she swung the garden pick down on Roger, striking him on the back of the head and killing him instantly. His body fell across the shallow trench he'd been digging, blood coursing into the dirt. She stood for a moment and let the anger subside, gazing down at the corpse of the young boy with disdain. She couldn't help but notice that she felt no real remorse for what she'd done. On the contrary, actually, she felt a sense of relief that had escaped her since Gerald died. She felt happy. Happiness eventually gave way to practicality, and Ms. Mary realized that she would have to not only dispose of the body but explain where the young boy had gone to the neighborhood. She covered the body with a mound of dirt and mulch, soaking it with water to pack it down and hopefully mask the stench of a rotting corpse. The next morning, she went to the butchers to buy some steaks and while she was there she nonchalantly asked him about disposing beef and pork bones.

"You could always throw them in the trash," replied the butcher, "but, if you wanted to avoid that then you could cut them into small pieces and put them in a compost pile. If you have one that's anaerobic then it'll break down the bones in about nine months to a year."

Ms. Mary went to the store and bought a sturdy saw and the best saw blades she could find. She went home and cut the body into very small pieces, shoving them deep into her mulch pile with a long stick.

As the year moved on, Ms. Mary used the mulch in her garden and her roses grew especially red. Their hue and size were almost enchanting and when she stared at them she felt as if she had fallen in a trance. As she looked around her garden Ms. Mary noticed that all of her plants had full, lush colors with strong, thick stems. All because of that organic, miracle mulch.

The next summer she took some of her roses to the city-wide gardening competition and easily won first place.

Ronin came out of the bodega bathroom higher than giraffe pussy. "Fuck, yeah." He rolled his neck and let the high scrawl its mark on his consciousness.

"HEY! YOU GETTING HIGH IN MY BATHROOM!?" the clerk yelled. "Get the hell out of my store!"

Ronin laughed. "Yeah man, high as hell. I'm gone." He walked out into the summer heat, which immediately slapped him in the face and killed his high.

"Goddam summer in the south," he grumbled, searching for some place shady to huff some more glue.

Ms. Mary came to from her daze and realized she had been sitting and staring at the empty chair across the table for almost twenty minutes. She shook her head and widened her eyes.

"I need to get started before I run out of daylight," she remarked to herself. Ms. Mary put forty dollars down on her twenty-dollar tab and got up, pushing her chair in. She scanned for Grady, who was talking to another table. She winked and waved at him, and he waved back as she made her way out the front door.

Ronin crossed the street and though his high had been diminished severely by the introduction of a sweltering southern summer heat, he was still only half sober. He noticed a computer hardware store and considered that he could definitely hide out in the alley behind that place and get another hit.

He was so busy looking up at the sign he didn't notice the old woman in front of him and he walked into her full force, knocking her to the ground.

"Shit!" he said.

"Oh!" Ms. Mary exclaimed, collapsing on the sidewalk.

"I'm so sorry," he mumbled, trying to help her up. "I was looking up and didn't see you."

She initially recoiled from his dirty hands, until she looked up and saw who bumped into her.

"It's no problem," she said confidently. "I wasn't paying attention either." She stood up and brushed herself off, eyeing Ronin as if he were a perfectly cooked steak.

"Ma'am, I really am sorry," he apologized in almost a whisper.

She smiled, "Please, don't worry about it. What's your name?"

"Ronin," he offered, however hesitantly.

"Ronin," she repeated, "that's a strong name. I'm sure you know the origin?"

"Yes ma'am, a warrior with no master," he said wryly, hoping this conversation would end soon so he could go take another hit.

"A Japanese Samurai whose master has died. My husband fought in Japan during World War II. He fell in love with the ancient country."

"That's interesting," Ronin said flatly. The lie slid halfway through his teeth before he realized he shouldn't have responded at all if he wanted this conversation to end.

"Tell me, Ronin, and be honest—do you have a home?" Ms. Mary asked, looking Ronin up and down.

Ronin paused. No one had ever asked him that. In fact, no normal person had ever taken an interest in him or cared to know anything about him.

"No ma'am," he said with a rare embarrassment.

Ms. Mary smiled. "Are you hungry?"

"Yes ma'am," he lied. His high hadn't quite subsided enough to reveal an appetite, but he thought if he said he wasn't hungry then she'd know he was high.

"I'd like to get you some food. Would you let me help you?"

Ronin didn't understand what was happening. Beyond the fact that he was stoned, this was a completely new experience to him—no one on the street had ever offered him a meal, much less taken an interest in him.

He stood, contemplating his options for a moment, all the while wishing he wasn't quite so messed up.

"Um, yeah, I suppose that would be nice," he finally muttered.

Ms. Mary heard the doorbell ring and got up from Gerald's recliner. She peered through the peephole and saw Petunia and Tom standing at her front door.

"Just a second," she said sweetly, grabbing a shawl from the coat hanger beside the door.

She swung the door open and noticed a solemn look on her friends standing on her doorstep.

"How can I help you? Is everything ok?" she asked, trying to contain her nervousness.

Petunia stepped forward and asked quietly, "May we come in, Ms. Mary? We would like to talk to you about something, but it would be better to discuss it privately."

"Oh my," Ms. Mary said worriedly, "please come in." She

opened the door and led them into her dining room, furnished with a large table and six chairs.

"Would either of you care for a drink?" she offered politely.

They shook their heads gently.

"Ms. Mary, please, have a seat," Tom said softly.

Ms. Mary sat at the head of the table; beneath it her legs shook from anxiety.

"Ms. Mary," Tom started to speak, only to be cut off by Petunia.

"Tom, please, let me," Petunia insisted.

Tom nodded and gestured for Petunia to take the lead.

"Ms. Mary, we want you to know that we all love you very much," Petunia started with a gentle tone. She took a deep breath before continuing. "We were talking about how beautiful your garden is and we began to discuss all the young men who have helped you throughout the years." She paused again, thinking carefully over her words. "And, well, we couldn't help but notice that none of them stayed." Another brief pause steadied her as she looked at Ms. Mary lovingly and spoke the following words, "And that there was really no mention of where any of them had gone."

Ms. Mary froze and the hair on her body stood up straight. In her heart of hearts, she knew this day would come; they knew and were going to turn her in. Panic started to set in.

"At first, we really didn't put the pieces together," Petunia continued. "We just accepted your story that each boy had moved on. It made perfect sense. However, as time went by, we couldn't help but notice that not long after each boy disappeared, your garden would bloom beautifully. Just like that. They would disappear, your garden would bloom, you would win the gardening competition, and then another boy would appear, and the pattern repeated itself."

Ms. Mary felt the fear and panic fill her body, completely consuming her. As the dam holding her emotions back burst, she erupted into tears in front of them.

"I'M SORRY!" she wailed. "I don't know what came over me! I lost Gerald and the first boy just stole his watch like some damned drug crazed fiend, and I killed him before I even had a chance to think! I'm so sorry! Jesus, please forgive me!" Her tears streamed and her head crashed onto her arms as she sobbed deeply, struggling for breath.

Petunia and Tom nodded to one another. They both got

up out of their seats and went over to Ms. Mary, wrapping their arms around her.

"It's OK," Tom whispered, "we are your friends and love you very much. "

"Yes," Petunia added, "we *are* your friends, and we love you *and* your garden."

They moved around beside Ms. Mary, placing their hands on her arms and back.

"Ms. Mary," Tom spoke delicately, "please calm down for a minute and listen to us. We aren't mad at you."

Petunia grabbed a tissue off the table and handed it to Ms. Mary.

"I … I don't … don't understand," Ms. Mary whimpered, trying to subdue her sorrow. "You're not mad at me?"

"No," Petunia reassured her, "not mad at all. In fact, we want you to keep going."

Ms. Mary raised her head to see the two of them standing next to her. She looked at Petunia quizzically. "What did you just say?"

Tom motioned for Petunia to sit back down. They took their seats next to Ms. Mary, each holding one of her hands.

"Ms. Mary," Petunia said, "your garden is so beautiful, and the entire neighborhood enjoys it *so* much."

Tom interjected, "Not to mention, you are the only one from the neighborhood who can win the city-wide gardening competition, which really helps bring more money in for the Neighborhood Association." He smiled wide and squeezed her hand.

Petunia leaned forward and explained, "We talked about it before we came over, and Tom and I came to the conclusion that if we had to choose between having you and your beautiful garden or the life of some transient addict, we would absolutely choose you every time."

Ms. Mary slowed her crying and wiped her face with the tissue Petunia had handed her. "So … you want me … you want me to keep doing what I've been doing?" She was apparently still trying to accept the curveball she had been thrown.

"We insist you keep going, Ms. Mary," Tom reinforced their request by again squeezing Ms. Mary's hand. "We *love* the beautiful garden, and we *love* having you in the neighborhood and we wouldn't trade those for ten thousand transients."

They hugged Ms. Mary, whispering reassurances of love and friendship in her ear. Giving her time to gather herself, they waited patiently.

"Now," Petunia stated matter-of-factly, "how will we address where these boys are going to keep everyone in the neighborhood on the same page?"

Tom stated, "We need to keep it simple so that it's easy to remember. They're transients, so we'll just say that they moved on. That's just the way of transients, right?"

Petunia smiled and raised her hand excitedly. "Oh, I have an idea! How about you send them off with a nice, cooked meal and a tray of muffins?"

"Yes," Tom added, "and we will simply leave it at that. It's easy to explain and understand."

Ms. Mary looked into the eyes of her friends and smiled as if a feeling of contentment had washed over her. "I love you both so much and this particular love will be our little secret."

As Tom and Petunia waved goodbye, holding hands, and empowered by the secret they held, Ms. Mary watched them giggle as they walked down the sidewalk. Now that they knew of her secret garden, the excitement of repeating the ritual was gone.

She walked over to the ten trophies she had won, each one representing the removal of another filthy addict who disgraced her beautiful town and who were so blessed to have been given a purpose by fertilizing her magnificent roses. As she scanned the inscriptions, her eyes stopped at the picture of Gerald. She picked it up, along with the deodorant and aftershave and held them closely to her panting chest.

"Oh, Gerald, they know our secret. I can't possibly carry on with them knowing. It ruins everything." She closed her eyes tightly and waited for her military husband to speak his words of wisdom as he always had then and now.

From a distance she heard his voice. "Remember what Benjamin Franklin said, my darling?"

"Oh, yes, he was your favorite for famous quotes. Let's see ... which quote are you referring to, my precious?" Ms. Mary held her breath, anticipating the perfect words that would set her free to continue with her perfect garden.

She felt her husband embrace her from behind and whisper gently in her ear as his hands slid around her waist and the goosebumps did a dance across her skin.

"Three may keep a secret, if two of them are dead."

After a long career in the corporate world, Don Tassone has returned to his creative writing roots. He is the author of two novels and eight short story collections. He lives in Loveland, Ohio.

# Rain Delay

BY DON TASSONE

David McMahon parked his car, looked up at the darkening sky and heard thunder in the distance. The forecast didn't call for rain until noon, but it sure looked like it would hit sooner.

He'd take his chances. He was meeting a friend for lunch and wanted to get his run in this morning.

Much of his five-mile route was under a canopy of trees anyway, and there was a covered picnic table two miles up the trail, just in case. He'd been running this stretch five days a week for nearly a year now, since he retired. The self discipline that had made him successful in business was still in his blood.

He stretched, then pressed the timer on his Apple watch. This morning he would aim for nine-minute miles, not bad for a 61 year old.

Within the first half mile, David felt a few drops of rain, but he kept going. By mile one, the rain was steady, and thunder boomed. He thought about turning around but pressed on.

By mile two, the rain was coming down hard, and David had to take cover. He sat atop the sheltered picnic table and wiped the rain from his face.

In every strength, there is a weakness. Within David's self discipline was an inflexibility that sometimes created problems. Now, dripping wet, he wished he had waited to run.

He was still adjusting to retirement, still learning how to live in the "real world." After years of being schedule-driven, he was finding it tough to relax. His days were still packed. He was still in a hurry.

Lightning flashed nearby, followed by a clap of thunder so strong it rattled the gable roof overhead. He was glad it wasn't made of metal.

I'd better let Theresa know I'm okay, he thought. He held his watch close to his face and sent his wife a verbal text that he had taken shelter and would head home after the storm.

Out of the corner of his eye, David saw a road bike approaching. Just before he reached the covered picnic table, the rider braked, but his bike slid on the wet pavement.

"Crap!" he yelled, pumping his brakes and bringing his bike under control.

He got off, walked his bike under the roof and leaned it against one end of the picnic table.

"Hope you don't mind some company," he said.

"Not at all," David said.

The metal cleats of the rider's cycling shoes crunched in the gravel. He took off his helmet and gloves and put them on the table. He was a young man, with long, black hair. His bright green Lycra jersey and black cycling shorts clung to his lean body. He too wiped the rain from his face. Then he hitched himself up on the table, leaving maximum space between him and David.

"So much for the rain starting at noon," he said.

"Amen," said David. "I started running two miles south of here. I thought I'd get five miles in well before this rain hit."

"And I started about 10 miles north of here. I thought I could get 25 miles in."

"I guess we're stuck."

"Guess so."

"I'm David," he said, extending his hand.

"Nick," the rider said, taking it.

"Do you ride a lot?"

"Just on weekends. What about you? You run a lot?"

"Five days a week," David said, hoping to impress.

"Wow! No wonder you're in such good shape."

"Thanks. I'm working on it."

The rain was coming down hard. Then it started to hail. Pea-sized hailstones pelted the roof and showered down all around them.

"Jesus!" Nick said. "I'm sure glad we're not out in that."

"Amen."

After a few minutes of awkward silence, Nick said, "So what you do for a living?"

"I'm retired," David said, feeling old.

He was still getting used to saying those words.

"I retired about a year ago."

"Good for you, man. I look forward to retirement."

"Well, that's a few years off for you," David said with a grin.

"Yeah, but I think about it a lot."

"What kind of work do you do?"

"I design video games."

"Sounds exciting."

"Not really. I mean it's okay, but most days I'm bored."

"I'm sorry to hear that. Do you think you'll stick with it?"

"Yeah, probably. I'm not sure what else I can do."

"Oh, I'm sure you have lots of options."

"I don't know."

"Well, what are your interests, if you don't mind me asking?"

"No problem. I like to design things, but I'm not crazy about video games. They used to be fun but not anymore. I thought this would be a great career. But most days, I feel like quitting."

"Do you have a degree?"

"Yeah, in software engineering."

"Well, we have that in common," David said. "Not the software part, but the engineering."

"You're an engineer?"

"Yeah."

"What kind?"

"Mechanical."

"What kind of work did you do?"

"I led a team of engineers. We designed, improved and fixed production systems."

"What kind of production?"

"Our systems made everything from jet engines to shampoo bottles."

"Sounds interesting. Who did you work for?"

"Reynolds."

"Wow. Big company. Were you in charge?"

"No," David said, flattered by the question. "I was a vice president."

"Cool. You must have loved it."

"Some days I did, especially early on."

"Yeah?"

"Yeah. I got into the field because I like to design things, but I ended up managing bureaucracy."

"But you were a vice president! That's pretty cool."

"Maybe. But I gave up a lot for that VP stripe."

"Like what?"

"Well, for starters, I didn't see my family as much as I should have. I worked long hours and traveled a lot."

"Do you have kids?"

"Yeah, two. They're both grown. They're married, and they've moved away. Unfortunately, we don't see them very often anymore."

"I'm sure you provided well for your family."

"Financially, yes. But I sacrificed too much. I worked all the time. I was convinced I was indispensable at Reynolds. But guess what? Since I retired, I haven't heard from anybody there. I realize now I was just a cog in a wheel."

"I'm sure you made a big impact."

"Yeah."

The hail had stopped, but the rain continued.

"How about you?" David said. "Are you married?"

"No. Not even a girlfriend."

"I see."

"I still live with my parents."

"Nothing wrong with that."

"I guess. To be honest, I spend so much time working that I don't have much of a social life."

"I hear you. You know what? In 35 years at Reynolds, nobody ever told me to work *less*. I think we've each got to set our own boundaries. In hindsight, I know I could have worked far less and done just fine, and I would have been there for my family a lot more."

"That's good advice," Nick said. "Set my own boundaries."

"Give it a try. What's the worst that can happen? They fire you? I doubt it. Employers want nothing more than to hold onto good people these days, and I'm sure you're good at what you do."

"Well, I hope I am. I'm just not sure I want to keep doing it."

"What made you decide to design video games?"

"I grew up playing them. But it really wasn't about the games themselves."

"What was it about?"

"I like to create."

"Well, with a degree in software engineering and the skills you've developed, I'm sure there a lot of other ways for you to create."

"Like what?"

"Well, off the top, I'd say you could be a city planner or a construction manager or a landscape designer."

"I hadn't thought of those."

"Look, I'm no expert in career planning. But I wish I'd tried some different things early in my career. How old are you, if you don't mind my asking?"

"I'm 25."

"What a great age. I think your twenties are your decade to experiment. People tend to converge too fast. I get that. You're supposed to know what you want to do. But I think you need to try different things and see what you really like and what you don't like and find out where you belong. When you hit 30 or 35, your life will be different. You might be married. You might have kids. You might have a house. You'll be settling down, taking fewer risks. So if you want to try your hand at landscape design, do it. But do it soon, before it's too late."

"Man, that's really good perspective. I do think I'm going to try something new."

"Good for you."

The storm had begun to let up, and most of the hailstones had melted.

"Well, I guess I'll get going," Nick said.

"Me too."

They got up. Nick grabbed his helmet and gloves.

"It was great to meet you," David said, extending his hand.

"You too. Thanks so much for all your good advice."

"I hope it's helpful. I know you're going to be very successful."

"Thanks."

David watched Nick as he pulled on his wet cycling gloves, strapped on his helmet and got back on his bike. He pointed it back the way he came.

"I'm heading home," Nick said. "Twenty miles is enough today."

"I think I'll head home too."

"Have a good one," Nick said as he rode off.

"You too," David called after him.

David looked at his watch. It was almost 11:00. He knew he'd never be able to make his lunch. Speaking into his watch, he sent his friend a message to apologize and reschedule.

He was about to resume his workout tracker but stopped and looked around. Sunlight streamed through the trees. Birds sang. The air was clean and still, and David felt a stillness within. He no longer felt like running. He decided to walk the two miles back to his car.

On his way, David reflected on his chance encounter that morning. He hoped the things he had shared would be helpful to Nick. He wished he'd had such a thoughtful conversation with his own children.

Maybe it's not too late, he thought. As he walked, he decided to take Theresa to dinner that evening. He wanted to talk with her about visiting their kids.

# Unseen

BY DON TASSONE

On November 4, 2035, 300 million miles from Earth, in a spaceship called Harmony, three astronauts—Mike Adams, Samantha Cristofori and Yuri Kubasov—descended through the thin Martian atmosphere toward the surface of the Red Planet.

All the exploratory missions had indicated conditions were safe for a landing. In ancient times, water had flowed on the surface of Mars, but no sign of life had ever been found there.

Adams, the crew commander, carefully guided the ship to a smooth area and safely touched down.

"Harmony has landed," he said.

The crew high-fived, and the whole world rejoiced.

"Well, let's suit up and take a walk," Adams said with a smile.

They all began putting on their sophisticated space suits. Adams would go first. The other two helped him secure his helmet.

"Good luck," Kubasov said.

"Godspeed," said Cristofori.

They both felt fortunate to be serving under such a brave man. To them, and to many, he was a hero.

Adams gave them a thumbs up. He pressed a button to slide open a hatch in the floor. Then he slowly descended the rungs of a metal ladder into the ship's lowest chamber and sealed the airlock above him.

Standing on the floor, Adams pressed a button, and an exterior door slid open. Outside, for as far as he could see, lay a flat, dusty, red desert. He steadied himself on grab bars along the doorframe before slowly descending the 10 rungs of the ladder to the foot pad. Then he stepped off the pad and onto the Martian surface and said, "Another step, another leap across the heavens."

It was elegant in its simplicity and a natural bridge from Neil Armstrong's eloquent words nearly seven decades earlier. Billions of people on Earth watched and listened in awe.

But no sooner did Adams step onto the gritty Martian surface than he saw something on the horizon that gave him pause. It was a faint but massive cloud. At first, Adams thought it was hovering in the distance, but then he realized it was slowly rolling toward him.

He had seen images of clouds in the Martian atmosphere, but this was different. Those clouds resembled clouds on Earth, billowy and floating on air. This one seemed to be moving with a force all its own. It was dark. As it got closer, Adams realized it was made up of countless tiny black spots, like a giant swarm of gnats. He didn't know what it was, but his gut told him it was a threat.

By now, he thought, his shipmates must be ready to exit the module.

"Go back!" he said into the microphone in his helmet. "Go back!"

His heart racing, Adams stepped back onto the foot pad and, as fast as his bulky suit would allow, made his way back up the rungs. At one point, he looked over his shoulder. The cloud was still moving toward him, now not so much rolling as swaying, like a ghost. It was probably a hundred yards away.

"Mike, what's going on?" Kubasov said.

"Get back in the module," Adams ordered. "Get ready to take off!"

He closed the exterior door behind him and pushed a button to pressurize the airlock. Then he climbed the rungs to the module, opened the hatch and nearly threw himself back inside.

His shipmates were in their seats, strapping themselves in. They wanted to know what was going on. So did the mission director in Houston.

"I'll explain later," Adams said. "We've got to take off. Now!"

The three of them pushed buttons and flipped switches furiously. The craft began to vibrate. At first, Adams wondered if the cloud had reached them. But then he felt the ship take off, picking up speed as it shot through the murky Martian atmosphere and back into space.

Adams guided the ship into the pull of the Martian orbit, past Phobos and Deimos, the planet's small, brown and white moons, and Harmony was on its way back to Earth. When things had settled down, he tried to explain what he'd seen to his shipmates and his colleagues at mission control.

Adams was known for his grace under pressure. It was one of the reasons he'd been put in charge of this mission. But no one else had seen what he claimed he'd seen, and people began to question Adams' competence and even his mental health.

But he remained insistent about what he had witnessed and confident in his judgment that it had represented a threat to Harmony. But the more he stuck with his story, the more concerned his shipmates became. A dark cloud that was alive? On a planet where no life had ever been observed? It was just too fantastic.

One night, when Adams had gone to sleep, Kubasov and Cristofori contacted mission control to ask that Adams be relieved of his command.

The mission director agreed. The following day, he called Adams to tell him he was putting Cristofori in charge for the remainder of the mission.

Adams was furious.

"Leo, I'm telling you there was something out there, and it was out to get us. I know it. I know it as surely as I know anything. You've got to believe me. I did what I had to do to save us."

"Mike, calm down. I know you think you saw something. But nobody else saw it."

"But —"

"Mike, try to put yourself in my position. You're upset, and the successful return of Harmony depends on a steady hand on the tiller. Now we can talk about everything when you get back. Until then, I'm putting Samantha in charge, and I'm asking you to do all you can to help her get the three of you back here safely."

Adams didn't know what to say. But as a former Navy pilot, he knew how to take an order.

"Okay, Leo. If that's what you think is best."

He signed off and switched places with Cristofori. Putting on a brave face, he told her, "I'm still here for you."

But Adams was shattered. In his 20 years as an astronaut, his competence had never before been questioned. Now he had been demoted and was being made to feel like a fool.

That night, when the others were sleeping, Adams held his head in his hands and quietly wept.

Seven months later, back on Earth, a small team from NASA greeted the three astronauts. There were no reporters present. NASA put out a statement and a photo of the astronauts, but there were no speeches, and there was no celebration.

After reuniting with his family, Adams was interviewed by NASA personnel, then admitted to a hospital for psychiatric evaluation.

He still didn't change his story, but no one believed him, and NASA itself came under fire. After all, the aborted Harmony mission had cost billions. Not only that, but the debacle put all other planned flights to Mars on ice.

In the meantime, the Harmony module sat dormant in a corner of a windowless NASA hanger, like some meaningless artifact tucked away in an old museum no one visits.

As Adams underwent another brain scan, no one could see the tiny microbes migrating from his ship's base across the concrete floor and out onto the tarmac. No one there could possibly have noticed because these microbes, remnants of water that flowed on a now-arid planet ages ago, can be seen only through the triple lens shield of an astronaut's helmet.

## *Tick~Tock*

BY DON TASSONE

I saw it on Google News. We Millennials have reached middle age.

I myself am 36, the so-called sweet spot of my generation. *Middle age.* I guess it could be worse. I could have been born a few years earlier. Then I'd be a Gen Xer. Those dudes are old.

I remember when we started coming into the workforce, how freaked out they got when we applied online, skipped our ties and actually took paternity leave. They called us slackers.

I wondered if "Gen X" was even a thing. Weren't Gen Xers just Boomers who took weekends off? I mean the guy who interviewed me for my first job had already been there for 10 years, and he wore a suit. I don't think he even had a cell phone. With a little less hair, he could have been my dad.

He offered me the job on the spot. I mean I actually knew how to do stuff online! When it came to social media, at least in those days, Gen Xers were clueless.

But I was gone in a year. The job was okay, but my

manager didn't seem to care about me. He'd send me emails at all hours, even on weekends. Not cool.

When I was starting out, it seemed like Gen Xers were everywhere. In a bar, I could spot one a mile away. He was probably drinking a light beer. Dude, it's craft beer or nothing. And you're leaving already? It's not even dark.

Once I was running a 10K, and I passed this guy from work. He was only about 10 years older than me, but he was walking. Walking! What's next? A cane? I made sure he saw me running by.

But things are changing. At work, the boomers are just about gone. There are fewer Gen Xers and more Gen Zers, the generation of snot-nosed kids coming up behind us.

They're a piece of work. They're hardly ever in the office. When Covid was over, our company went hybrid. I guess they think hybrid means they can work from home.

A couple of Gen Zers work for me now. I can never find them. I'm not sure when they work. When I try to tell them we have office hours, they laugh.

One of them sent me a TikTok clip the other day. I'm not on TikTok, so I had to ask her to show it to me. It was a riff on office hours. It made her laugh.

At least I've got a couple of Gen Zers on my team. Other folks have set up interviews with these kids only to be ghosted. Of course, since I haven't actually seen my Gen Z employees in a while, maybe they really are ghosts.

When they do see fit to come into the office, all they want to talk about is social issues. I wonder if they think they work for a non-profit.

These younger employees are wearing me out. In fact, I've been pretty tired lately. I've been putting on weight and losing my hair too. When I look in the mirror, I see my dad staring back. The baggy clothes I've begun wearing don't help.

My wife and I used to love to go out with friends. Now we go to bed early, even on the weekends. I seldom go to bars anymore because they're so loud. Plus, all that craft beer has given me a gut.

I don't love my job, but it pays well, and the healthcare benefits are good. I've got a mortgage, and I have to think about saving for my kids' education and my retirement. I work too much, but I'll probably stay.

My only respite these days is taking my family to my parents' house for dinner on Sundays. It's so quiet there I can hear their grandfather clock. Tick-tock, tick-tock, tick-tock.

That's the sound of time passing, not the app.

John Young is the author of two literary novels: *Getting Huge* and *When the Coin Is in the Air,* as well as *Fire in the Field & Other Stories*. When he was eight years old, John told his mother he wanted to be a scientist or a clown. So he went into advertising and figures he got pretty close. Along the way, he graduated from Indiana University and earned an MFA from Emerson College, Boston. He lives in Cincinnati, Ohio.

# Sleep Stories

BY JOHN YOUNG

"Daddy?"

Patrick's eyes flutter open. "Hi buddy," he whispers and glances at the clock a few minutes after 3:00 in the morning.

"I had a bad dream." Marcus's little fingers tease the remaining fur on Bunny's ear.

"Yeah?"

"Yeah," Marcus says.

He waits for Patrick to ask what it was, but in this second wakeup tonight, Patrick thinks how the boy used to be an all-night sleeper. How they both were.

"A monster was chasing me and roaring at me."

"Remember? In your dreams, you can turn around and tell the monster to stop."

"Yeah, and I did."

"Did the monster stop?"

"Yeah."

"And then what happened?" Patrick whispers.

"And then the monster sat down and cried."

"Why did he cry?"

"Because he was a monster."

Am I the monster? Patrick wonders. Or Rachel? After their vicious arguments, he pondered the impact on their four-year-old, but in those moments, that concern fell away, and he roared and screamed as much as Rachel did. Maybe more. Definitely more.

When Rachel left, what Patrick felt most was a relief from the slights, fights, and shame. What he misses most is sleep.

Every day after school, Marcus asks where Momma is and when she'll be home. It's hard on Patrick raising a child alone. Teaching high school biology, rushing out the door in the morning, just getting to the grocery—it's all hard.

Rachel's departure also left Patrick financially stretched until the lease ran out in South Boston, and he found this one-bedroom in Braintree. A couple of old library partitions, harvested from the school basement, define a 4-year-old's bedroom from a corner of Daddy's bedroom. It works for a preschooler, who's sad and confused about his mother, and nervous about kindergarten, or as Marcus calls it, "kitty-garden." A lover of dogs, but wary of cats, it's another reason to fear kitty-garden. "Are there a lot of cats there? Or just kittens?"

Nightmares of monsters, missing mothers, and mean teachers wake Marcus at least twice a night. Usually it means climbing into bed with Patrick where those cold little feet keep him awake if worry and anger don't.

Patrick lifts the boy into the queen bed now and slides over to the cold sheets, Rachel's side, to give Marcus the warm spot. The boy soon falls asleep, but Patrick can't stop thinking about his wife's affair. How long did it go on before he became suspicious? When the thong underwear fell from their hiding spot as he pulled out a towel? When she kept talking about that guy? When she asked him to stroke her hair this way during sex? How many men before this one? So many nights working late in the PR department. Really working? Or something very different? How does it start? What are the first words, and the ones that cross the bridge?

And him, the trusting, loyal idiot. The clueless cuckold.

Did she laugh at him with her lover? Laying naked and oozing after sex, laughing at Patrick?

Maybe he deserved it somehow. Why did he follow her back to Boston?

The alarm jolts Patrick awake, and he turns it off. The boy doesn't stir. He falls back on the pillow and closes his eyes, wishing for another hour but gets up. He takes a quick shower. No time to dry his hair. It's cold outside, cold in the apartment, but always hot at the high school. He has to get Marcus up and dressed. The preschool gave Patrick a written warning for bringing Marcus in pajamas once. Christ on a bike, one day, one time. They should see how teachers dress at school—half of them look like they're in pajamas. The women wear tights and long flannel shirts like PJ tops. He's no better, in zip-up hoodies over a polo and jeans. With Mrs.

Daniels Preschool right on the way to work, he can't screw it up.

Marcus is pretty good at dressing himself now, while Patrick slams together lunch for both of them: peanut butter-and-jelly sandwich, apple slices, cut carrots, one cupcake. Snack of cheese and cracker for Marcus, granola bar for Patrick. Rachel valued variety, in food, and in other things it appears. But identical lunches and the same every day make life easier.

Patrick dashes off a quick doodle on the brown-paper bag for Marcus every morning—a tree, a dog, a silly face, a bird. Today, it's a little fish followed by a big fish. Could it trigger the monster nightmare again? Too late. Into the bag lunches go.

Marcus starts crying and yelling from his kid-sized bed.

"What? What's wrong?"

"I don't like these socks!"

"You love those socks. With the black dogs like Jasper? Those are awesome."

"I *hate* them," and Marcus hurls the socks which land gently on the floor. "Dinosaurs. Dinosaur socks."

Patrick wants himself to laugh, but there is no time for it. They have to roll.

"Come on, Marcus, you wore those yesterday. They're in the wash. Wear the Jasper-dog socks."

"I want dino socks! Mommy would know where they are."

Rachel probably did buy a second pair, crammed in a box Patrick hasn't unpacked yet.

Pick your battles, he tells himself and takes a breath. He searches the hamper, pulls one dino sock out and throws it to Marcus. Rushing now, he can't find the other.

"Hey, here's a fun idea, wear dinosaurs on one foot, Jasper-dogs on the other. They can race!"

The boy screams, "Noooo-wwwaaa," and throws himself on his bed.

Patrick dumps the hamper on the floor, something else to clean up when he gets home, and drops to his knees scrambling through the stinky laundry. Why is everything such a big deal? He finds the blasted sock and throws it to Marcus, looks at the clock, no time for breakfast now. Rachel would hate it, but Rachel ain't here, so Patrick grabs another package of chocolate cupcakes.

"Breakfast in the car, Buddy. Let's roll."

"My shoes!"

Patrick helps with the shoes, ties them fast. Thank god it's April—Boston winter takes ten more minutes. On a good day.

"To Mrs. D's," Patrick says. "Let's go, go, *go*!"

While he explains the role of mitochondria in mammal cells, Patrick's phone vibrates in his pocket. It stops. Then starts again a few seconds later. It stops. Then vibrates again.

He pulls the phone out. It's preschool.

Worst-fears leap to mind before he can tell the kids to review cell components and slips into the hall to answer. Marcus is okay. But he bit a boy after lunch. Yesterday, he kicked a girl on the playground. And two days earlier he pushed a boy to the ground. The preschool knows about Rachel leaving—it feels like everyone does—and they're trying to help, but this crosses the line. They tell him to come and get Marcus now.

But he can't he's teaching.

Now.

Patrick finishes the class and runs for the office—a teacher, not a friendly one, yells: "No running in the hall." He resists flipping her the bird—just barely—but he doesn't stop running.

In the principal's office, he explains as briefly as possible, that he has to pick up Marcus at preschool, skipping over the biting because, well, who wants to admit their kid's a biter? After an eyeroll the principal grants it.

On his way to Mrs. Daniel's Preschool, Patrick calls Dr. Izensen, the pediatrician, who's in his 50s and has become something of a father-figure to Patrick. Especially since his own family is a thousand miles away in Nashville, and his father a million miles away, emotionally speaking. The pediatrician is busy, but he calls back when Patrick has Marcus in the car. Izensen suggests he and Patrick meet alone at a Dunkin Donuts near South Shore Hospital after rounds.

The young woman downstairs agrees to watch Marcus. When they meet, Izensen seems happy to see Patrick. And Patrick speaks openly as he does with no one else about Marcus's trouble sleeping and his preschool behavior. Patrick also opens up about his own troubles and the effects of sleep loss.

Izensen says he's reluctant to try medication—and Patrick says, "Good." Then Izensen says what Patrick knows in his heart; the behaviors are more about instability at home and his fears of what might happen next.

"Just like us, kids are stressed out by big changes. And you've both faced a lot of change recently. Marcus also senses your sadness, concerns, and anger—all of which are normal—but it scares him. He's acting out because he can't control any of it."

Izensen lets that sink in for a minute, takes a drink of coffee, watches two cops come in and chat-up the young woman at the counter who wears her wavy, chestnut hair in a thick ponytail exactly like Rachel.

"So here's the hard part, my friend," Izensen says, "as the solo parent, you need to make some changes—even as you struggle with other changes. You're doing your best, but you need new tools."

"And here I thought, I just needed more dinosaur socks."

Izensen laughs. "Those will help too. I was going to prescribe a few pairs."

"Commit to a new evening routine," Izensen says. No electronics, no-TV, no-phone, no-computer for least an hour and a half before bed. For both of you."

Patrick pulls out his phone, "Let me write this down."

Izensen puts his hand over the phone. "I'll email you the details. For now, just listen."

Patrick turns his phone over and slides it aside.

"Make evenings low-stress. Just be with Marcus. No grading papers, preparing lessons, or talking to your wife. Especially no talking to her. If possible, go for a walk—fresh air calms us and helps us sleep. And then read to him, or tell him a made-up story in a calm tone."

"I've never made up a story for him before."

"Give it a try. Even if you're lousy, he'll love it. Maybe you can make them up together."

That night, after a dinner of chicken nuggets and maco-cheese, they wash dishes together, with Marcus drying and putting away pans, and they go for a walk around the block, counting April robins and stopping to pet Jasper outside the

Johnsons' house. Back home they both brush their teeth. Patrick helps Marcus with a final trip around the railroad tracks of molars. Then pajamas, a bedtime jazz playlist, and a reading of *I Love You to the Moon and Back*.

When it ends: "Another one."

"Tonight, something different," Patrick whispers. "I'll tell you a story."

"But I like when you read to me."

"Me too, but this could be fun." Patrick hasn't worked it out, but he notices Stegman, the small, plastic stegosaurus clutched in Marcus's hand.

Dinosaurs supplanted trains for top interest. And Stegman lives in Marcus's pockets, surviving several rides through the washer and dryer. To avoid the drama of the inevitable disappearance of Stegman, Patrick bought two more and squirreled them away in a sock drawer.

"This is story about young dinosaurs."

Marcus is hooked.

"Gretta is a blue diplodocus, and she lives in Sauropod City with her father."

"Where's her Momma?"

Where's her momma? Probably ran off with some jerk T-rex and abandoned her family. "She took a new job in another city and had to move. But Gretta will get to see her, just as soon as things settle down." Patrick wonders if this is anxiety provoking. "The nice thing is Gretta's best friend, Bonnie, lives across the street. She's a brontosaurus."

"No such thing as a brontosaurus, Dad. It's apatosaurus."

"Right," Patrick whispers, "but let's not tell Bonnie because she thinks she's a brontosaurus, and it might upset her to learn she's really an apatosaurus."

Marcus nods, and Patrick continues. Turns out Stegman

lives just down the street and has a dog named Jasper. And Tripper, a clumsy triceratops, lives a block away in the second floor apartment of a three-family house (just like the one Patrick and Marcus live in).

Over the first week, Gretta emerges as the central figure. She's a little afraid of the dark, of third-floor neighbors who argue a lot, and of cats and kitty-garden starting in the fall.

In one story, Gretta is not invited to Bonnie's birthday party. But it wasn't a snub; the invitation fell under the seat of Bonnie's mother's car, and they call Gretta to come over.

In another, Tripper shows Gretta a secret waterfall. She shows others, and it gets overrun with dinosaurs who trample flowers and leave litter. Marcus asks about the waterfall place on the way home from school the next day, and Patrick tells a follow-up story of Gretta getting Sauropod City to make it a park. Then Gretta and her friends help clean it up and replant wildflowers.

Jasper Johnson, the neighbor's black lab, makes appearances in the stories as do a many other dinosaurs.

Patrick keeps notes and brief outlines of the stories because Marcus asks to go back and revisit stories from the previous nights, and if Patrick gets a detail wrong, Marcus is quick to correct. In the retellings, Patrick often pauses to ask Marcus for additional depth— "and what kind of pizza did they order?" Or "What color is Tripper's bike? And Stegman's skateboard?"

Rather than add to Patrick's exhaustion, the stories energize him. And they emerge as a way for Patrick to advise Marcus—when a velociraptor bites Stegman on the playground, how does that make Stegman feel? What should he do? As the stories and days stretch on, Marcus talks about Greta and her friends, and Gretta becomes a guide for stressful or scary moments.

"What would Gretta do?" Patrick asks.

"She'd tell the teacher Jimmy left some toys out."

"Really? But what about that time Gretta helped Stegman figure out how to close the stuck gate on the fence so Jasper wouldn't run away?"

"Yeah, maybe she'd help Jimmy put away the toys."

"I think she would too. What about you, Marcus, what will you do next time?"

"Yeah, I can help Jimmy put the toys away."

As Marcus continues to learn more about dinosaurs, the cast expands to include Roger, an ichthyosaurus, and Emma a baryonyx and many more.

And sleep, which started this story experiment, improves. On the back of the bathroom door, Patrick charts Marcus's slumber. Under the new routine, the graph is rising, rising like the dream of an optimistic economist, more sleep, longer sleep, deeper sleep.

After six weeks, Marcus sleeps through the night more. Which, of course, means Patrick does too. And he feels lighter, more patient with students, quicker to laugh with Marcus, and telling better Gretta stories.

One Friday morning, Patrick gets up early. He wants the weekend to start off well, with a sit-down breakfast and a calm start. Patrick takes the luxury of a medium-length shower, and before shaving, he charts Marcus's sleep for last night. For the first time, he sees Marcus has slept through the night for a full week. When did that last happen?

Next he lathers up and begins to shave. After a couple of swipes he looks at himself in the mirror. With a towel around his waist, he's almost unrecognizable to himself. Too skinny and long, shaggy hair. He can't remember his hair this long —no cuts since Rachel left, eight months ago. Can it be that long, the hair *and* the time? He gets out scissors and trims the hair around his face, then the sides, the top. He cuts the back by feel, measuring length against a finger and snipping. He knows he's doing a hatchet job, but now that he's started, he can't turn back. When he stops, it's mangled, but it looks new. And new carries its own weight, in biology, in parenthood, in life. With a few last snips, in an effort to balance the cut, Patrick is ready to embrace the new as best he can. The hair? Well, time to find a barber in Braintree.

# The Judge and His Dog
## BY JOHN YOUNG

In Nema, Indiana there was not a more proud man than the retired federal judge, Duncan Howe, nor a more proud dog than his lion-sized collie, Mr. Thomas Jefferson. It was as if the beautiful dog knew his champion pedigree as well as the judge knew his own. When these two strolled the streets of Nema, they carried an air of royalty. And were treated as such. Duncan Howe had been a distinguished lawyer and Federal Judge in

Chicago before retiring to, if not the largest, certainly the most elegant limestone stone house in the county. Judge Howe and Mr. Jefferson lived there alone, a widower for 20 years now, with a daytime housekeeper named Madeline Patch.

No one dared boss Judge Howe as 49-year-old Madeline did. And she was the only person in Nema who called him Duncan. Likewise, he was the only one who called her Madeline instead of Maddie. Early each morning Maddie walked from her street of simple, wood-frame houses to the elegant end of Elm Street to make Duncan's coffee and breakfast. She worked until two o'clock when she left to meet her four children after school, then returned to prepare Duncan's dinner.

Twice a day, late-morning and evening, Judge Howe and Mr. Jefferson took a walk around town—both of them perfectly groomed: Judge Howe in his bow ties, starched white shirts, and wool suits; Mr. Jefferson with his thick tan, black, and white coat. Their manners were as impeccable as their appearance. Judge Howe gave a slight bow and a, "How do you do?" to women, and to men a clear wave or a firm handshake. And Mr. Thomas Jefferson kept his tongue in (even on the hottest days). He ignored other dogs, never barked unnecessarily, and never relieved himself in an embarrassing place. They were a singular sight in Nema, Indiana.

At the age of 75, Judge Howe still drove his Cadillac to Bloomington once a week to lecture at Indiana University's School of Law where he held a post as Distinguished Lecturer. When he spoke, words were clear and sharp, without hesitance or doubt, opinion imparted as fact. And people acted on his words without question. That was as true at Dairy Queen or Dodd's Drugstore as when he told the Law School dean to scrap a plan for a joint law/environmental degree ("There's a place for progressive ideas, but a law school of standing is one in pursuit of quality students and classic training.") Simply put, people did as the judge said.

And that is what got him in trouble.

Every May, Judge Howe had Mr. Thomas Jefferson professionally shampooed and groomed at The Happy Groomer in Bloomington to remove the rest of his considerable

winter coat. On his way to a Law School faculty meeting,

Judge Duncan Howe stopped at The Happy Groomer. Before going inside, Judge Howe carefully lifted a small Band-Aid from his chin where he'd cut himself shaving and checked it in the rearview mirror. When he entered The Happy Groomer, bells rang overhead, and a woman's voice sang from the back, "Be out in a sec."

From behind a curtain a woman emerged like a highly groomed poodle herself with high arching peroxide blonde hair tied back by an oversized pink bow, false eyelashes, and excessive eye shadow, long red fingernails and matching lipstick. "Oh, Judge Howe," she said, "sorry to keep you waiting, sir. How may I help you?"

Judge Howe, having just pressed his thumb to his chin and found a dab of blood, said, "Shave and groom."

"Shave and groom?" the woman's voice echoed weakly.

On his way out the door, Judge Howe repeated, "Right. I will pick him up this afternoon."

As he left he heard the woman's saccharine voice speaking to the collie, "I forgot you was coming to see us this morning, Mr. Jefferson. Yes I did, you big boo-boo."

When Judge Howe returned to pick up Mr. Jefferson, he couldn't believe what he saw. Had it not been for the eyes and the long thin nose, he'd have not believed the rat-like animal before him was Mr. Thomas Jefferson. The dog, so ashamed of his lost coat, had to be carried to the car. He stood on the back seat of Duncan Howe's Cadillac, with his shaved tail between his legs, his knees half bent, his head and ears low.

Duncan drove numbly home and carried the dog to the house. When he called for Madeline to open the door, she yelled, "Oh, my God. What happened?"

But Duncan didn't answer. He took the dog to the library and slid the heavy walnut doors closed behind him. Inside,

Duncan lifted Thomas Jefferson onto the sofa where the dog maintained his posture from the car. The judge, stroking the stubby coat, told the dog he was sorry, that it was an accident. Mr. Jefferson's lowered head did not move. Only the eyes strained to look up to the face of his master. Then those sad, brown eyes searched the room for the darkest corner, and the dog crawled off the sofa and walked with his belly inches from the parquet floor into that corner. Duncan dragged the plush

oriental rug from in front of his desk, and Mr. Jefferson laid on it.

Duncan lay on the floor next to his once beautiful collie, and tears pooled at the edge of his wire rim glasses and flowed down his cheeks. Hugging Mr. Jefferson, Duncan asked the dog to forgive him, to please forgive him.

Duncan heard the heavy walnut library doors slide open. "Get out. Get out," he ordered.

But Madeline did not. She came to him and kneeled on the floor to stroke Duncan's gray head which hung just above the sad dog. Duncan's arms found Madeline's thick waist and gripped her tightly, his head in her lap.

"There, there now," Madeline said, rocking him back and forth, a breast pressed to the side of his face. She worked her hand up and down his suit jacket, and whispered "There, there now," as she wiped the tears from his wrinkled and liver-spotted face.

"It was an accident, Duncan. Mr. Jefferson will be okay." But he knew that she knew better. Anyone could see the depth of shame and loss in the dog's eyes. His pride, his dignity, his identity, had been shaved. From the front of her apron, Madeline drew a Kleenex, shook out the folds, and handed it to Duncan.

When he blew his nose, it seemed to clear his head, and

the judge recoiled from his housekeeper and rose to his feet where he pulled down his jacket and buttoned it. He sat behind his large walnut desk, taking up a book, chair squeaking as he swiveled away from her.

"Duncan, let's go in the kitchen, and I'll make you some tea."

"No, I'll stay here. Thank you, Madeline."

"Judge, this doesn't help a thing. Come and have some tea." With that Madeline Patch got up and walked from the dark library.

He heard her banging around the kitchen and slide the pocket doors closed. When she returned with tea, she spoke from the other side of the doors. "Duncan, your tea is here in

the parlor. My kids'll be home from school soon, so I gotta go. I'll be back to fix your supper." She paused, nothing. "Now you come and drink this tea." Then she left.

When Madeline Patch returned, earlier than usual because she worried about Duncan, the tea had been moved into the library, and Duncan Howe was asleep in his leather chair beside Mr. Jefferson. Untouched on the floor before the dog was a plate heaped with cooked and uncooked hamburger, a bowl of milk, a bowl with two raw eggs, and bits of cheese. Mr. Jefferson lifted his eyes but not his head when Madeline entered the room; then the dog turned away. She tried to call Mr. Jefferson from the corner to take him out but he wouldn't come.

In the kitchen, sticky egg shells, bloody hamburger wrappers, and uncapped milk cluttered the counter. Madeline cleaned up and prepared dinner: baked potato,

Cornish hen, tossed salad. Duncan insisted if he must eat when he wasn't hungry, he'd be served at his desk in the library.

The next morning, Madeline found Duncan asleep in the library on the tufted leather couch dragged over near Mr. Jefferson who remained curled in his dark corner. The food before the dog remained untouched, and now included pieces of Cornish hen. Duncan's own dinner had been more picked over than eaten.

That morning he drank coffee but ate nothing.

Neither Duncan Howe nor Mr. Jefferson left the library all day. For the first time in the six years that Madeline Patch had worked for Judge Howe, he did not shave or put on a clean white shirt.

The next day was much the same as the days before.

When Judge Howe and Mr. Jefferson twice failed to make either of their daily walks, people in Nema feared for Judge Howe or his dog. They asked Maddie, but she said the collie was, "a little under the weather." But that didn't put an end to talk.

On the third morning, Madeline found Mr. Thomas Jefferson dead in the corner, shamefully curled. Madeline kneeled next to Duncan with a hand on his shoulder and softly whispered to the old man sleeping on the sofa, "Duncan, Duncan." When his tired eyes opened, she said, "It's over now. Mr. Jefferson has gone in his sleep."

Words about the death of his nine year companion, his best and most loyal friend, sucked the strength from Duncan Howe, causing him to draw his knees up and pull the blanket over his shoulder to his nose. Tears eased from the old man's eyes and dripped off the bridge of his nose onto the leather sofa. Madeline said nothing more but sat next to him and stroked Duncan's back.

He whispered to Maddie, "I keep asking myself how he would have felt if he'd inflicted a similar shame on me. But it is inconceivable, even by accident. Oh, I know he was just a dog, but he was a special dog and a dear friend to me."

"That he was," Maddie said. "You loved him, and he loved you. It's always hard to lose someone you love."

Maddie was making coffee when she heard Duncan go out the back door to the garage where he took out a rusted, round-point shovel. Under the branches of the large cottonwood in the back yard he began to dig. When he hit roots, he hacked at them with the shovel until Madeline went out and said, "Duncan, stop this." But he went on without acknowledging her.

"You'll give yourself a heart attack," she said. "You're digging your own grave." She watched then added, "I'll send my boys over after school to dig the grave." Again Duncan ignored her and went on digging. She went back inside but kept an eye on him from the kitchen window.

He sweated in the warm morning sun, so he stripped off his shirt and undershirt and threw them aside. Madeline had never seen him bare chested, the pale, thinly muscled arms, the white hair on his narrow chest. He'd not dug but a small hole when he stopped to lean on his shovel—the pale chest heaved for air, thin white hair tousled, glasses down on his long thin nose, white stubble showing on his chin for the first time since she'd met him. He looked more like a bespectacled rat than a distinguished federal judge. She came out and stood on the back porch but neither spoke. He checked his hands, and they were red with pain, blisters already forming. Then he turned them over and Madeline Patch saw they were spotted as autumn apples fallen from the tree.

Judge Howe turned to Madeline, and she watched the

recognition fall over him before he crossed his arms to cover himself as a woman might. Then he grabbed his shirts and strode past her.

"Send your boys over after school," Judge Howe said and went inside.

Madeline heard the shower running when she went upstairs on her way to the attic for an old blanket. Part of her wondered if the old man might shave his own head in apology.

When Duncan came downstairs and walked into the kitchen, Maddie hardly recognized him. He wore dungarees, work shoes, and a plaid short-sleeved shirt. In six years, she'd never seen these clothes or shoes. And he looked, well, he looked common, as common as the men who frequented Liars Bench outside the courthouse.

"I hope to return in time to help Neal and Brad finish the hole, but back by dinner if not," he said. He started out the back door, then paused by the form bundled in the blanket, and turned to her. "And, Maddie, thank you for your kindness."

By the time Duncan returned, Maddie had straightened up the library, and the boys were finishing the burial. He stopped to see if he could help, but they waived him off like Maddie had told them to do.

Then Maddie saw another first as the Cadillac backed past the kitchen window right into the grass and stopped under the cottonwood. He opened the trunk, and the boys put aside their shovels.

When Maddie went out to see what the fuss was about, she saw a concrete molded statue of a collie about one-fourth life-size on a concrete base with inset letters, "Mr. Thomas Jefferson March 1980—May 1989."

BY JOHN YOUNG

"Go home if you want, Richard," I say, "but you can't take the ball. I'll bring it to your house when we're done."

"I'm taking my ball."

"I don't think so."

I don't like this. It's the end of a fringe friendship, but I never really liked Ricky anyway. Especially when he insisted we call him Richard. Dick would be more fitting.

"First of all Ricky, Mike didn't foul you, and you know it. All ball. If you can't take Mike blocking your shot, fine go home. But you're not taking the ball."

Mike says it doesn't matter. And I say it does.

"It's my ball."

Any wonder I hate rich kids? "Ricky, you try to take that ball, and you're going to take a bloody nose with you, because I'm going to punch your face."

"I'm going to tell my dad."

"Go cry to your daddy, Ricky. I'll punch him in the nose too."

Ricky left, and we played three-on-three with the one guy waiting. Then, I'll be damned if Ricky and his daddy don't show up. His dad screeches to a stop, drove from two blocks away in a big SUV and charges across the park toward me.

"I told Ricky I'd bring the ball to your house when we're done."

"But it's his ball, and—"

"Seven guys want to play. One," I resist saying pussy, "One wants to go home."

"Give me that ball."

Chuck tosses it to him, and I knock it away before he catches it.

"Did you threaten my son?"

"I said I'd punch him in the nose if he took the ball. I also said I'd punch you in the nose if you try to take it. Not like we're gonna wear it out."

"Richard, wait in the car. Give me that ball!"

And I do it, consequences be damned, I hit him right in the middle of the face. It knocks him back a step and a half, and then he lunges at me. I sidestep him, and he keeps coming. It's like a game of tag. I juke and run, duck and dodge. Hell, I'm fourteen, I can do this all day. Next thing, I'm laughing. I'm scared too, but it's funny, and I can't stop laughing—fat, middle-aged dude trying to catch me. He's huffing and puffing, blood running out of his nose, and pretty soon, I'm like running circles, and he lunges at me red-faced as I pass. The rest of the guys are laughing too—except Mike, he keeps saying to cool it. A couple of guys encourage me, a couple encourage Fatso.

Then something clicks in me, a mean streak, and I want to hurt Ricky's dad. I adopt a boxer's stance, dancing around him. He's half bent, panting, struggling just to stand up straight and keep me in front of him. His white shirt untucked, spots of blood on it. I pounce forward, cocking my arm for a blow, and he ducks throwing his arms over his head with a howl. I laugh and spring back.

Then I decide to hit Fatso, just one more time. I pounce in the evening light, cocking my fist. And he punches, catches me hard under the ribs, right in the solar plexus—and I go down on the asphalt, bam, down like a wet towel. My mouth open, I can't breathe. Am I gonna die?

I hear the old man grunt to my friends, "Gimme the ball."

# Meet the Moondust Gatherers

## LIBBY BELLE

Libby Belle is the editor of *Gathering Moondust* and the author of several books of short stories featuring quirky, eclectic characters. Please visit her website for more information.

LibbyBelle.com

## CAROL BETH ANDERSON

Carol Beth Anderson formatted the interior of *Gathering Moondust*. She's an author of fantasy novels and very short stories, and she narrates audiobooks. To find out more, please visit her websites.

Author/Formatting Site: CarolBethAnderson.com
Narration Site: AndersonNarration.com